A DESIRE AS OLD AS TIME . . .

"My God!" James exclaimed. "You infuriating little twit, will you listen to me. I *am* happy. I have been happy for a number of years. I just want to be left alone. Why can't females understand that term. Left alone. A-L-O-N-E."

James halted abruptly and drew a deep breath. He heard the muted voices of the couples on the terrace and realized that he and Hilary had walked a good distance away from them. He felt assaulted by the scents of the night air. It was the scent of Hilary, however—that unidentifiable blend of flowers and spice and forest pungency—that filled his senses and made them swim. The fire of her hair was silvered in the moonlight, and gazing into her eyes, he felt as though he were being drawn into a golden vortex.

He seemed about to explode with the maelstrom of emotions that seethed in him, when without volition—almost as though he were being compelled—he bent his head. When his mouth met her~ in a crushing, angry kiss, he felt her stiff͏ is-tance. The next moment, h~ ~o melt into his embra~

Lady Hilary's Halloween

by

Anne Barbour

A SIGNET BOOK

SIGNET
Published by the Penguin Group
Penguin Putnam Inc., 375 Hudson Street,
New York, New York 10014, U.S.A.
Penguin Books Ltd, 27 Wrights Lane,
London W8 5TZ, England
Penguin Books Australia Ltd, Ringwood,
Victoria, Australia
Penguin Books Canada Ltd, 10 Alcorn Avenue,
Toronto, Ontario, Canada M4V 3B2
Penguin Books (N.Z.) Ltd, 182-190 Wairau Road,
Auckland 10, New Zealand

Penguin Books Ltd, Registered Offices:
Harmondsworth, Middlesex, England

First published by Signet, an imprint of Dutton NAL,
a member of Penguin Putnam Inc.

First Printing, September, 1998
10 9 8 7 6 5 4 3 2 1

ACKNOWLEDGMENTS

I would like to thank two people who have given me inestimable assistance in the preparation of this book. First, Sister Carol Kovarik, of St. Martin's Benedictine Monastery of Rapid City, South Dakota, for translating the initial dialogue between my hapless Roman soldier and those he encountered in Regency England into acceptable Latin.

Second to Susan Lantz, Ph.D., Associate Professor of Mechanical and Biomedical Engineering at the Ross-Hulman Institute of Technology of Terre Haute, Indiana, for sharing her knowledge and that of her colleagues on electricity and the formation and artificial creation of lightning.

Any errors I committed in either of these fields are solely my own.

Chapter One

"Jasper! You wretched beast!" Lady Hilary Merton sighed. Tossing down her trowel, she moved toward her dog. She eyed with disapprobation the rapidly enlarging hole in the soft soil enclosed by what might once have been stone walls. "Now look what you've done."

The animal thus addressed glanced up reproachfully from the patch of ground he'd been excavating. Well, yes, it must be admitted he was on the large side, and more than somewhat disreputable in appearance. Theoretically a cross between a lurcher and an Irish wolfhound, he looked more a mixture of Shetland goat and Welsh pony. Shrugging philosophically, he twitched his tail and continued digging.

"We will have no unauthorized quarrying, Jasper," said Hilary, belying the severity of her words by scratching him affectionately behind his ragged, platter-sized ears.

"We are here on sufferance," she continued, scolding gently, "and must mind our manners."

She made an odd picture, a small, slight figure shaking her finger in reproof at an animal the size of a moose calf. Jasper hung his head, but the next moment destroyed the effect by jumping up to lick her face with an entirely unreciprocated enthusiasm.

Hilary mopped her cheeks with her sleeve and, straightening her bonnet, glanced around with some satisfaction. She had, she felt, accomplished a great deal in the last few months. It was too bad the Roman villa, discovered some years earlier, was not on her father's property, but the boundaries of Whiteleaves lay just a few hundred yards away. In any event, Sir William had given her his tacit permission to work here. Now, she thought with a small surge of excitement, if only the new owner of the property would be so amenable. Surely, such a noted antiquary as Mr. James Wincanon would applaud her efforts and seek her out for further assistance in uncovering the remains.

Hilary stood for a moment in the stillness of the forest. A slant-

ing ray of afternoon sun bathed her in a welcoming warmth, for the
late September air was chill.

Mm, she reflected inconsequentially. It would be Halloween
soon, her favorite festival of the year. Not just because it occurred
during autumn and harvest time, but because of the hint of magic
and ancient mystery that hung over the countryside. Best of all,
one need not believe in any of it to enjoy the fun.

But never mind that now. She turned her attention back to the
ruined villa and in her mind's eye, she pictured it, whole and pros-
pering—a homestead for an owner and his family. A retired legionary, perhaps, who had decided to settle in Britannia after a
lifetime of service to the emperor. There would no doubt have been
a porch to welcome visitors, and spacious rooms inside where the
estate holder and his family conducted the business of their lives.
She had already found a few artifacts and surely there would be
more—mosaics, and sculptures, and pottery, as well as coins and
traces of all the other objects that made a house a home. She could
hardly wait to begin working under Mr. Wincanon's guidance.

She became aware that the sun's rays were lengthening. Goodness! She should be home right now preparing for this evening's
dinner party—and she had promised the vicar's wife she would
stop for tea. She gathered the trowel and the other utensils she used
for her digging and placed them carefully inside the small shed
nearby that she had ordered constructed for this purpose. Then,
Jasper loping after her like a fur rug caught in a windstorm, she
mounted the little gig parked at the edge of the site. She slapped
the reins against the horse's flanks and clattered off toward the ancient Roman boundary road, now known as the Fosse Way, that ran
near the villa site.

The vicar's wife, Mrs. Thomlinson, awaited her on the front
porch of the vicarage.

"I'm so glad you made time to stop, Hilary, for I know you're
probably anxious to get home to ready yourself for the dinner party
tonight. Goodness," she concluded, glancing about, "did you come
out alone—again?"

Hilary smiled. She took no affront at Mrs. Thomlinson's tone of
admonishment, for the older woman had, over the years since her
mother's death, taken up a position as her surrogate mother. "Now,

Mrs. T., you know Jasper is all the company I need when I go out—particularly on such a short jaunt as the one to Goodhurst."

Indeed, with a set of splendidly efficient teeth, Jasper was well-known throughout the neighborhood and provided a strong deterrent against any evildoer unwise enough to so much as consider an assault on the person of Lady Hilary.

"He certainly is devoted to you," said Mrs. Thomlinson, shutting the door gently but firmly in Jasper's face.

She led the way in to the vicarage parlor and ushered Hilary to a chair near the fire. Murmuring instructions to the maid who entered the room on their heels, she seated herself nearby.

Hilary laughed in agreement with Mrs. Thomlinson's words. "Still," continued the vicar's wife, "now that Goodhurst has a new owner—a bachelor—it really is not the thing for you to be haring off there on your own. I know you don't care what people think—"

"No, I don't, Mrs. T.," Hilary interposed with some asperity. "In any event, the villa is some distance away from the main house. In fact, it is much closer to my home than to Mr. Wincanon's, and since I haven't even met the gentleman, I don't see where my visits provide any grist for the gossip mill. Tell me," she continued in an effort to turn the subject, "have you decided on a costume for the Halloween Ball? You and the vicar are so inventive every year."

Mrs. Thomlinson laughed. "Oh, we're still mulling over the possibilities. I did tell the vicar that he'd make a splendid Henry the Eighth, but he said he thought Mr. Fenwick had already chosen that one."

"Well, Mr. Fenwick is a trifle on the spindly side for Bluff King Hal, but—oh! Did you notice, by the by, that he escorted Miss Shelburton home from church last Sunday? I do believe they're going to make a match of it."

Mrs. Thomlinson chuckled. "And I can see that you're immensely set up over *that* development. Ah, thank you, Betty," she said to the maid, who brought a tray of tea and cakes.

"Well, it was time someone took a hand." Hilary accepted a steaming cup from her hostess and selected a cake. "Anna Shelburton was not happy as the Bardrake's governess, for she is not the type of female to make a career of minding other people's children. And poor Walter Fenwick has been at loose ends since his mother passed away last year. He needs a woman to look after him, and Anna is the perfect candidate. Mr. Fenwick just needed someone to give him a push."

"So, that's what you did. Literally. The poor man—it was lucky he didn't end up in Holiday Pond with the shove you gave him, almost into Anna's lap."

"Well, it plunged them into a conversation, didn't it?" Hilary laughed unrepentantly. "I know I'm a terrible busybody, but I just cannot abide seeing people living unhappily all for the want of a little determination. I mean, just look at Meg. She's my sister and I love her dearly, but she and Richard were making *such* a mull of their lives."

"Until you convinced Lord Willerton to hire Richard as his agent."

"Precisely." Hilary inclined her head smugly. "Meg professes her gratitude every time she comes home to visit."

She swallowed the last her of tea and rose to her feet.

"And now, I know this has been a shabby short of visit, but you and I do not stand on ceremony and I really must leave. As you said, I must hie me home and don my finery for the party this evening—and I suppose you will be doing the same."

"Gracious, yes. We don't want Mr. Wincanon to think his new neighbors a parcel of bumpkins."

"Even though that's what we are," Hilary replied prosaically. Kissing Mrs. Thomlinson lightly on the cheek, she left the vicarage, a packet containing one of the lady's famous seedcakes in her hand. With a mild remonstrance, she suffered Jasper's exuberant expressions of joy at their reunion.

Back in the gig, Hilary contemplated the evening that lay ahead. Little was known of Mr. Wincanon except that he was the favored nephew of the Duke of Dolmain and related to half the noble houses in the country. He was also a wealthy man, being worth not a penny less than thirty thousand a year, if reports could be believed. And, though no one hereabouts except herself was interested, James Wincanon was considered one of the foremost antiquarians in the country.

In a few moments she entered the bounds of her father's estate. The Earl of Clarendon's country seat, Whiteleaves, was not vast, but it was, as he always stated with ill-concealed pride, large enough and beautifully situated.

Just inside the wall that surrounded the estate, Hilary passed a crumbling stone tower. She smiled. It was not far from the villa, and it, too dated from the time of the Roman occupation of Britain. Oddly, it had been constructed inside the perimeter of a "dance," one of the many circles of standing stones that were scattered about England, created thousands of years before the advent of the Romans.

She had always been interested in the stone circle, having divined that one of the huge, recumbent stones set between two upright boulders had been intended as an altar. In her fanciful teens she had even laid offerings of fruit and flowers there. However, it was the tower that had fascinated her. How many times had she played there, picturing in her mind the Roman troops, banners flying, marching and fighting so far from home? It was at this time that she had conceived a burning interest in the ancient empire and the men who had guarded its frontiers. Over the years, despite other demands on her time and energy, she had perused the works of historians such as Tacitus and Livy. She had even studied Latin with the vicar, and could translate a funerary inscription or a scrawled prayer without assistance. Now, at the ripe age of four and twenty, she felt confident in calling herself a skilled antiquary.

Not that she did not face some difficulties in the pursuit of her passion. Her family, consisting of her father and her brothers and sisters and their progeny, felt that she was in danger of turning into a bluestocking. In addition, her studies and her fieldwork took time away from what they considered her primary duties as chatelaine of Whiteleaves and resident relative-on-call for whatever crises might appear on the family's horizon.

She certainly did not resent her role as mistress of her father's house, but she longed to accomplish something just for herself, to attain some small measure of competency and recognition in an area outside her domestic domain.

Perhaps, Hilary thought with another glance at the tower, she might gain that recognition through an association with the renowned James Wincanon.

"For I am certain," she said briskly to Jasper, who sat beside her, ears flying and half a yard of tongue lolling from his mouth, "that he will appreciate the contribution I can make to his efforts."

She nodded hopefully at Jasper's bark of agreement, then, on a whim, she paused and dismounted from the gig. She did not enter the tower, but ran to the altar stone at the edge of the circle where she uttered a small prayer to whatever spirits might have lingered there through the millennia. Quickly, almost furtively, she broke off a piece of the seedcake and laid it on the altar. Feeling remarkably foolish, but somehow strengthened, she hurried back to the gig, unnoticing of the breeze that, just for a moment, sighed through the clearing and rustled the trees that hung over the altar stone. Nor did she observe the shadowy presence that watched for a moment before sliding silently away through the trees. Smoothing the skirts of her serviceable and sadly mud-stained muslin, she slapped the reins and resumed her journey.

An hour or so later, she sat, bathed and gowned before her dressing table.

"If you don't hold still, my lady, you're going to get this here pin stuck in your ear."

Emma Barker spoke as severely as she was able with her mouth full of hairpins. Her admonition, however, produced little result. Hilary wriggled impatiently under her maid's ministrations.

"Emma, for heaven's sake, you're not rigging me out for an audience with the Queen. It's only a dinner party."

Emma snorted. "Only a dinner party, indeed. As if you've talked of anything else for days. Now sit still. Do you want this Winkum-whatsizzname feller to see you looking as though you'd just crawled through a knothole?"

"His name is Wincanon," retorted Hilary with dignity. "James Wincanon, and I am not trying to impress him with my hairstyle."

"No? You'll snare him with your big, brown eyes, then?"

Really, thought Hilary. She had allowed Emma too much freedom of expression of late. That's what came of employing as a lady's maid a young woman with whom she'd made daisy chains as a child.

"I am not," she said with some asperity, "trying to snare him at all. I hope he and I will become colleagues—nothing else."

"Hmph." Emma snorted again, unfazed.

In fact, mused Hilary, contemplating her image in the mirror, it was a very good thing she was not planning to ensnare Mr. Wincanon, for her physical assets would certainly never promote such a goal. She eyed her hair with disfavor. Through the years she had tried to think of it as auburn, or titian, or even strawberry, but it was none of these exotic tints. It was, to describe it in painful truth, an unattractive, orangey-red. As in underdone bricks, or carrots, or a blazing conflagration. In addition, it was absolutely unmanageable. No amount of brushing and anointing it with pomade could tame its tendency to escape in undisciplined tendrils that sprang in all directions at once. Hilary felt that by right she should have been endowed with heavy, darkly mysterious tresses, fashioned into one of those polished chignons that lent one such dignity and poise. Her eyes were a disappointment, too. They could at least have been an exotic green; instead they were an indeterminate shade of light brown, with odd flecks of a lighter color. And, while she was cataloging her list of dissatisfactions, she could use a few more inches as well. Lord, she was such a dab of a woman, skinny as a bed slat and just as sadly lacking in curves.

James Wincanon, she considered in disgust, would take one look at her and dismiss her as a scatterbrained tomboy. And who could blame him? How could he know that beneath her hoydenish exterior reposed the soul of a scholar?

It would help, she supposed, if she could dress in clothing more suitable to a female of superior intellect, but her father insisted she affect the frills and furbelows he considered appropriate to a gently bred maiden on the hunt for a husband. She was not always so dutiful, but Papa had been supportive of her academic interests, so that she felt she must give in on what was, after all, a fairly minor point. Still, she hated appearing before the world looking like a circus pony in a gown of pale blue sarcenet, trimmed with several tiers of ruffles and embroidered with enough flowers to deck a church.

She jerked as yet another hairpin was thrust into the arrangement of curls that teetered unsteadily atop her head.

"Emma," she said at last through gritted teeth, "I am as presentable as you can make me. Mister Wincanon has probably already arrived, along with all the other guests, and Father will be wondering what has become of me."

"Humph," grumbled Emma. "I don't see that you can afford to pass him over sight unseen, for you're not getting any younger."

Hilary bit back a retort. Really, this was most unbecoming—brangling in such a manner with her own maid.

"If you're quite finished with me," she said frigidly, glancing into the mirror once more, "I'll take my aging, decrepit self off. Mister Wincanon is probably striding up the front steps right this minute."

Turning a darkling glance on her maid, she hurried from the room.

As it happened, James Wincanon was still some distance from the front steps of Whiteleaves, to which stately residence he had been invited for dinner. He was, in fact, traveling in his curricle at a somewhat desultory speed along the road that connected his new home, Goodhurst, to that of the earl. It was apparent from the slight frown that marred the gentleman's aquiline features, that he was not looking forward to the evening's festivities.

And why should he? he mused sourly. It was bound to be a replica of a hundred other evenings he had suffered through since he had come in to his majority some ten years ago. Among the phalanx of neighbors to which he would be presented there would be at least three unmarried females present—eager young damsels, attended by calculating mamas, all of them ready to pounce like vixens on a plump rooster dropped in their midst.

His unease did not spring from an inflated estimation of his own attractions. He knew himself to be endowed with an eminently ordinary set of features. He was of reasonably upright moral character, and possessed of a personality that could hardly be called scintillating. Thus it might be difficult for some to account for his unvarying success with the fair sex. He smiled cynically. Ah, the blessings of wealth and exalted connections.

He sighed. He had been pleased at the opportunity to purchase Goodhurst. He had been after the estate for years, ever since he'd learned of the Roman villa that lay in its forested hills. Having now acquired the property, he anticipated bringing his treasure to light.

His plans for his stay in Gloucestershire did not include socializing with the local gentry. He would lose no time in donning the aspect that had served him so well over the years—that of an eccentric recluse. He would make it clear that while he would accept whatever community responsibilities were required of him, he was not in the market for a bride, and, after these few initial forays, he would not be available for appearances on the social scene.

"Ho, guv'nor, that looks to be the place, up ahead."

Thus recalled by his tiger, James turned his curricle at a massive set of gates, flanked by stone pillars. A few moments later, after traversing a winding drive, bordered by flourishing beeches, he arrived at his destination, a sprawling manor house of Tudor origin. As he mounted the front steps, the door swung wide before he could lift his hand to the bronze knocker that adorned it, and a butler of imposing mien ushered him into a hall that, while it featured the requisite suits of armor and the odd halberd or two on the walls, bore a welcoming air.

Smiling benignly, the butler guided him up the staircase that ascended in a flowing crescendo of marble and wood, and, ushering him into a spacious salon, announced him in mellifluous tones to those assembled inside.

He recognized his host immediately, one of the few persons in the room he had already met. The earl hurried toward him with hand outhrust. He was a tall, hearty man with graying hair and a benevolent expression. As he moved across the room, he beckoned to a young woman who stood near a window, chatting with a group of ladies. A very young woman, indeed, surmised James as she approached. She could not possibly be his hostess, was his next thought, unless—A sense of foreboding swept over him.

"Mister Wincanon!" exclaimed Lord Clarendon. "Welcome to Whiteleaves. May I present my daughter, Lady Hilary?"

Chapter Two

"Charmed," James murmured colorlessly, brushing the girl's fingertips with his lips. Was there no Lady Clarendon, then? Was this infant one of that most dreaded of species, an unmarried daughter?

"Mr. Wincanon," said the girl in a high, breathless voice, "I have been so looking forward to meeting you."

James groaned inwardly. He might have known. No wonder Lord Clarendon had made such a point of inviting him to his home. Lord, was this awkward little gamine with the incendiary hair and huge amber-colored eyes the earl's only daughter, or were there more lurking, waiting to pounce? To his vast relief, a matronly female approached, with a young man in tow. She was introduced to James as Mrs. Horace Clapham, wife of a neighboring squire.

"Pleased to make your acquaintance, sir," Mrs. Clapham bellowed jovially. "Say hello to my son, Freddie. He ain't good for much yet, but he's a decent lad."

Freddie Clapham's cheeks flushed dully.

"Mama, please," he whispered in an anguished tone.

"Well, and you are, then," his parent roared. "Or at least you will be, as soon as you give over wearing those ridiculous clothes."

James surveyed the young man. His high shirt points were wilting visibly under the weight of his mortification, and his fobs clinked disconsolately from where they dangled in ornate profusion from a brilliantly embroidered waistcoat.

"I think you're looking quite fine today, Freddie," interposed Lady Hilary.

James smiled inwardly. Naturally, a damsel raised in the depths of Gloucestershire would consider this unformed sprig the epitome of manly perfection.

Actually, Hilary's motive in speaking so to Freddie was one of simple kindness. Privately, she thought him absurd in his sartorial excesses, but she had been acquainted with him since his birth and knew him to be a nice young man. His parents, a rough-hewn squire and his wife, were the bane of his existence.

Having attempted to see Freddie at his ease, she turned back to Mr. Wincanon, whose gaze traversed the room in obvious boredom. Her eyes narrowed. He looked remarkably as she had pictured him. Tall and angular, and definitely scholarly. On second glance, however, he seemed surprisingly authoritative for one whose passion was intellectual pursuits. He bore an air of strength—almost of command—that was both reassuring and vaguely unsettling. He was slender of build, but by no means slight, for she could not help but be aware of the muscled frame beneath his evening dress. His brown hair waved over a wide brow and aquiline features. His eyes, of a deep, velvety, chocolate brown, were penetrating and oddly compelling, and contained an expression of disillusionment. A disdainful smile curved lips that were surprisingly full and sensual. Altogether, he did not give the appearance of a pleasant gentleman, but then, she was not looking for charm in a prospective colleague.

For some minutes, the conversation was dominated by Mrs. Clapham, who attempted unsuccessfully to bludgeon Mr. Wincanon into a promise of participation in an upcoming church fête. Eventually, the lady accepted defeat, propelling her hapless off-spring toward another group of guests.

She was replaced almost immediately at Mr. Wincanon's side by Mrs. Horace Strindham and her daughter, Evangeline. Evangeline was some five years Hilary's junior and had recently returned from a successful Season in London. She was acknowledged as the neighborhood's reigning beauty, possessing the luxuriant dark hair currently in fashion. Her eyes, too, were dark, and her lashes swept in flirtatious profusion over exquisitely curved cheekbones.

Both Evangeline and her mother, after a single glance at Hilary, apparently forgot her existence.

"I believe I am acquainted with your aunt, Mr. Wincanon," said Mrs. Strindham, in the manner of one firing an opening salvo.

"And which aunt would that be, ma'am?" the gentleman queried, his gaze resting on Evangeline in bored appreciation. "I have so many, you see."

Mrs. Strindham remained unscathed. "Why, Lady Mary Waters, of course. We met not long ago when we were in London. Of course, we met so many people. My little girl"—she gestured fondly toward Evangeline—"was such a gadabout, we scarcely spent one night in our own home the whole time we were there. At any rate, I think it must have been at Lady Wolverhampton's ball—or no, perhaps at one of the Duchess of Mortlake's at-homes." She tapped Mr. Wincanon's wrist playfully with her fan. "You know how it is when one's daughter becomes wildly popular."

"Mm, no, I'm afraid I do not, ma'am," Mr. Wincanon replied with such blatant disinterest that Mrs. Strindham flushed.

"At any rate," she continued hastily, "Lady Mary is such a

lovely person." She turned to propel Evangeline forward. "By the by, may I present you to my daughter, Mr. Wincanon?"

Evangeline extended her hand, treating Mr. Wincanon to the full force of a blatantly coquettish gaze. Mr. Wincanon smiled dutifully.

"Charmed," he murmured again, releasing fingers that remained in his a fraction of a second too long.

"I am so pleased to make your acquaintance, sir." Evangeline's voice was sweet, yet slightly husky, belying the blush that spread over her cheeks. "My papa says that you are a renowned scholar." She breathed the words reverently, as though scholarship was the quality she sought above all in a man.

Mr. Wincanon merely inclined his head.

In the awkward pause that ensued, Mrs. Strindham hastily drew aim once more. "We are having a musicale in two weeks' time, Mr. Wincanon. Nothing elaborate, of course, just a few friends, but we would be delighted if you would join us."

"Oh, yes," added Evangeline shyly, allowing her incredible lashes full rein. "Do please come."

"I am afraid that will not be possible." Mr. Wincanon's voice was smooth but very firm. "I find that there is much to which I must attend right now, so that I cannot permit myself any social distractions."

Evangeline's expression of blank disbelief was almost comical. It had no doubt been a very long time since a man had refused her beckoning.

"Oh, but—" began Mrs. Strindham.

"Surely you can't mean that, my dear man!" The voice came from a lady who had inserted herself into the small group that now encircled Mr. Wincanon. She placed a graceful hand on her breast. "Emily Houghton," she said, smiling coquettishly. "We met the other day in the village. My Charlotte and I came in to choose some embroidery floss."

"Of course."

"Charlotte is right over there, speaking to the vicar's wife." Mrs. Houghton waggled her fingers to attract her daughter's attention.

Was she only imagining it, thought Hilary, or had a certain desperation crept into Mr. Wincanon's expression?

"I do hope you are not serious about avoiding social obligations," continued Mrs. Houghton, "for I am planning an alfresco breakfast for a week Tuesday. I do hope the weather will continue fine, for—"

"No!" The word burst from Mr. Wincanon like an expletive. "That is"—he went on in a milder tone—"I appreciate your, er, kindness, but I really must refuse. Now, if you will excuse me . . ." He turned away abruptly.

What a very rude gentleman, Hilary thought with some asperity. At least, she reflected somewhat smugly, she herself would not suffer such a rebuff when she approached Mr. Wincanon. The gentleman would, of course, be pleased that at least one female present was not a simpering lack-wit.

But never mind that now. Hilary bustled to where Mr. Wincanon had once more taken up a position, this time in conversation with Mr. Roger Whittlesham and two other men. His expression was pained as Whittlesham threw back his head in laughter at what was no doubt an extremely coarse witticism.

Hilary sighed, but, persevering, she made her way forward. As she reached Mr. Wincanon's side, the laughter suddenly ceased. Mr. Whittlesham and his friends drifted off for conversation elsewhere, leaving Hilary alone with her prey.

"I understand, Mr. Wincanon," she began, "that you have come here to—"

She was interrupted by the entrance of Dunston, the butler, who announced in stentorian tones that dinner was served. Blast! Mr. Wincanon, she knew, would be seated at her father's right hand during the meal, while she would take her place at the foot of the table. Between them would lie yards of napery, tableware, and guests. She would just have to wait until later to engage the famed antiquary in a meaningful discussion of her efforts at his villa.

Later proved to be well after dinner. As the gentlemen joined the ladies in the drawing room, Hilary, by dint of some extraordinarily deft footwork, outmaneuvered no less than four female guests to seat herself next to Mr. Wincanon. Marshaling her patience once more, she turned her attention to the pianoforte, where a procession of ladies and gentlemen, herself included, participated in a musical program. It was many minutes before Miss Cecily Broom lifted her fingers from the pianoforte, signaling the conclusion of the program. The guests, including Mr. Wincanon, applauded politely as one by one they rose, some drifting off to play cards, some to gather in conversational groups around the chamber.

Hilary stood and grasped Mr. Wincanon by the arm.

"Would you care for a turn on the terrace, sir?" she inquired, lifting her gaze to his rather forbidding features. "It is a very fine night."

A wary expression crossed his face. He glanced toward the long terrace doors, seeming to relax somewhat as he observed the number of ladies and gentlemen proceeding through them. Hilary thought she noted a flash of resignation in his eyes as he inclined his head and proffered his arm.

Once outside, they paced the stone paving in silence for some moments until Hilary turned to him impulsively.

"Actually, Mr. Wincanon, I asked you out here because there is something I wish to discuss with you."

The wary expression increased in magnitude and intensity. Mr. Wincanon halted abruptly.

"And what would that be, Lady Hilary?"

"Do call me Hilary. Everyone does."

"Oh, no. Surely not everyone." Hilary's eyes widened at the clearly discernible antipathy in his tone. "I prefer to maintain the proprieties, if you do not mind. What is it that you wished to discuss?"

Goodness, thought Hilary, startled. Even for an academic, the gentleman seemed inordinately stuffy. She shook her head impatiently.

"I want to talk to you about your Roman villa."

Mr. Wincanon's brows snapped together. "My Ro—! What about my Roman villa? How do you—?"

Hilary produced her sunniest smile. "Come, Mr. Wincanon. Your interest—and expertise—in Roman antiquities is well known, as is the reason you purchased Goodhurst. Everyone hereabouts has known of the villa's existence since Sir William's gamekeeper stumbled onto it, oh—it must be seven or eight years ago. No one paid much attention, except for me, of course, but—"

"You?" interposed Mr. Wincanon sharply.

"Yes." She smiled shyly. "You see, I share your passion. For antiquities," she added hastily as he frowned. "I have made a thorough study on the subject, and I have been conducting a—a scientific investigation of the remains at Goodhurst," she finished in a rush. "You are aware, of course, that your estate marches with Whiteleaves."

She halted, observing that Mr. Wincanon was staring at her with undisguised hostility.

"Let me get this straight, Lady Hilary." His voice was flint striking steel. "You have been digging in—in *my* Roman remains?"

"Um, yes." Hilary faltered. "But they were not yours at the time. Sir William—"

"Never mind Sir William!" snapped Mr. Wincanon, and Hilary gaped at him in astonishment. Never had a gentleman spoken to her in such a tone.

Mr. Wincanon drew a deep breath. "Forgive me, Lady Hilary. Allow me to complement you on your inventiveness, if not your originality, but I assure you your efforts are unnecessary. Now, just tell me. Have you truly visited the site of the Roman villa?"

An unpleasant sensation was beginning to churn in Hilary's interior. "Well, of course, I have. Didn't I just say so? And, as I also just said, I did not do so without permission."

"But not *my* permission."

"No, but—"

"Good God, I have not even had the opportunity to visit the place myself, and you"—he drew in another deep breath—"you have actually been digging up the site with a shovel?"

"Of course not," Hilary replied indignantly, watching with disfavor as Mr. Wincanon relaxed fractionally. "I used a trowel."

"Oh, my God." Mr. Wincanon rang long fingers through his hair. "Do you realize what damage you may have caused, you little—that is—Lady Hilary?"

Hilary, now thoroughly irritated, stamped her foot. "I did *not* do any damage. I was extremely careful, both in my excavations and in the handling of my finds. Now, if you—"

Mr. Wincannon grasped her shoulders.

"Your finds?" he echoed in a sibilant whisper.

"Yes. Not many, of course, but I have turned up several coins and some pottery shards—which I believe are Samian ware—as well as a shoe, and a comb," she added eagerly.

"Oh, my God," he murmured again. "And what did you do with

these finds? Are they now adorning a table in a drawing room, along with an imitation Egyptian vase or two?"

A tide of anger swept over Hilary. What a perfectly odious man! She drew herself up to her full five feet two inches and spoke through gritted teeth.

"I have placed all the artifacts from *your* villa in a locked cabinet, and I will be pleased to return them to you at your convenience."

"That's something, at any rate," said Mr. Wincanon, ignoring her wrathful demeanor. "I shall collect them within the week. In the meantime, concerning your mucking about in my villa—"

Hilary wrenched herself from his grasp. "I do not muck, Mr. Wincanon," she said with great precision. "I am trained in modern excavation—" She ignored his muffled snort. "I have read Lyson and Benhurst, and employ their methods. You will find that, having used such care, I have disturbed only a small section of the villa. In the future—"

"There will be no future for you in my villa, Lady Hilary. I must congratulate you, for you have succeeded admirably in your little plan. You have certainly gained my undivided attention. However, I must ask you to cease and desist your activities there."

"Cease and desist!" gasped Hilary furiously. "My little plan! Why, you arrogant, conceited, pompous fop!"

At this point, the Lady Hilary Merton, a redhead in every sense of the word, gave vent to her temper. Without further thought, in a manner taught to her by her brothers, she brought up her fist. The ensuing crack as it connected with Mr. Wincanon's jaw echoed in the cool serenity of the late summer evening.

Chapter Three

"All right," James muttered irritably to the reflection that stared accusingly at him from his shaving mirror. "I was a trifle rude last night."

Receiving no reply, he sighed.

"Oh, very well, I behaved like an unmitigated boor."

His reflection merely continued to glare. He swung away as his valet entered the room, and, accepting shirt and cravat, he pondered the events of the evening before.

"Not," he barked at Friske, "that I did not have just cause."

"Of course not, sir," murmured his valet soothingly.

"The rig she tried on me has not only been perpetrated unsuccessfully on many occasions, but, given her age and appearance, was ludicrous. Good God, she must be, what—sixteen?—and obviously has the brains of an underdeveloped parsnip."

"Quite so, sir."

Friske, having tenderly buttoned his master into his shirt, proffered a cravat and stood reverently aside. Mr. Wincanon, while regrettably lacking in a true sense of fashion, was possessed of a slender, elegant form. That the underlying frame seemed to be composed, to Friske's mind, of coiled steel, in no way impinged on the fit of his clothes. Better yet, Mr. Wincanon was particular about his appearance. The daily ritual of Tying the Cravat was always performed with due respect.

On this morning, however, his master disappointed him. Snatching the length of linen from Friske's fingers, James wrapped it perfunctorily around his throat and secured it with a knot that was little short of careless. Friske allowed his features to fall into an expression of pained disapproval. Which Mr. Wincanon ignored.

A knock sounded at the door, followed almost instantaneously by the entrance of a tall young man, meticulously garbed in a modest ensemble. His dark hair was clipped somewhat shorter than the current mode, and his eyes, also dark, were lit with a hint of laughter.

"Ah, Robert," said James to his secretary. "You're up and about early."

"As always, sir," replied Robert Newhouse primly. His lips quirked in a wry smile that contradicted his virtuous words. "I have brought the papers you requested."

"You are a jewel of promptness and efficiency, Robert—as always. You must have swotted into the small hours on these."

"You said you wanted them as soon as possible. In addition, I was hoping to creep off for a few hours this afternoon. Max Wentworth, your bailiff's son, has offered to show me some of the prime fishing spots on your land, with dinner at his home afterwards."

"Ah, plundering my resources, are you?"

Robert, who had come to know James Wincanon well over the two years he had been in the gentleman's employ, grinned.

"Well, it's not as though you'll likely be doing much plundering yourself, sir. Not that it wouldn't do you good to use God's fresh air and sunshine for something besides rummaging about in piles of old bricks. Speaking of which," he continued, "have you had a chance to commune with your Roman remains?"

James's lips tightened. "No. I have been busy with Wentworth and a hundred other things I would rather not be doing. I plan to look them over straightaway after breakfast this morning."

"Mm. It looks as though it's going to come on to mizzle momentarily."

"I shan't be deterred by a few drops of rain, Robert. I've definitely earned a treat. Particularly," he added with a grimace, "after last night."

Robert grinned. "Ah, yes. How went the dinner party?"

James snorted. "You were wise to make other plans. It was as deadly as predicted. I think the mamas of Gloucestershire are even more predatory than their London counterparts."

"Attacked on all sides, were you? Did not your host—an earl, isn't he?—protect you?"

James snorted again. "Protect me! He is a widower with an unwed daughter, and she more or less led the charge."

"Mmm. I think Max told me about her. Something of an original, I understand."

"To say the least. She seems the complete hoyden. She trotted out the breathless-interest-in-antiquities humbug. I'm afraid I deflated her rather rudely. Although I paid dearly for my transgression." Ruefully, he rubbed the shadowed bruise on his jaw and described for Robert the scene that had occurred in the darkness at Whiteleaves.

"Lord," he concluded. "Even in the moonlight, I could see those amber eyes, flecked with golden sparks and spitting like little volcanoes."

Robert chuckled. "She sounds most, er, unusual. However, she's somewhat older than she looks, and Max said she is known to be an aficionado. She's even been seen pottering in the villa remains. I understand Sir William allowed her free rein."

"So she says. She must have known for some months of my efforts to purchase Goodhurst and grasped the opportunity to begin an early campaign. Lord, out here in the wilds of Gloucesterhire, I had hoped to escaped the machinations of scheming females."

Robert smiled. He was well versed in his employer's problems with the gentle sex. He had stared unbelievingly at balls and dinner parties where Mr. Wincanon had been positively swarmed on by avaricious mamas and their daughters. They waylaid him on the streets, for God's sake. He had once seen a young woman fall to the ground in front of his horse in the park, so she could pretend the animal had run her down. And she was the daughter of an earl! Another female hired a street urchin to snatch her reticule so that Mr. Wincanon would rush to her assistance in Oxford Street.

"Well, it sounds as though you made short work of her." Robert continued offhandedly. "By the by, have you seen the current issue of *The Gentleman's Magazine*?" Receiving a negative head shake, he continued. "It seems as though your friend Mordecai Cheeke has scored another triumph."

"Cheeke!" exclaimed James. "Now what?"

"According to the article, he claims to have uncovered a temple to Ceres in Kent—near Tenterden."

"Oh, that. He mentioned it the last time we met—at a meeting of the Antiquarian Society, I believe."

Robert uttered a muffled snort and James raised his brows.

"You disapprove of the eminent Mr. Cheeke?"

Robert flushed. "It is not my place to approve or disapprove, sir, but I wouldn't be surprised if this Ceres thing is all a hum. Of course, I have only met him a few times, in company with other of your colleagues, but"—he blurted—"the man strikes me as a self-aggrandizing buffoon. In fact, I'm not so sure he wouldn't stoop to fraud to get his name in the newspapers."

"I must admit I've suspected the same," replied James mildly.

Robert continued somewhat belligerently. "It's my belief the fellow has, in the past, stolen some of your theories. Lord knows he's always sniffing around anytime you embark on a new project. In fact, I wouldn't be surprised to see him turn up here, once word of the villa circulates in antiquarian circles."

"Like a ferret," James agreed with some amusement. "With nose and whiskers aquiver. And now," he concluded briskly, donning the coat held out to him by Friske, "enough of this unpleasantness. The ancient past awaits. Have you breakfasted?"

The two gentlemen swung from the room, and an hour or so later, fortified with steak, eggs, and a tankard of ale, James departed from the house astride a mettlesome bay.

At about the same time, Hilary left her own abode, gowned in yet another serviceable muslin and sturdy boots, Jasper at her side in the gig. She had been advised by both her father and their housekeeper, Mrs. Fimble, against going out today on the grounds that the weather looked extremely threatening. She had ignored these warnings, however, not to be put off from the unpleasant task that lay ahead of her. In the seat between her and Jasper reposed a sturdy umbrella of oiled silk.

"Can you believe that anyone would act in such a rude, overbearing manner?" she demanded of the dog, whose only reply was a short, sharp bark.

"The nerve of the man, implying that . . ." She paused uncertainly. Just what was it that he had implied? What was all that about her plan? He seemed to think that she had lied about her interest in the ancient world, and that she was trying to perpetrate some sort of fraud on him. How perfectly ludicrous, to say nothing of insulting! Well, he would think twice before offering her such an indignity again.

She squirmed uncomfortably. Perhaps she had been a bit hasty in striking him. Fortunately, their quarrel had been unobserved, but certainly she had destroyed any chance of working with him. Of course, he had already ruined that opportunity.

She went over his words again. Inventive but unoriginal? And what had he meant about her efforts to gain his attention? Surely, he could not believe she would engage in a complicated fraud simply to attract his notice? The man must be possessed of a monumental conceit!

She glanced over her shoulder at the wooden box affixed to the rear of the gig. In it were packed the artifacts she had removed from the villa site over the past months. It had cost her a pang to give them up, for she had not thoroughly examined them or sketched them as she had planned to do, but she was determined to restore them to their legal owner at the earliest possible moment. She had no intention of taking them personally to the odious Mr. Wincanon. She would simply travel to the site, remove her tools from the little shed, and replace them with the boxful of artifacts. She would then send him a dignified note apprising him of her actions.

"With any luck," she confided icily to her companion, "I shan't be obliged to see or speak to the wretched creature ever again. Hopefully, as soon as he has completed his work at the site, he'll return to London, or wherever it is he resides permanently."

Again, Jasper had little to say in response beyond an obliging woof.

Passing the tower, she grimaced at the stone altar, which could be glimpsed through the trees. So much for the efficacy of offerings to ancient spirits. A mutter of thunder echoed her reflections.

Upon arriving at her destination, she was surprised to behold a handsome bay tethered to a tree nearby.

"Oh, no," she breathed, whereupon Jasper stiffened to attention. He bent his attention on the horse, but being trained not to offer gratuitous insults to neighboring equines, he merely sniffed the air inquiringly.

Halting the gig, Hilary glanced about before stepping down cautiously from the vehicle. Her feet had no sooner touched the ground than the sound of footsteps caused her to twist suddenly. She stumbled and fell to the ground in an ignominious heap. Her faithful hound, of course, sprang immediately to give her succor, subjecting her face to a thorough licking.

In the meantime, she found herself gathered into an embrace. At least, it might have been called that by some. To Hilary, it seemed as though she had been grasped by a piece of farm equipment. Two strong arms plucked her from the soil, dusted her off in a brisk fashion, and set her on her feet in a manner that fairly jarred her teeth.

Mr. Wincanon's greeting was no more courteous.

"What the devil are you doing here?" he growled. "I thought I told you—"

"And good morning to you, Mr. Wincanon," Hilary replied coldly, removing his fingers from her shoulders. "I did not expect to see you here."

"No, I don't suppose you did," said James peremptorily. "I thought I told you—" he began again.

At this point, Jasper, recalled to a sense of duty, took umbrage at this stranger in his domain, and the tone the man was taking with his personal human. He bared his teeth and uttered his most intimidating growl. The stranger merely glared at him.

"What the devil is that?" he inquired of Hilary.

"He is my dog, Jasper." Her tone by now had become positively glacial, but Mr. Wincanon merely grunted.

"That's not a dog. It's something that fell off a cathedral." He glanced around. "Is this animal your only companion, Lady Hilary? I wonder you should be careering about the countryside unaccompanied."

"Jasper provides all the protection I need," Hilary said stiffly. "What he lacks in beauty and form he more than makes up for in intelligence and devotion. I am perfectly safe in his company. In any event—"

Mr. Wincanon interrupted with a wave of his hand. "I thought I requested that you desist your activities on my site."

"No, you did not request—you ordered, Mr. Wincanon." She placed a hand on Jasper's head. The dog was becoming increasingly hostile and, although she was almost tempted to bite the insufferable Wincanon herself, she did not wish to escalate the already high level of antagonism. "I am merely here to retrieve my tools and to return the artifacts I found here." She indicated the wooden box with a disdainful sweep of her arm.

His interest in her presence abruptly evaporating, Mr. Wincanon swung about to approach the gig.

"Good Lord!" he exclaimed. "This container is completely unsuitable. Whatever is in here must be completely shattered."

"I think not," said Hilary through clenched teeth. "I wrapped each of the items individually and placed them very carefully. I believe you will find them to be in the same condition as when I turned them up from the earth."

"It would be better if you had not turned them up at all," snapped her antagonist. "Now, I have no idea where they were found—information that would have told me a great deal, for—"

"On the contrary, Mr. Wincanon. If you would take the time to look before indulging in ill-timed accusations, you will see that I have begun a set of grid lines with string. I noted in my log where each artifact was found and made a sketch of its position in the ground." She pulled a small notebook from her reticule and handed it to him.

"Ah," said Mr. Wincanon, looking more nonplussed than pleased. He swung about once more to the box.

"It's locked," he snapped.

Drawing a deep breath, Hilary dug once more into her reticule, this time dredging a key from its depths. This she also handed to him. Snatching it from her, he applied himself to the sturdy lock that guarded the contents of the box. Removing some of the packing, he uttered an involuntary grunt of satisfaction.

"Yes," he could be heard, muttering to himself. "Unmistakably Samian ware. Excellent specimens. And the coins . . . mm, yes."

"The earliest of them dates back to the reign of Trajan and I did not find any later than the early years of Postumas, so I'm assuming so far that the villa was built around 100 A.D. and abandoned some time after 250."

"Yes, yes," he said impatiently, then straightened abruptly to look at her.

"Who figured that out for you?"

Hilary stiffened. "I calculated it for myself, Mr. Wincanon. It was quite simple, actually—as you must know."

"Of course it is, to one who is familiar with Roman coinage and with the dates of the reigns of the Roman emperors."

"Precisely."

Unable to ignore the asperity in her tone, Mr. Wincanon grinned. Hilary almost gasped involuntarily at the change that swept over his features. Why, who would think that his appearance could be so improved with a smile or that it could take several years from his perceived age.

"Very well, Lady Hilary, I will concede, you have apparently learned a great deal in the few months you have studied Roman history."

Hilary stiffened. "Mr. Wincanon," she began carefully, "you seem to be laboring under the delusion that I was lying when I told you that I am a student of ancient history—particularly of the period when the Romans ruled Britain. I cannot understand why you think I would do this. Are you under the impression that I seek to curry favor with you?" Her gaze swept him over him contemptuously. "May I ask on what you base that assumption? I have been interested in antiquities since I was a child. In fact, long before I ever so much as heard your name.

"I will admit that I was pleased when I heard we were to be neighbors. I actually looked forward to meeting you, but this was solely because of your reputation in the antiquarian world. I have so longed to know someone with whom I could share my interest and further my education." Her voice wavered for a moment, but she continued swiftly. "Can you imagine? In my ignorance, I thought we might become colleagues. Allow me to apologize for my temerity. Had I any idea that you are a boorish, conceited clod, believe me, I would never so much as spoken to you."

She swiveled on her heel and hastened to the gig, followed by Jasper, who, though bewildered by this hostility on the part of his mistress toward an apparently nonthreatening fellow human, growled his support. Mounting the gig, Hilary turned once more toward Mr. Wincanon, who stood motionless with shock.

"I wish you joy of your remains, Mr. Wincanon. They possess neither warmth nor life, but then neither does their owner." With which Parthian shot, she signaled her horse to move forward and sped from the scene.

Chapter Four

James stared after the rapidly diminishing vehicle.

Phew! he thought dazedly. What a little termagant! And Robert was right. She certainly did not seem lacking in intelligence. In addition, given the apparent sincerity of the imprecations she had hurled at him, one might almost believe she was, as she claimed, a devotee of the burgeoning science of archaeology. He smiled grimly. He had met females of this persuasion, but they were plain, no-nonsense sort of women, usually on the far side of forty and austere in appearance and demeanor. None of them were in the first blush of youth, nor were they possessed of eyes of molten gold, or hair like drifting fire. James shook himself irritably. She was merely another simpering damsel bent on acquiring his wealth and status for herself, and now she was furious with him for confronting her with this fact.

Which was a good thing. He certainly did not need any distractions in the work he had laid out for himself.

A rumble of thunder caught his attention and he frowned. The sky had become distinctly ominous, with low, roiling clouds the color of ill-polished pewter. He supposed he should not have let Lady Hilary set out on her return journey. The minx was likely to return home soaking wet, a fate perhaps well-deserved, but being a gentleman of sensibility, he hoped he was not the sort who would take pleasure in her misfortune. Ah well, it was too late to overtake her now. At any rate, with luck she would arrive home before the storm broke.

Speeding toward Whiteleaves, Hilary was immersed in the same sort of reflection. Peering at the sky, she was dismayed to observe flashes of lightning accompanying the thunder that had phased from ominous mutterings to muted booms. An unladylike expletive escaped her as the first drops of rain spattered in the dust of the road.

To be truthful, a good measure of her invective was directed at James Wincanon. Not only had he practically driven her from his land with a fiery sword, but he had accused her of trying to hoodwink him in the most underhanded manner! Lord, he must think himself a combination of the god Apollo, King Solomon, and—and Ball Hughes, reputedly the richest man in England. Well, Mr. Wincanon *was* wealthy, but surely—dear heaven, did he think she was after his money?

Another crash of thunder wrenched her thoughts from this unpromising path and she unfolded her umbrella against the worsening rain. The protection afforded by this convenience, however, proved meager. The wind had picked up, driving the rain into her face, and even by dint of tilting the umbrella, she was soaked through within a few minutes.

She glanced at Jasper, seated beside her, seemingly unaware that it was raining at all, though water streamed into his eyes and through his shaggy coat. How fortunate it was that he was unafraid of thunder and lightning, thought Hilary. When another bolt flashed, Jasper merely opened his cavernous jaw in a doggy grin and thumped his tail soddenly on the seat.

Hilary peered into the curtain of rain. Goodness, it was only eleven o'clock in the morning, but the world had darkened to an unhealthy twilight. The wind increased, producing an odd, keening sound that seemed to writhe through the heavy air in an ominous warning. Sylvia, the placid mare that pulled her gig, snorted suddenly and reared on her hind legs. She whinnied loudly in agitation and it was with difficulty that Hilary forced her to her task.

The wind rose to an even higher pitch. The air felt thick. It was hard to breathe, and in a few moments Hilary felt herself engulfed in the same primal, instinctive fear that affected Sylvia. Her pulse pounded. It was becoming harder and harder to control the horse. The wind was a howling, destructive entity that tore at her clothes and the umbrella.

The Roman tower loomed in the near distance, and making a decision, Hilary drew on the reins. The tower would not afford much protection, but she determined to take shelter in its crumbling remains at least until the rain abated a little.

She was able to see now only by the lightning flashes that lit the scene in eerie, jagged images. Clutching her umbrella in one trembling hand, she descended from the gig. Jasper scrambled after her. Hilary led Sylvia, still harnessed to the gig, to the side of the road. Leaves whipped at her face and tree limbs tore at her skirts. Tying Sylvia to a sturdy oak, she gathered Jasper in her arms and attempted without success to lift him from the ground. Giving up, she tugged at his collar and began to lead him toward the tower.

At that moment, a bolt of lightning rent the sky with such force that it seemed the whole universe must be shattered with its force. It arced overhead, in a blinding, sizzling crackle that culminated in a fiery explosion at the top of the tower. In the next instant a cataclysmic crack of thunder sounded. It shook the ground in a roar that seemed to presage the end of the world.

With a shriek, Hilary flung herself to the ground and scrambled under the gig, with Jasper, at last as terrified as his mistress, plunging right behind her. Throwing an arm about him, she buried her face in his coat, almost sobbing in her fright. For what seemed an eternity she remained thus, listening to the reverberations of the lightning strike. A sharp, pungent odor filled the air, which fairly throbbed. Hilary's heart pounded an accompaniment to its electric rhythm.

Then, suddenly, all was still.

After a few moments, Hilary cautiously poked her head out from under the gig. Oddly, the rain had completely stopped, although a heavy mist clung to the surrounding trees. The wind had died and once more birds twittered as they went about their business. The only other sound to be heard was an abrupt clink of metal, coming from the tower, and the cry of a human voice raised in obvious fear and startlement.

The next moment, through the mist, an apparition hurtled from the narrow aperture at the bottom of the tower, his mouth open in a terrified scream. Hilary stared in disbelief. It was not the figure itself that riveted her attention. He was apparently middle-aged and somewhat overfed. It was his style of dress that caused her eyes to start from her head. The man was clothed in some sort of armor! In fact, he looked like . . . She halted, dazed, unable to complete her thought.

He continued toward her, scattering tatters of fog in his wake. The momentum of his headlong flight from the tower carried him to within a few feet of her, where he stopped abruptly. Hilary caught her breath. The man wore a short, woolen tunic underneath a metal corselet fashioned from strips of metal. The strips lay horizontally across his chest and dropped vertically from his waist to his knees. The whole was cinched with two leather belts, crossed over his waist and hips. From one of these, on his right, hung a sheathed dagger, and from his left, another leather sheath, no doubt crafted to contain the sword that he waved threateningly above his head. Over all, he wore a heavy woolen cloak, affixed at his shoulder with an ornate pin. His feet were shod with sturdy, heavily studded sandals, laced with leather thongs. His head was bare, and pink skin shone through a sparse covering of graying brown hair.

What did he think he was got up as? wondered Hilary dazedly. What was a stranger doing stumbling about in the rain in this ludicrous fashion, dressed in the garb of a Roman soldier and wielding what looked like an eminently serviceable sword? Hilary shrank farther beneath the meager shelter of the gig, pulling Jasper with her.

At her movement, the man jerked his head in her direction. He stared wildly at the gig for a moment, perceiving Hilary almost immediately. He stumbled toward her, bellowing incomprehensibly. Reaching beneath the gig, he grasped her by one shoulder, and began pulling her from her shelter.

Jasper took immediate exception. With a snarl of outrage, he wriggled free from Hilary's arms and lunged at the man, who raised his arm as though to cleave the hapless animal in two with his sword. With a cry, Hilary wrenched herself from the man's grip and flung herself protectively over her pet. For an instant, she simply stared upward, her gaze a combination of supplication, fear, and anger.

The man stared back, and Hilary was surprised to find her emotions mirrored in his eyes. Except, perhaps for the supplication. For a long moment he stood above her, sword upraised, droplets of moisture flying from its blade. What seemed to be a stream of threats poured from his lips. At last, the sword wavered uncertainly. The next moment, he sheathed it and, silent at last, gestured for Hilary to come out from under the gig. When she merely thrust herself backward, he shook his head and put his hand out in a gesture that was more impatient than threatening.

"Ego tibi non nocebo," he said, in a tone whose volume was measurably reduced.

Good God, she could not understand a word he was saying!

"Who are you?" she asked in a quavering voice. "And what are you doing here?"

"Unh?"

Well, she understand that, at least.

"Who are you?" she said again, slowly and clearly.

She received the same response, followed by another gesture. At last, Hilary accepted the hand extended to her, shushing Jasper, whose suspicions were in no way allayed.

She noted distractedly that the man was fairly tall, and very broad. He was not obese precisely, but his style of dress certainly emphasized his barrel chest and considerable paunch. He surveyed her curiously, and glancing down at her gown, she blushed. Goodness, she must look like a drowned chicken, drenched through as she was, with her bonnet dripping into her eyes and her hair lying in sodden strands over her shoulders.

His gaze next moved to the gig and his eyes widened. Stepping closer to it, he ran his hands over the frame, then approached her horse, which still displayed its anxiety over the recent lightning strike.

"Quis tu es, et ubi hoc vehiculum insolitum nanciscisti?" he asked in a rumbling voice.

Hilary bit her lip in exasperation. Why was the man speaking in gibberish? But . . . There was a faint familiarity in his words.

"I'm sorry," she replied. "I don't understand you." She pointed to herself. "I am Lady—that is, I am Hilary Merton." She swiveled her finger in the opposite direction. "What is your name?"

"Cur in nugis dices, tu femina stulta?" the man inquired irritably. *"Ubi hoc plaustrum nanciscistie? Et equus . . . Quid genus est?"*

Hilary's ears pricked up. Yes, she knew some of the words he spoke. *Femina.* Woman? And—*equus* meant horse—in Latin! What was going on here? Was he some sort of lunatic? An educated lunatic, perhaps. Although, he certainly did not give the appearance of an intellectual.

Clearing her throat, Hilary said, *"Ego sum Hilary Merton. Quid nomen tibi est?"*

A look of satisfaction sprang into the man's small brown eyes. He thumped his chest. *"Ego sum Marcus Minimus Rufus,"* he announced proudly.

He *was* speaking Latin, Hilary concluded disbelievingly.

"Where do you live?" she asked, in the same tongue.

"I am from—what is the matter?" the man queried abruptly as Hilary waved her hand.

"You must either speak more slowly," she said haltingly, "or couch your words in English, please, or I shall not be able to understand you."

"Ing-glish? Is that some sort of local, tribal jargon? It must be, for your Latin is awful. Are you from beyond the frontier then?"

"N-no, I—Where did you say you live?"

"I am stationed at Isca."

The world seemed to spin in great, wobbling circles. Isca? That was the old Roman name for Caerleon.

"However," continued Rufus, "I am currently part of a detachment maintained at Corinium."

"Corinium," echoed Hilary in a hollow voice. Corinium, in Roman times had been the second largest city in Britain after London and was now the quiet little town of Cirencester, located just a few miles from Whiteleaves. Walking unsteadily to the side of the road, she sat down with a thump on a handy boulder.

Rufus, meanwhile, was gazing about him once more. "I don't understand," he said slowly. "I had a horse tethered, but I don't—" He stopped suddenly, his jaw dropping and his eyes bulging. "The tower. Gods, what has happened to my tower?"

He pointed a trembling finger at the tower, which had sustained remarkably little damage from the lightning strike and stood as it had always done, a lone, ruined sentinel near the Fosse Way.

"Your tower?" she asked.

"Yes. Well, no, not *my* tower, but—Gods, never mind that. What happened to it? It looks as though it was hit by a thousand loads of *ballista*. And my detachment—where are they?"

Hilary was having difficulty following all this, but she caught the gist. Evidently, Rufus knew the tower as a whole structure and was astonished to find that it was now a ruin. An uncomfortable train of thought was gearing up in her mind.

"Ah, Mr. Minimus—" she began hesitantly, uncertain as to how to proceed. "Can you tell me today's date?"

He stared at her blankly.

"Ump, now that I come to think of it, it is the *nones* of *Septembrius* already."

September. The *nones* . . . that would be the fifth, which was a little off, but still . . .

"What year?" she continued, holding her breath.

"Why, it is the second year of the consulship of Trajan."

Again, the surrounding scene spun before Hilary. Good God, the man thought he was living in the year 100 A.D. or so! She was in the presence of a dangerous lunatic. She darted a glance at Jasper, glad of the protection of his size and his teeth.

"Listen," said Rufus suddenly. "I seem to have lost my transportation. I must get into Corinium and report the destruction of the tower and my missing men. Your rig seems serviceable. Will you take me into the city?"

"Me?" Hilary squeaked. "Oh, no. That would be—"

Rufus advanced on her and Hilary jumped nervously. Jasper bared his teeth. Rufus, however, merely removed a leather pouch hanging from his knife belt. Seating himself on another boulder, he opened it and withdrew a handful of coins. "I will pay you for your trouble, of course," he said, picking through the coins. He finally proffered two of them, and Hilary gasped. Though not precisely new-minted, they were obviously recent in issue, and on them could be clearly discerned the heads of Roman emperors. Vespasian COS II, read one, and Titus, IMP XIII the other. Accepting them in trembling fingers, she examined them carefully.

"May I see the rest?" she asked, her voice ragged.

Rufus glared at her suspiciously, but he dropped the coins into her hand. Hilary turned them over carefully, one by one. She had seen their like many times, but mostly in sketches in history tomes. One was a duplicate of a specimen she had unearthed at Goodhurst. The coins she held in her hand, however, bore no trace of the ravages of centuries.

These were undoubtedly genuine and they had undoubtedly been minted within the last few years. Despite all reasoning to the contrary, they appeared to be ancient Roman coins, but they were not ancient. They were new. The implications of this concept surged through Hilary.

No, it was impossible. It was ludicrous. She was as crazy as the man standing before her to so much as consider such a notion. The idea of someone traveling through time from Roman Britain to pop up unannounced in the nineteenth century was—was insane. And yet . . . Her thoughts returned to the earth-shattering bolt of lightning that had struck the tower. Could such an eruption of a natural force have produced a rent in the fabric of time itself?

No, of course not.

Still . . .

She gazed dubiously at the man calling himself Minimus Rufus, noting with dismay that his returning stare was increasingly wrathful. She wished above all things to be away from him, but she did not feel she could leave him here. He was obviously all about in this head and could not be left alone. Besides, what if he really—? She clamped her mind shut on this frightening line of thought and returned her attention to Rufus. With a muttered oath, he rose from his boulder and strode down the lane toward the Fosse Way.

"No!" she cried. "Wait!"

Rufus halted and turned expectantly. Hilary nodded her head and the problematic legionary hurried back to her. She hastened to the gig, and untied Sylvia from the oak. She led horse and vehicle back to the road, but when the soldier would have seated himself in the driver's place, she indicated vigorously that she would take the reins. She gestured to Jasper, who sprang up into the seat, re-inforcing his mistress' wishes with one or two succinct growls. Scowling, Rufus slid his ample posterior toward the other side of the seat and Hilary took her place. She pulled the gig about, and in a moment, the two, with Jasper between them, moved smartly down the lane.

At this point, Rufus took umbrage once more. He might be con-fused as to his correct place in time, but he realized clearly that they were not headed toward his desired destination.

"No!" he roared, reaching across Jasper to grasp at the reins. "Corinium!"

Jasper promptly solved this contretemps by sinking his teeth into Rufus' arm. It was protected by the leather wristlets he wore, but still the action proved effective. Rufus jerked back into his seat, reaching for the dagger at his belt, but, to Hilary's vast relief, he seemed to think better of his action and subsided with a rumble of ancient oaths.

As they crossed the Fosse Way, Rufus looked up and down the highway, but Hilary proceeded straight across it.

"Via Martius?" he queried, swiveling his head around to keep it in sight.

"Via Fosse," Hilary stated. Surely, if Rufus was pretending to be a visitor from Roman Britain, he would know the correct name of this most important highway. Then she recalled with a sinking feeling, that the Fosse Way was a fairly modern denotation. The road's name in Roman times was no longer known.

Wordless, she concentrated her attention on her driving. She had turned the gig around without thought. She did not stop to ponder her reason for doing so. She did not know what to make of Mar-cus Minimus Rufus and his preposterous claim. She knew only, with an instinct as strong as it was inexplicable, where she must go now.

Chapter Five

The short journey with Minimus Rufus proved astonishing and informative, if one could be brought to believe his tale. To Hilary's incredulous ears, he had divulged that he was an armorer in the Spanish Cohort of the Second Augusta Legion, and he was a Roman citizen. She felt herself growing positively dizzy as he told her that he was married—not legally, for under Roman law, legionaries were not allowed to wed until after retirement. However, he had lived with his Maia, a woman from Aquae Sulis, for a number of years and considered her his wife.

Against her will, Hilary was coming to believe that the man calling himself Minimus Rufus was neither a lunatic nor a fraud. Not only did he possess information shared by a very small minority of scholars, but it would have taken an actor of almost superhuman skill to portray a man from another time so skillfully. She watched as he seemed to grow more puzzled during the remainder of their journey. After awhile, his chatter stilled and he gazed about him in increasing unease until they pulled up at James Wincanon's villa site in a spray of gravel.

To Hilary's relief, Mr. Wincanon's horse was still tethered there, and as they approached, the gentleman himself emerged from the shed. His eyes narrowed as Hilary drew the gig to a halt. They widened as his gaze shifted to her companion.

"What the devil—?" he began.

"Please, Mr. Wincanon. I know this looks a little odd, but—"

"My good woman," he said gratingly, his gaze sweeping over her companion, "a little odd does not cover it by half. If you have some idea of further expounding on your expertise in antiquities—"

Hilary stamped her foot. "My good man," she blurted, "if you can bring yourself to suppress your absurd prejudices for a moment, I have something of interest to relate—and someone I would like you to meet." She gestured toward Rufus, who had descended somewhat stiffly from the gig. Jasper, who had evidently decided the stranger posed no further threat, romped at his heels.

"Mr. Wincanon," she said formally, "may I present Marcus Minimus Rufus? He is a visitor from—from a great way off."

James gaped at the man who approached him, right arm slightly raised in a salute. He turned to glare at Lady Hilary, noting irritably that even in her disreputable, sodden state, she looked like a youthful sprite out for a morning frolic in the forest.

A visitor? Good God, what kind of May game was she playing with him now?

Was the fellow got up for a fancy dress ball? If so, he'd done a bang-up job. Was he an antiquary? What had she called him? Minimus Something.

James observed that the stranger was gazing at him with what seemed to him an exaggerated curiosity. Tentatively, he fingered one of James's brass coat buttons and muttered something under his breath. James started. Was that Latin?

"Now, see here," he began, slapping away the stranger's hands. At this, however, the man stiffened and—yes, he actually growled.

The man turned to Lady Hilary and spoke again. Or, rather, bellowed.

"Ego tempun satis effundi cum te et tus amico absurdis. Me oportet ire!"

James stared at him, stunned, as he stalked away in the direction of the gig. Before he could mount the vehicle, however, Lady Hilary spoke softly.

"Jasper."

Immediately, the dog sprang to his feet and raced to stand before the armored stranger, growling far more menacingly than had the man. Since Jasper stood waist-high, James was not surprised when the stranger halted. He swore, but he halted.

Lady Hilary approached him. She spoke falteringly—and, thought James uncharitably—ungrammatically in Latin.

"Minimus, I know this must seem very—odd to you, but please be patient. Something has apparently happened. Something very strange, and you are going to need help. Please let me confer with this gentleman." She waved a somewhat disdainful arm toward James.

Leading the unwilling stranger, precisely, thought James in some amusement, as though he were a recalcitrant guest at a formal reception, toward a low stone wall, she bade him be seated, leaving Jasper to guard him. The man subsided with a sullen air, glaring balefully at the dog standing purposefully before him. She then turned back to James.

"Now, then, Mr. Wincanon," she said crisply. "Please sit down. I know I am banished from your precious site, but I believe that what I have to tell you will change your mind."

She drew a deep breath. "You see, as I was on my way home, lightning struck the—"

"Yes, I heard the crash from here. Surely it didn't—Are you all right? It sounded as though it must have brought the sky down."

"Well, it didn't. But it did bring something almost as astonishing."

Lady Hilary described the events following the lightning strike in succinct but complete detail. At the end of her narrative, she put her hand to her head, as though suddenly overwhelmed.

"I know this all sounds incredible, but I simply didn't know what to do next—so I brought him to you."

James stiffened, but said not unkindly. "And just what is it you wish me to do?"

At this, Lady Hilary stared up at him. "Why—why, talk to him, I suppose. Try to ascertain—"

"Come, come now, dear lady." Mr. Wincanon smiled in what Hilary could only describe as a patronizing manner. "I acquit you of any part in this—this faradiddle, but surely you cannot expect me to take this charlatan's tale seriously."

Hilary sighed. "I can't blame you for your skepticism. I certainly felt the same myself. But to what purpose would a man perpetrate such a monumental—and complex—fraud?"

"I'm sure I don't know, but he must have some nefarious plan in mind. People, after all, do not stroll about the corridors of time as they would on an afternoon tour of the British Museum. Or, perhaps he is mentally deranged."

"If he is, he possesses a great deal of knowledge about the Roman occupation of Britain. Does he look like a scholar to you? And the coins—oh yes, wait until you see the coins." Briefly she described their apparent veracity. "Where could he have come by them? When you see them, I am sure you will judge them quite authentic—and recently minted. Mr. Wincanon," she finished, "all I'm asking is that you talk to him and draw your own conclusions."

She grinned suddenly. "And just think. What if he really was hurled from the first century to the nineteenth by a lightning bolt? Would you not enjoy a conversation or two with him?"

James gazed thoughtfully at the young woman before him. Good Lord, she must be all about in her head to approach him with such a piece of nonsense. Or perhaps simply gullible. Just look at her. She moved with a youthful, coltish grace and her wide, amber eyes were those of a complete innocent. She claimed to be an expert in antiquities, yet she gave the appearance of the veriest schoolchild. On the other hand, she seemed to have some familiarity with the subject. And she did speak fair Latin.

He thought back to the lightning that had rent the sky. The resulting thunder had shaken the ground beneath his feet. According to Lady Hilary, Rufus had described a similar occurrence just before his alleged transference through time. If a man in another era were to be the victim of such a strike on the same spot where lightning would again strike a number of centuries later, was it possible . . . ?

No, of course it wasn't. But James glanced speculatively at the older man, still fulminating where he sat near the gig. His gaze wandered over the armor plating and thickly studded boots. His garb was undoubtedly that of a Roman legionary stationed perhaps in Caerleon circa 100 A.D. In addition, his garments and the metal strips that made up his armor showed signs of everyday wear.

James sighed. At any rate, it did not look as though he would be rid of either one of his visitors until he probed the matter further. He approached the old warrior, who glared at him with obvious suspicion.

"My dear sir," began James in his best classical Latin, "we seem to have a most unusual situation here. The young lady"—he gestured toward Hilary—"says that you are in possession of a small quantity of coins. May I see them?"

Rufus' expression of suspicion deepened. It took some effort on James's part to assure him that he had no designs on the legionary's pocket change. Grudgingly, the warrior pulled out his pouch and emptied it into James's palm. Seating himself on the gig's mounting step, James examined the little hoard.

"Mmp," he grunted. The coins certainly did look authentic. One by one, he turned them over in his hand. There were two sestercii, six denarii, ten aes, and twenty quandrans. Just what one might expect a soldier to carry with him on a routine outing. All bore the heads of various emperors from Augustus to Trajan with appropriate details on the reverses.

James lifted his head to gaze penetratingly at the man who called himself Marcus Minimus Rufus. The older man did not flinch, but thrust forward an already pugnacious chin and stared back.

"My good fellow," said James, only to be rewarded with a surly grunt.

"Minimus Rufus," James began again. "May I ask you—what year is this?"

Minimum grunted again, this time in exasperation. "The little wench there asked me the same thing. It is the second year of the consulship of the Imperator, Trajan."

"Oh, God." James drew a deep breath. "Minimus Rufus, old man, I think you'd better sit down."

At this, Minimus stiffened.

"Who are you calling old?" he asked belligerently. "I am in my prime—my forty-eighth year, if you must know. I've been—"

"Yes, yes," interposed James placatingly. "I only meant— Please. Sit." The legionary seated himself with a great show of reluctance on the remains of a stone wall. "Rufus, I must tell you that the year is actually eighteen hundred and eighteen in the Year of our Lord."

Obviously, James's words meant nothing to Minimus, for his response was a vacant stare.

"Um," said James by way of explanation.

Hilary spoke up in irritation. "What he means to say, Minimus Rufus, is that the lightning strike you suffered some moments ago apparently propelled you forward in time. You have made a leap of approximately seventeen hundred years."

Not unnaturally, this statement deprived Minimus of speech. His eyes bulged alarmingly and his mouth opened and closed several times.

"Lunatics!" he cried at last. "I am fallen in with lunatics! Leave me!" He struggled to his feet, ignoring Jasper's minatory growls. "Let me be on my way!"

Casting a "now-see-what-you've-done" glance at James, Hilary stepped forward and set a hand on Minimus' brawny shoulder.

Jasper stepped up to offer his enthusiastic assistance, but it was several moments before Minimus subsided enough for James to resume speaking.

"No, no," he said soothingly. "It is all true, and I believe I can prove it to your satisfaction. You stand now on my land. Come with me to my, er, villa."

This produced another burst of invective from Minimus and this time it took much persuasion on the part of both Hilary and James, to say nothing of Jasper's persistent urging, to propel him into the gig.

James, still unconvinced of Minimus' authenticity, rode beside the gig as Hilary drove the short distance to the manor house. He did not speak, but listened carefully as Hilary interrogated the legionary. He did not know whether he was more astonished at the perspicacity of Hilary's questions, and her ability to calm Rufus' sensibilities or the man's almost offhandedly correct answers. Answers that revealed a comprehensive knowledge of the world of ancient Rome and its colony, Britannia. James watched Minimus carefully as they rounded the last bend of the drive and the house came into full view.

Once more, the warrior's mouth fell open. He gaped vacantly at the structure, constructed of the famous Bath stone that seemed to gather all the light of the afternoon into itself. After a long moment, he turned first to Hilary and then to James, fairly gabbling in consternation.

"It's all right, Rufus," said Hilary hastily. "This is what grand houses look like now. I know it must seem very large to you, but you need not be frightened."

Immediately, Rufus jerked upright. "Frightened? I? A soldier of the empire? I have seen many buildings of this size, of course. Nero's Golden House in Rome would make this place look like a thatched hut. However, I've not seen many so tall. And with so many windows. They appear to be glazed," he concluded in some awe.

James chuckled. "Yes, we can make glass easily now, and quite cheaply. Of course, we have to pay a tax on our windows, but that is another problem."

Rufus settled back in the gig, for the first time seeming to accept the possibility that James had told him the truth. His expression deepened to one of dismay and an age-old fear of the unknown.

When the odd little party drew up to the manor's front door, James dismounted from his horse and assisted Hilary from the gig. Rufus also clambered down from the gig, and stood, with Jasper at his heels, surveying the manor house.

Hilary stepped up to him, murmuring encouragement. Watching her, James was forced to admit once again, that if one took the time to really look at Lady Hilary she was not unattractive. Her features were well-formed and that mop of red hair lent them a certain incandescent charm.

He frowned. Not that he was even slightly susceptible to feminine charm, no mater the erudition that lay behind it.

Not to his surprise, Rufus huffed for a moment, then allowed Hilary to place her hand on his arm. She smiled encouragingly as she led him up the stairs and, when the door was swung open by Burnside, the awe-inspiring butler inherited by James from Sir William, Rufus allowed himself to be ushered into the house with no further demur. Burnside, on his part, refrained from displaying so much as a flicker of ill-bred curiosity regarding the extremely odd appearance of one of his master's guests, nor the fact that the other, though she was well known to him, should really not have been here at all sans chaperon.

"Send Mrs. Armbruster to me, if you please, Burnside," were James's first words to the butler. "And please send someone to Whiteleaves to fetch Lady Hilary's abigail. As you can see, she was caught in the rainstorm that occurred awhile ago."

"Very good, sir. And the, er, animal, sir?" Burnside indicated Jasper, who was attempting to insert his large form through the door as unobtrusively as possible.

"You may have it removed to the stables," said James firmly. "Although he is not, as one might suppose, to be ridden."

At a gesture from Burnside, a hovering footman ran to grasp Jasper by the collar, but the dog forestalled this indignity by the simple expedient of once more baring his teeth. The footman retreated to a prudent distance.

"We can simply leave Jasper outside," said Hilary icily. "He will be no trouble—though he may howl a little." She swept past James and the butler into the house.

Rufus, on his part, remained silent, absorbing his surroundings with fearful curiosity. Silently, his gaze wide, he took in damask hangings, crystal chandeliers, armorial bearings and heavily upholstered furnishings. By the time James ushered him into the library, Hilary trailing in their wake, he appeared ready to explode.

"Gods!" he exclaimed as James shut the door. "Tell me again where in time I am. And what is the language you speak now? Am I still in Britannia? Who are you? You cannot be citizens of Rome, but you do not look like Dobunnii. What—"

James raised a hand. "We will answer all your questions, Rufus, in good time. But first I wish you would answer some of mine."

Rufus snarled. "I have done nothing but answer your questions since we met. Now, it is my turn."

James remained unmoved. "I will tell you anything you wish to know, but I must also tell you that I am not at all convinced that you are the genuine article."

"What?" gasped Hilary. "Good heavens, Mr. Wincanon, how can you doubt him? I will very readily admit that the situation is difficult to comprehend, but it must be apparent to the meanest intelligence that Rufus is precisely who he says he is—a simple soldier who somehow has been hurled through time."

James's chocolate-brown eyes narrowed, and once more Hilary was struck by the unnerving strength in his gaze. "But you see, my girl, I flatter myself that I possess a bit more than the meanest intelligence, and I am not easily duped. Anyone can craft the garb of a legionary, and—"

"Oh, really?" Hilary smiled thinly. "And just who of your acquaintance has the knowledge to do such a thing with such minute, correct detail? Aside from your colleagues, of course, but do you really think Professor Barnstaple or—or Lord Emsbrooke or any of the other members of the Antiquarian Society would lend themselves to such a lark?"

"I can think of one who might," muttered James, "but I cannot see him spending his valuable time on a mere prank."

Hilary glanced at him curiously but said nothing.

Since this interchange had been conducted in English, Rufus had turned his attention elsewhere. Moving to one of the bookshelves, he removed a volume and held it gingerly in his hands. He riffled through the pages for a moment before turning an inquiring look toward James.

"It is a book," said James. "We use them now in the place of parchment scrolls. They are more durable and easier to read."

"Ah," said Rufus. "But I cannot read this."

"You can read?" asked Hilary interestedly.

"Of course, I can read. Do you think me an ignorant barbarian?"

James went to another shelf and plucked a volume from the shelf. "Here, try this."

He handed the book to Rufus, who examined it carefully.

"Histories"—he read aloud—"by P. Cornelius Tacitus. Mmpfh. Never heard of him."

"He was Agricola's son-in-law." Rufus stared at him blankly. "Julius Agricola." James's tone was dry. If the man had never heard the name of one of Britain's most famous governors, there could be little doubt he was a fraud.

"Yes, of course I know who he is," retorted Rufus testily. "He was some years before my time, though. I understand he was a good man, but I know nothing of his son-in-law, or his daughter, for that matter."

"Oh?" James asked quickly. "And what about Agricola's predecessor?"

Let us now see how much the fellow really knows about first-century Britain.

"Ah well then, I know even less about Julius Frontinius. He brought the Silurians to heel in Wales, and seemed to have a bug up his arse about public works. Never plant a garden when you can put up a building, was his motto. No skin off my nose, of course, except that he set a precedent, and it's us soldiers who are expected to provide the grunt work. That's what I was doing in the tower, by the way."

James and Hilary exchanged glances and James knew a twinge of surprise. Lady Hilary might be young and flighty, but she had an unsettling pair of eyes. They were huge and, he decided, not so much amber as a deep gold, although sometimes they seemed more copper—and they displayed a bright intelligence that, despite himself, he found fascinating. He shook himself and looked away quickly.

To Rufus, he said, "Yes? What about the tower?"

"Construction was started about fifty years ago, before the frontier was secured. It was to be a watchtower—being right on the Via Martius—with a small fort attached. For some reason it was never completed, but it was never dismantled. So, now, what with Corinium developing into a major city—maybe a *colonia* some day—Quietus—he's the present governor—Avidius Quietus—came in a year ago—apparently decided a theater would be nice— I hear he's something of an intellectual, and ordered that the stones from the old tower should be brought to Corinium for that purpose.

"I was among a small detail sent to do the job. And a back-breaker it was, too."

"I thought you were an armorer," interposed Hilary.

"Well and I am, and a good one. I was sent along to Corinium to service the troops there, but, as I said, the detachment is a small one, and there's been little tribal activity for years, so there is not much need for my skills, at least for the moment. I was standing in the wrong place at the wrong time, unfortunately, and got volunteered for the job." He grunted disgustedly. "You'd think I'd know better by now after twenty years. I guess I must be getting slow on my feet."

Despite himself, James grinned, and Hilary was made dismayingly aware of the stirring in her insides thus engendered. "I understand the problem," he said. "I've been caught that way, myself."

Rufus' brows lifted. "You are in the army?"

"I was."

Turning at a small sound from Hilary, he directed a frown at her. "Yes?"

"Nothing," said Hilary hastily. "I was only surprised—that is, I did not know you had served. Were you at Waterloo?"

"No," answered James shortly. "I sold out in '14, when we thought we had Boney safely kenneled on St. Helena. I served on the Peninsula."

Hilary's mouth formed a small, round O. "I had no idea," she murmured.

"Is it impossible," asked James irritably, "that a scholar can be a soldier, as well?"

"Of course not," replied Hilary, her surprise still evident in her tone. "But you must admit, it is an unusual combination. I suppose," she added carefully, "that it only proves that one should not be too quick to judge on appearances."

James glanced at her sharply, but said nothing. He turned his attention to Rufus, who circled the room, tapping lightly on the windowpanes.

"Now, then," he said, only to be interrupted by a scratching at the door, followed by the entrance of a plump, middle-aged woman, who wore a cluster of keys at her waist.

"Ah, Mrs. Armbruster," he said as the housekeeper advanced into the room. "We have a visitor, for whom we'll need accommodations for, er, an extended period." He paused, indicating with a dubious gesture his guest, over whom Mrs. Armbruster had cast one startled glance before averting her eyes. "He is assisting me in a—ah—project for the Antiquarian Society."

"Very good, sir," said Mrs. Armbruster expressionlessly. To Rufus, she said, "If you will follow me, sir?"

She turned, swinging back in some surprise when Rufus did not follow her.

"That's all right, Mrs. Armbruster," said James. "I'll show him up myself later."

"Very good, sir. And will the gentleman be joining you for lunch? And Lady Hilary?"

"Lunch? Ah—it is that time, is it not? Just send in some sandwiches, please."

He sank into a nearby chair when the door closed behind the housekeeper.

"Whew! I can see this entire situation is going to be fraught with peril."

"Does this mean that you believe Rufus' story?" asked Hilary eagerly.

James rose slowly and stared at Rufus. He sighed. "I just don't know. He spins a good yarn, but the whole thing is so preposterous—

"Devil take it," he said to Rufus in Latin. "Are you telling me the truth?"

Again, Rufus thrust forth his jaw. "Are you calling me a liar, you underfed barbarian? Do you think it possible to rig a strike of lightning?" He waved his arms in indignation.

"No, but—" James's eyes widened as his gaze fell on the dagger exposed at Rufus' waist. "Where did you get that?" he breathed reverently.

Withdrawing it from its leather sheath with every evidence of pride, Rufus caressed the blade.

"A beauty, isn't it? Case-hardened bronze from the finest craftsman in Lugdunum."

"That's Lyons," said James in an aside to Hilary.

She nodded. "Yes, and known for the fine metalworkers there."

Again, James experienced a surge of surprise.

"It was a gift from my father when I went into the army. I was just a boy, then."

"May I?"

James extended his hand and Rufus grudgingly placed the knife in his palm. A footman entered with a tray of sandwiches just then, accompanied by wine and cakes. Munching thoughtfully, James examined the knife. He had seen similar specimens, unearthed after centuries in graves or river mud, but they were all in advanced stages of deterioration. This blade was whole and shining and beautiful, the handle carved from fine ivory. Engraved on the shaft was a hunting scene, portraying hounds closing in on an agile wolf. The detail was remarkable, the workmanship exquisite. The conclusion to be drawn from the knife, in its authentic construction and materials, was inescapable.

"All right," James said at last, almost breathless with the implication of his words. "I believe you have been transferred from the end of the first century to this present year of 1817. The question now, I suppose, is how did you get here? And how do we return you to your proper time?"

"Oh, I know that," replied Rufus, almost offhandedly. "At least, the part about how I got here."

Chapter Six

"What?" gasped Hilary and James in unison.

"It was the old Druid," asserted Rufus, helping himself to a sandwich after a cautious perusal of the tray and its contents. "It must have been."

"What old Druid?" Again, his listeners spoke as one.

"He lives in a little cave near the tower. Crotchety old buzzard. Says he's the Guardian of the Stones. You know, the circle where the tower sits."

Hilary nodded in fascination.

"At any rate, I understand he nearly foamed at the mouth when the tower was built. Sacrilege, he screamed. Claimed it was due to his curses that the thing was never finished. When I met him—when our lads showed up to begin removing the stones—he flew into a rage. Mm, what is this? Some kind of ham? It's good, but how do you slice the bread so thin? Anyway, since I was in charge of the detail, he turned his temper on me. Told me to take my pack of desecrating savages and leave. Can you believe? That filthy old heathen calling Roman soldiers savages? I sorted him out in brief order, of course. Every day, though, he's shown up at the fifth hour or so, hurling curses and making a general nuisance of himself. Yesterday, I finally cuffed him up the side of his head and told him to push off. He swelled up like a poisoned pig and let loose with what must have been the biggest, ugliest curse in his bag of tricks. Then, he just shuffled off.

"I think, though," he concluded, "that the old gopher's incantation must have held more juice than I credited him for. I mean, here I am."

"Indeed," said James, unable to control the broad smile that spread across his features. What a find! The old warrior's theory on the cause of his remarkable journey was ludicrous, but no matter. The important thing was the journey itself. He, James Wincanon, most ordinary of mortals, was actually entertaining in his study a denizen of first-century Roman Britain. What unimaginable nuggets of information could be gleaned from this citizen of the ancient empire? Why, Rufus could no doubt provide him with more information on the Roman occupation of Britain than he could discover in a lifetime of digging. Here was history on the hoof! He could travel the length and breadth of England with Rufus, and the warrior could simply tell him where to excavate.

James smiled. Mordecai Cheeke would be ready to chew bricks. Suppressing an ignoble chuckle, he said to Rufus, "We must get you settled in here. Please consider my home as your own. We'll have to get you out of those clothes, of course. I think my head coachman is about your build, though a little taller. His clothes should do until we can get something made up for you. Then, we'll—"

"Hold on," interposed Rufus abruptly. "I can't stay here."

"Of course, you can. As you can see, I have plenty of room."

"No, no," continued Rufus impatiently. "I mean I can't stay here in your year 1870 or whatever. I must go back to where I belong. Now."

He moved toward the door as though to leave, but Hilary, who was in his path, laid a hand on his arm.

"Of course, you must return to your home, Rufus," she said hurriedly. "But how are you to do that? Do you know how to, um, reverse the Druid's curse?"

Rufus paused uncertainly and James stepped up.

"Besides, your theory is absolutely absurd. Do you honestly believe an old Druid, muttering in his beard, could send you hurtling eighteen centuries ahead of yourself?"

Rufus bent a look of outrage upon his host, but his reply was interrupted by Hilary, who said witheringly to James in English, "Well, of course he does! This is a man who probably believes one can tell the future by staring into sheeps' insides." To Rufus, she said placatingly, "Never mind him, he speaks without thinking sometimes. The thing is, you must have somewhere to stay while we sort all this out. We'd like to help you figure out how to get back, if you will let us."

James knew an urge to grasp Rufus by his shoulder plates to keep him in the house, but he knew such a move would be foolish. Time traveler or not, he couldn't keep the fellow chained up in the basement. Although, that was at present very much his inclination. No, he could only hope that Minimus Rufus would accept his hospitality. He held his breath as Rufus considered, and then at last allowed Hilary to shepherd him back toward his chair.

"Ah." James exhaled. "Now, then, let us get you up in your own chamber. I'll show you about, and at dinner we can discuss what is to be done next."

Rubbing his hands briskly, he ushered Rufus into the corridor, only to be told by a footman that Lady Hilary's maid had arrived and awaited her instructions in the hall.

"Oh!" Hilary, who had followed the gentlemen into the corridor, started guiltily. "I suppose—that is, I must get home." She glanced down at her gown, drying into a wrinkled, misshapen mess.

"Yes," agreed James promptly. Hilary flushed. "Unless you'd care to stay for dinner," he added in a more courteous tone.

"No. That is, no thank you," she replied coldly.

James knew a twinge of shame. She was so very earnest and she could not, of course, be faulted for trying to take advantage of the situation. Having parlayed a nice little display of antiquarian knowledgeability into what she must now see as a winning proposition, she would be foolish to abandon the scene.

"I should prefer," continued Hilary in a voice that could have chipped diamonds, "to keep our—our arrangements on a businesslike basis, Mr. Wincanon. To be perfectly frank, I have no desire to spend any more time in your company than necessary. Perhaps we can work out a schedule, alternating the time we spend with Rufus. We can both ponder on the problem of getting him back to his own time."

James, startled by the depth of her anger, could find nothing to say in response. They had by now reached the hall, and Hilary gestured to the maid awaiting her. To Rufus, she added in her halting Latin, "I hope to see you again, soon, Minimus Rufus. Perhaps tomorrow, if Mr. Wincanon can spare you, you will do me the favor of some conversation."

Rufus nodded benignly and with a regal nod to her host Hilary swept from the house. The dignity of her exit was somewhat marred as Jasper greeted her with all the enthusiasm of a dog forcibly restrained in chains to keep him from his beloved mistress. Accepting a footman's assistance, she climbed aboard her gig, bundling the dog into the vehicle with her. Assuring Jasper of her continued well-being, she slapped the reins smartly and clattered briskly away.

Whew! James watched her out of sight. He grinned despite himself. It was hard to believe so much spirit could be contained in one small female. What, he wondered the next moment, had been her purpose in speaking of him so? It was not the first time he'd had his hair combed, of course, but often he'd discovered that such a show of antipathy was merely meant to pique his interest.

Lord, he sounded like an insufferable coxcomb, but in truth he spoke only from experience. He sighed inwardly. It grew wearying, this necessity to view every damsel who crossed his path as a threat to his well-being. There were times when he wished to consign his wealth and his connections to perdition. He supposed women—even the best of them, he thought with a familiar ache, could not be blamed for looking out for the main chance, he simply wished that they did not see him as their personal ticket to a life of luxury. Why couldn't they just leave him alone?

But Lady Hilary . . . What was there, he wondered moodily, about this particular booby trap in skirts that made him feel ashamed of his suspicions? Granted, she bore the appearance of a complete innocent, from her fiery hair to her pretty silk slippers. At least, he supposed they had been pretty before being exposed to a raging thunderstorm.

He was forced to admit that it was beginning to look more and more as though her knowledge of antiquities was the result of a genuine interest in the subject. It would no doubt be pleasant to have someone in the neighborhood who shared his passion, particularly such an appealing someone. Not that he was interested in anything but her scholarly attributes. She could be of inestimable help, since there was no question that a knowledgeable assistant could take many of the more mundane tasks of his work at the villa off his shoulders—the cataloging, the sketching, laying out the grid, perhaps even some of the lighter digging, if she were so inclined. Yes, he would permit the earnest Lady Hilary to assist him, within her limited capabilities, and he would allow her a judicious amount of time with Minimus Rufus.

Of course, at the first sign that her young ladyship harbored ulterior designs on his bachelor status she would be returned posthaste to her dutiful life on her father's estate. James expelled a satisfied grunt before bending his attention once more to Rufus.

The important thing, he mused as he led the soldier up the stairs, was to keep Rufus' identity a secret. If anyone got wind of the notion that James Wincanon was entertaining a visitor whom he believed had traveled through time from another age, he'd find himself thrust into the nearest madhouse before the cat could lick her ear. Well, that should be no problem. Even if Rufus were to announce his identity to the neighborhood at large, he would be speaking, after all, in Latin. Of course, if Mordecai Cheeke somehow got wind of the situation, no matter how absurd the story, he would investigate.

On the other hand, there was little or no chance that Mordecai Cheeke, even if he did seem to possess a genius for sniffing out James's plans, would hear about the unorthodox gentleman currently residing in James's house. In short, there was no impediment to a minute investigation into the life and times of M. Minimus Rufus, a *tessarius* in the army of the Emperor Trajan.

The next couple of hours were spent outfitting the legionary in a suit of clothing that, while perhaps not suitable for the guest of a renowned scholar, at least allowed him to fit into his new setting. He looked surprisingly at home in the leisure garb of a coachman, though he complained bitterly about the necessity of wearing trousers, which he seemed to feel labeled him as a barbarian. He also objected vigorously to the cumbersome, confining footwear provided him. Otherwise, he seemed agreeable to maintaining his new wardrobe, at least for a short space of time.

With wide-eyed interest, he accompanied James on a tour of the house. This took longer than James had expected, since Rufus paused frequently to investigate furnishings and such wonders as bellpulls, gas lamps, and clocks. The latter seemed to fascinate him—not only the dials with their moving hands, but the glass that covered them.

At dinner, this amicable state of affairs deteriorated somewhat. James began to stem the flow of Rufus' questions with some of his own—with a marked lack of success.

"No, I don't know anything about the agrarian policies of Quietus. Or the proposed withdrawal from the Scottish border. Gods, do you think the governor or the province consults me on such things? What I want to know is how long you plan to keep me cooped up here."

"I certainly do not intend to keep you here at all," replied James rather testily. "However, as Lady Hilary explained—"

"The lady explained that I need a place to stay—and clothes, which is true, but I cannot be spending all my time here. I must get back to my own time, and it seems to me I should make my way back to the tower. That's where I was snatched up, and that must be where the answer lies to getting me back home."

"Yes," said James soothingly, "but you need not get back home right this minute, do you? You seem interested in the changes that have come about over the centuries. Have you no desire to see more? Does not the prospect of spending, say, a few weeks in another time period appeal to you?"

"No, by the gods, it does not!" bellowed Rufus, rising from the table to throw down his napkin. "Do you think I have no life of my own? You seem to look at me as a—a portable history book. Well, let me tell you—I find this whole situation damned—unsettling—and inconvenient."

"My good fellow," began James hastily, "of course, I have no wish to detain you against your will. I only meant—"

"And don't 'my good fellow' me." Rufus began to pace the area just behind his chair. "Let me explain something to you. I've been in this man's army for almost twenty years. I'll be receiving my retirement certificate soon. Maia and I have it all planned out. I've been setting money aside for years now to buy my own business. I'm a good craftsman and there isn't anything I can't do with metal. I've got my sights on a little place just off the forum in Corinium. Folks there want silver for their tableware, and the ladies must have lamps of bronze or tin to light their homes and fine *fibulae* to pin their cloaks.

"Even with my savings, though, I've had to borrow from Maia's brother, Felix. I hated to do it, because just between you and me, Felix is a snake. Which is where my problem comes in. The final payment on the shop is due in a few days, and in a moment of weakness, I gave my portion to Felix so that he could pay the entire sum, just in case I couldn't be there. Well, of course, I had every intention of showing up with my hair in a braid, but, I don't, it's a dead cert that Felix will put something over. I don't know what, exactly, but I suspect he'll have the whole place put in his name. Or, worse yet, take the money and simply head for parts unknown."

"But that would be stealing!" exclaimed James, fascinated despite himself.

Rufus laughed shortly. "Oh, would it now? Well, that wouldn't bother Felix. He's just the sort of man as would diddle his own sister."

"Well, old fell—that is, Rufus, I understand your problem, and you certainly have my sympathy, but I don't see what I can do right at the moment. Frankly, I have no idea how you got here—aside from the Druid curse," he added hastily. "And I have no idea how to get you back where you belong. I'll certainly do my best to help you, though, and if it's possible to somehow whisk you back to your own century, we'll bring you about. In the meantime, perhaps you could see your way clear to helping me. That is, I've devoted a good bit of my life to unearthing the details of your time. There is much I could learn from you, if you would let me." James eyed the legionary shrewdly. "And the Lady Hilary, too. She shares my interest and I know she would also be glad of your, er, tutelage."

"Mmp. She's a nice little thing." Rufus' voice softened. "Are you and she betrothed?"

"What?" James paled. "I hardly know the chit! Why would you say—?"

"Oh, I don't know," Rufus replied vaguely. "She reminds me of my oldest daughter," he added, apropos of nothing.

"You have children?" James began breathing again.

"None of my own, but Maia was a widow when I married her. She had three daughters, all good, biddable lasses. The oldest is married with a babe of her own now. I'm hoping Maia will give me a son," he added somewhat wistfully. "Eh, how the time flies." He chuckled. "Or, in my case, I guess you'd say, time flies and takes me with it."

James's eyes lit. "Indeed, you have taken wings for a flight such as no man has undertaken before."

Rufus turned back to his meal. "This stuff is good." He pointed to his plate. "What is it?"

"It's called beef Wellington, named after one of our national heroes," he said, gesturing toward a footman. "And try some of these potatoes, as well. I think you may never have tasted them before."

Rufus pronounced the potatoes acceptable, though as a rule he didn't care much for foreign dishes. The meal progressed and Rufus declared himself eminently pleased with the pupton of fruit with which it closed. Later, they sat over a decanter of port and Rufus exhaled in loud satisfaction.

"As good a meal as ever Maia put before me," he declared, unburdening himself of a monumental belch. "Now, if only these outlandish clothes weren't so tight. These cursed trousers are even more uncomfortable than they look. And for the gods' sake, why do the men of this time strangle themselves with these great, long pieces of cloth?" He struggled with his cravat for several moments before proceeding to dismantle it. James lifted a hand in protest, but at this point Burnside entered the room.

"You have a visitor, sir," he said, staring at Rufus in some disapprobation.

"At this time of night?" asked James, startled. "Well, tell whoever it is that I am not at home to visitors. I—I'm indisposed."

"But, he said to tell you that he has come a long way, sir. He is a Mr. Mordecai Cheeke and he has come to Gloucestershire specifically to see you."

Chapter Seven

James's mind raced. Mordecai Cheeke? What in God's name could have brought him here?

To Burnside, he said merely, "Put him in the blue saloon, and tell him I'll be with him in a moment."

He turned to Rufus. "I'm sorry to cut our conversation short, but I would just as soon you not meet this man. I can't explain right now," he said, urging Rufus toward the door, "but you must go up to your chamber. Stay in your bedchamber until I come to you. Trust me on this, Minimus Rufus. If Mordecai Cheeke gets wind of your presence here, there is a very real possibility he will muck up any chance you have of returning to your home."

On his way to the blue saloon, he was met by Robert, just returning from his day's outing with the bailiff's son.

"My boy, you are come just in the nick." He grasped the aston-

ished young man by the arm and propelled him toward the staircase.

"I don't have time to explain, but—how much Latin have you?"

"Latin?" Robert gaped at his employer. "Well, um, it's adequate,
I suppose. I can toss off a tag now and then if required, but I don't
suppose I could converse like a native." He smiled quizzically.
"What's toward, sir?"

"As I said, I don't have time—but I need you to bustle upstairs
and entertain a guest. You'll find him in the chamber next to mine.
He speaks only Latin, and everything he's liable to say to you is
true, no matter how incredible it sounds. Tell him you are my
friend—although I don't know if that will help. His name is Marcus Minimus Rufus, and it is imperative that you keep him occupied, for he mustn't stir from his chamber. Mordecai Cheeke is
here, and—"

Once again Robert interrupted with an astonished query, which
James waved aside with what he felt was a creditable aplomb.

"I don't know what he's doing here, but I imagine he's up to no
good. I'll get rid of him with all possible speed, and then I'll come
upstairs. Remember, keep Rufus where he is even if you have to
summon a squad of footmen to tie him down."

So saying, he turned and proceeded down one of the corridors
that led from the hall. A moment later, he entered the blue saloon.

The gentleman standing at a display case turned swiftly at
James's footstep. The case contained artifacts culled from various
archaeological sites throughout Britain, and its door was now
open. From it, the gentleman had removed a small, but exquisitely
crafted statue of the goddess Minerva.

The man did not look like a scholar. He was short in stature, and
given to dandyism. His high shirt points were the most prominent
feature of an ensemble that featured pale lavender pantaloons,
topped by a coat of mauve, under which lay a startling waistcoat
of a virulent rose, lavishly embroidered with fanciful designs in
every hue of the rainbow.

He seemed to be given to sweets as well, for he was plump, with
a ruddy face, and round, slightly protuberant eyes, so that he bore
the appearance of a fashionable cherub. His hair fell about his
childishly curved cheeks in glossy, brown ringlets, further com-
pleting the illusion.

"James! My dear fellow!" crowed the gentleman with every appearance of delight.

"Mordecai," murmured James, inclining his head slightly. "What brings you to the wilds of Gloucestershire? You're just passing through, you say?"

Mordecai lifted his hand in a deprecating gesture. "I've come down for a bit of rustication, dear boy. I'm on my way to see Sir Harvey Winslow. He's been after me to visit him for some time now. He's a crashing bore, of course, but he informs me that he's turned up a mosaic on his property. It doesn't sound like anything of importance, but you must know, Sir Harvey's chef is an absolute artist. How could I refuse? He lives some fifteen miles distant, near Stratton. Needless to say, I could not pass by without stopping to see how you go on."

Thank God, thought James, relieved that Cheeke's visit would be brief.

"I must say," continued Mordecai, all ingenuous interest, "I was surprised to learn that you had left the metropolis for the pastoral scene. What drew you here, James?"

"As you say, a bit of rustication," murmured James. Wordlessly, he removed the figure of Minerva from Mordecai's acquisitive grasp and locked the cabinet door before leading his guest to a satin-striped chair near the fire. Pouring wine into two glasses, he handed one to Cheeke and took the second to another chair on the opposite side of the fire. Mordecai sipped appreciatively before cocking his head. His eyes widened innocently.

"But did I not hear you have discovered the remains of a villa hereabouts? On your newly purchased estate, in fact?"

"Mm, yes," James replied casually. "Certainly the remains provided an additional incentive for purchasing Goodhurst. However, I had already decided to buy a place in the country. My collection"—he swept an arm toward the cabinet—"has grown somewhat extensive. Unlike Sir John Soane, I did not wish to turn my house in London into a clutter of odds and ends gathered from the corners of the earth, so I elected to place my things in a more, er, commodious setting."

"I see."

A silence fell, as Mordecai continued to drink his wine.

"Have you turned up any artifacts of interest?"

James affixed a lazy smile to his lips. "A few bits and pieces, merely."

Mordecai waved an admonishing finger. "You don't fool me, my boy," he said playfully. "Despite your secretive ways, I know your propensity—nay, your very genius—for sniffing out major finds. You're onto something here, James. I can smell it. And I want to know what it is."

James stiffened warily. He was tempted to simply deny Cheeke's ludicrous suspicions. Unfortunately, this would not serve to allay them. Indeed, denial would simply inflame Cheeke's acquisitive instincts even further. He bent a bland smile on his adversary. "Even if such an absurd assumption were true, do you think I would be likely to confide in you?"

"Ah, my dear colleague, you refer to the brisk, not to say, fervent spirit of competition that has sprung up between us over the years. I understand perfectly, but surely, something of this magnitude should be shared."

"And so it would be—if there were something to share—at the proper time."

He transferred a meditative gaze to a point beyond the window.

Mordecai sighed. "I see you mean to be difficult, but I shall not give up. I know there must have been a compelling reason for you to abandon your snug digs in Duke Street, and I mean to discover what it is."

The words were spoken in a tone of light badinage, but James had no difficulty in discerning the predatory glitter in Cheeke's pale gray eyes.

"Really, Mordecai"—James tipped up the last of his wine—"I must not keep you. The daylight hours are still lengthy, but the sun set some time ago, and it is growing quite dark. If you wish to make Stratton before nightfall, you had best be on your way."

Somewhat reluctantly, Mordecai emptied his own glass and rose, smoothing a hand over his blinding waistcoat. "Yes, yes. There will be a moon tonight, but one requires some daylight to travel, given the state of the roads these days. One wonders if any improvements have been made to the Fosse Way since the Romans departed, eh?"

He chuckled at his own witticism and James smiled dutifully. Within a few minutes Mordecai had taken his leave, promising a return betimes to ". . . look in on your progress, old man—at your villa."

When the door had closed behind him, James moved across the hall to the staircase, where he sank thoughtfully onto the bottom step. He had apparently allayed Cheeke's suspicions, but as surely as the showers of spring would follow the snows of winter, Mordecai Cheeke would return to Goodhurst. Keeping him out of Rufus' orbit would be the devil's own work.

Upon entering the bedchamber allotted to Minimus Rufus, James stepped into a scene of mild chaos. Robert and Rufus stood in the center of the room, facing each other in a confrontational stance. Each spoke at peak volume, neither apparently listening to what the other was saying. The dissonance was further augmented by the fact that the dispute was being conducted in two languages.

"Nullam notionem habuisti de quibus hablis!" bellowed Rufus.

"What the devil is the matter with you?" returned Robert at full roar. *"Esne non dicere potens instar hominis prudentis?* Or, no, that's not right," he added in English, in response to Rufus' expression of puzzlement. "Can't you speak like a reasonable man? That's what I meant. Not a reasonable cabbage. *Hominem,* not *holinem. Rationem."*

"I *am* being reasonable!" The dialogue continued in Latin. "It is you and your barbarian master who are committing the unconscionable crime of laying hands on a soldier of the emperor's army."

"Oh, for God's sake, nobody's laid a hand on you, but I'm liable to land you a facer if you don't stop screeching like a ravished maiden."

At this point, James, who had been trying to make himself heard above the roar of combat, brought his fist down on a nearby table, causing the various accoutrements set on it to rattle impressively.

"Please, gentlemen," he said calmly as Rufus and Robert whirled about simultaneously.

It was some moments before order was restored, but at last, Rufus, breathing heavily, sat gingerly on the edge of a chair and Robert flung himself into one nearby.

"Now then," said James. He raised an admonishing hand to Robert, who opened his mouth in obvious indignation. "I shall explain all in a moment. First allow me to make peace with our guest."

He turned to Rufus. "Minimus Rufus," he began in Latin, "I have no intention of keeping you here against your will."

Rufus snorted and rose from his chair.

"However," continued James coolly, "if you will but listen a moment, I believe you must see that it is to your best interest to remain in my home—at least for the time being."

He paused for a moment, eyeing the warrior. Rufus, while not precisely subsiding, looked as though he was prepared to give ear to James's arguments.

"As the Lady Hilary said awhile ago, you are in a difficult position. You have traveled from your own time to one that is completely foreign to you. You have no money and no clothes, except for what you are wearing, and you don't speak the language."

Behind him, Robert gave utterance to a choked gasp.

"If you travel thus into the world, I think you will eventually find yourself taken up by the constabulary and placed in a facility very much less pleasant than your present lodgings.

"On the other hand, if you agree to stay here and follow my direction, I will do everything I can to return you to your proper place in the cosmos. Frankly," he said again, "I haven't the slightest notion how you got here, or how to get you back where you belong, but I'll do everything I can for you. Now, what do you say?"

Rufus bent a hard stare on him. Robert seemed to have stopped breathing, and the only sound to be heard in the room was—appropriately enough, thought James—the ticking of a little clock on the table by Rufus' bed.

"You will allow me to come and go as I please?" asked Rufus, his suspicions obviously not completely allayed.

"Of course, although I suggest that you not leave the premises without me."

"And you will help me escape this benighted time period?"

"I will, indeed, although I hope to demonstrate to you that we are not such a bad lot here in the nineteenth century."

"Very well, then. I wish to go to the tower right now. Or, no," he amended glancing out of the window, where darkness pressed against the panes, "first thing tomorrow morning."

James bowed. "As you wish. As for the rest of the evening, would you care to peruse some of the books in my library? I have quite a few in Latin. Or perhaps we could embark on a program of English for you. As I think I have told you, that is the language everyone hereabouts speaks now. It is descended from Latin and Celtic and a few other tongues with which you are probably unfamiliar."

Rufus grunted. "If it's all the same to you, I think I'm for bed. It's been a long day. I'd like to look at a couple of your books, though—the Latin." He paused for a moment as an idea struck him. "Do you have any written a few years ahead of my own time? It might be interesting to know who the next few emperors will be."

James frowned. "I had not thought of that—of the repercussions of sending you back to your own time with a foreknowledge of the future. I'm not sure that's such a good idea."

Rufus stared at him, uncomprehending.

"If you know what's going to happen in your future, you might be able to change what is to come."

"Mm," replied Rufus, rubbing his chin. "But," he said slowly, "I would have already done that if it were possible—if you see what I mean. And the future—or rather, your present—is already changed. No?"

"I—I have no idea," said James. "You may be right, or"—he tapped his chin thoughtfully—"in any event, the histories of Tacitus should provide you with some interesting reading material. By the by," he continued, an arrested expression in his eyes, "where did you say you were from?"

"I was born in Italica—in Iberia."

"Ah, Spain. Italica is near Seville, I believe. Tell me, are you familiar with the name Hadrian?"

"Of course. He is a protégé of Trajan the Imperator, you know, and he, too, is from Italica. In fact, my father worked on the estate of Hadrian's family, and we played together as children." Rufus chuckled. "You know, I saved his neck when he was just a pup. One day we went fishing and he took a tumble in the river. I pulled him out. I don't suppose he remembers."

"Hmm," replied James. "One never knows. We'll have to discuss this further. At any rate, I shall see you in the morning. When you arise, ring the bell—here it is—and I shall instruct someone to send for me. Robert?"

He gestured to his secretary, who followed him dazedly from the room.

"Wh—wha—?" he mumbled as the door closed behind them. "D'you mean to tell me that the fellow we just left back there is—is—" He seemed unable to finish the thought, but followed, unresisting as James led him downstairs to the library.

"Yes, Robert. 'The fellow' is Marcus Minimus Rufus, late of the Emperor Trajan's army and he comes to us from approximately seventeen hundred years ago."

"My God!" Robert gaped at his employer. "With all due respect, sir, I think someone around here has gone round the bend. To tell you the truth, I'm not sure if it's that old walrus or you or me, but I'm pretty sure it isn't me."

James grinned. "I don't wonder at your, er, skepticism, Robert. Allow me to allay your fears."

Briefly, he recounted the remarkable appearance of Minimus Rufus, detailing the old soldier's knowledge of the period and his finely crafted dagger. Of Lady Hilary's part in the fantastic tale, he said little, for some reason reluctant to discuss her with his secretary.

"Well!" exclaimed Robert at last. "Well. It is difficult to see how a mere lightning bolt—although Max and I heard it, too, and it certainly was a stunner—could effect the transportation of a man from one century to another. On the other hand, I cannot imagine anyone pulling such a rig so successfully, especially on someone like you. I mean, you're not stupid to begin with—"

"Thank you, my boy," said James solemnly.

Robert flushed. "Yes, sir, but you know what I mean. You're known to be a downy one. I'd think it would be just about impossible to fool you. Besides, what would the man gain?"

"The same conclusion I've reached myself. I may be all wrong, of course, but I've decided to proceed as though our friend upstairs is the genuine article."

Robert's eyes lit. "If that's the case, sir, imagine what he can tell you!"

"I have thought of little else since his appearance. My only concern right now is Mordecai Cheeke."

"Good God, yes. If he should get wind of this—wait a minute. Did you say he was here? What did he want?"

"Merely to pass the time of day, if he was to be believed. I bundled him away from here with all possible speed, but his instincts are in full cry. I don't know what got his wind up, but he apparently thinks my Roman villa will prove to be the archaeological find of the century. Which, it might, of course, for one never knows what might turn up, but—"

"And now you have two reasons for keeping him away from here."

"Precisely. He said he was on his way to visit Sir Harvey Winslow, who lives some fifteen miles from here, but it takes barely two hours to traverse that distance. From what he said, I imagine he will be buzzing around here like a starving honeybee—and just as much of a nuisance."

"I'll instruct the servants that you will not be home when he calls."

"Good. And now, in the words of Minimus Rufus, it's been a long day, and tomorrow will come early. I shall want to send word first thing to Lady Hilary, inviting her to participate in my first real conversation with that gentleman."

Robert's brows lifted in surprise.

"Ordinarily, I would not allow a female within miles of either our guest or the villa, but I do not see how, under the circumstances, I can keep her away. In addition, as you remarked earlier, she is something of an original. I have decided to permit her limited access to Rufus and to allow her to assist in the excavation of the villa—on a strictly circumscribed basis, of course."

Robert's lips twitched. "Of course."

James bade his secretary a dignified good night, and made his way toward his bedchamber. Later, he gazed at the ceiling in the cool darkness, reflecting on the extraordinary day that had just come to a close.

Who would have thought that a slender young hoyden, who looked to be barely out of the schoolroom, could have been responsible for the good fortune that had just befallen him? It was as though someone had just handed him the deed to a gold mine. No—much better than a gold mine, for the information that he would glean from Minimus Rufus was a thousand times more valuable than any paltry metal that one might dig from the earth.

His thoughts drifted to Lady Hilary. She was not what one could call a tempting morsel to be sure—even if he were the sort of man to be tempted by feminine charms. That there might be something beneath her bonnet besides that tumble of incendiary curls made her more interesting, but not likely to charm him into a proposal of marriage. He was not a monk, of course, but his preferred female companions had always been voluptuous in form and mature in outlook. They clearly understood that all he wanted or needed was a physical relationship based on clearly stated boundaries and expectations.

He liked women well enough—in their place and as long as they did not look for a permanent union. He was forced to admit that, despite his earlier assumptions, the little Merton seemed to pose no threat in that direction. Actually, she appeared to have formed an aversion to him. Despite that fact, he looked forward to an association with the lady. How fortunate that she had established such a rapport with Rufus. She would no doubt be of help in prying all sorts of informational nuggets from the ancient soldier.

His mind drifted toward sleep, still mulling over the possibilities that dwelt in the bulky form of Minimus Rufus, but as his eyes finally closed, his thoughts were of the little gamine with whom he would begin work on the morrow.

Chapter Eight

"Humph!" exclaimed Hilary with an unladylike sniff. She had risen from her bed not an hour before and now sat at the breakfast table with her father, a note in her hand. "How very condescending of Mr. Wincanon." She scanned the note. "He requests the pleasure of my company at his home today, at my earliest convenience, so that we might proceed with the excavation in his villa."

She always relished this time of day, usually spent in companionable chatter with her father over morning toast and kippers. Today, after the rain, the sun fairly blazed on meadow and parkland as though to make up for its previous lapse. Hilary basked in the warmth streaming through the tall windows that overlooked the manor's terrace.

"Goodness," she remarked. "With harvest over and done with, Halloween will be on us soon. Has Mr. Archer seen about the bogeys for the ball? Everyone was so pleased with our celebration last year that it wouldn't do to provide anything less this year."

Lord Clarendon looked up from his paper. "It seems to me it's getting so we make a great deal too much fuss over Halloween. According to the vicar, it's turning into nothing more than a pagan romp. Bogeys, indeed. As though our steward had nothing better to do with his time. The night is not even a proper feast day, merely the eve of one, and I don't see why we must borrow a barbarous Scottish custom merely to please our staff and tenants."

Hilary laughed. "Because it's not just the tenants who enjoy creating odd-looking lanterns from turnips. They add a festive touch to the ball, as well. In addition, the good reverend's words would bear more weight if he did not always try to outdo everyone else with the ingenuity of his costume."

The earl's lips curved upward. "Yes, indeed. What was it last year? Ivan the Terrible? No, that was the year before."

"Last year he and his wife came as shocks of wheat. It was very effective, except they kept dropping bits of chaff all over the ballroom. It made the dancing quite hazardous."

Hilary spread a liberal dollop of butter on her toast.

"But what is this about Mr. Wincanon?" asked the earl. "I thought you and he did not hit it off."

"Well, we didn't," responded Hilary tartly. "The man was an absolute boor. However—" She hesitated, uncertain as to how much she should divulge about yesterday's adventure. Nothing, was her instant decision. Papa could be counted on to maintain a certain discretion, but he would no doubt assume his youngest daughter had taken leave of her senses if she began babbling of time-traveling Roman soldiers. "However"—she continued brightly— "I saw him again yesterday morning at his estate. I drove there to bring him the artifacts I had found earlier. On that occasion, he was more pleasant. Papa, do you know what I think? I believe he sees me as an empty-headed flibbertigibbet who is on the prowl for a husband."

"Bless my soul!" exclaimed the earl. "The fellow must have rats in his attic. You have less interest in getting married than any other female of my acquaintance. As I know only too well," he concluded with some asperity. "You ain't interested in him, are you?" he added hopefully. "As a prospective husband?"

"Of course not. Mr. Wincanon may not be as unpleasant as I first thought him, but he is the last man in the world I would think of marrying."

The earl sighed. "Seems to me that's what you say about every man of your acquaintance."

"Papa, you know I have no objection to marriage per se. Winifred and Susan and Meg seem very happy with their chosen mates, and William and Dickon, as well. I simply feel that if I'm going to give up my independence to some man, he'd better be one whom I can trust not to button it into a tight little box made of his own prejudices."

"Yes, yes," said her father with the air of a man who had heard all this many times before. "If you're going to spend the day with Wincanon, however, be sure you take your maid."

His paternal duty performed to his satisfaction, he returned to his paper.

Well, of course, there was no question, thought Hilary, finishing the last of her toast. She would accept Mr. Wincanon's invitation, much as it galled her to do so. She was determined to be among those present when an interrogation of that gentleman took place.

The first thing she would ask was whether or not a vast bath complex actually lay beneath the pump room in the city of Bath. There was some controversy raging over this matter, Samuel Lysons and his followers declaring that the site contained not only the baths but no doubt a temple to Minerva. Others pooh-poohed the whole notion. Then, of course, closer to home, there was the matter of the fort at Caerleon. And then . . . fairly shivering with anticipation, she gulped the last of her coffee and hurried from the room.

Unknown to her, a few miles away James was indulging in the same sort of reflections. He had been closeted with Minimus Rufus in his study for the better part of two hours, and the soldier's descriptions of the layout of Cirencester made his mouth water.

"It's as impressive a city as any in the empire," declared Rufus, "as I've been telling Maia. She's all for setting up shop in Glevum when I retire, but I told her, 'No, no, it's in Corinium where the money's going to be.' We'll make a mint!" His face darkened. "If, that is, her oily brother doesn't filch my savings." He twisted to face James. "I must get back," he said, for perhaps the twentieth time that morning. "When are you going to take me to the tower?"

"As soon as Lady Hilary arrives."

Rufus seemed to relax fractionally. "Ah, good. I shall be glad to see her again."

"In the meantime," continued James, "what can you tell me about your fort at Caerleon?"

Rufus heaved a sigh of one much put upon. "I've told you already. We have fifty-five hundred men there, divided into twelve cohorts—all of the Second Legion."

"The Second was formed during the reign of Augustus, was it not?"

"Of course. That's why it's called the Second Augusta. Best outfit in the army, if you ask me."

At this point, a footman scratched at the door with the announcement that Lady Hilary had arrived. He was followed closely by the lady herself, and the next few moments were occupied in seeing to a replenishment of the coffeepot from which James and Rufus had been refreshing themselves.

"I've been meaning to ask you"—Rufus indicated his cup with a disdainful sweep of his hand—"what is this swill, anyway? It tastes like bull piss. Don't you have a good honest soldier's drink about? Some beer, maybe, or even a little wine? That stuff we had last night was good. Is it local? The Dobunni make a decent red. Well, not exactly decent, maybe, but drinkable. I think they concoct it out of apples and honey and some kind of berries. At any rate, it's better than what we get at Isca, except for once in awhile when somebody gets in some good Mosel or even a Bordeaux. I remember a couple of weeks ago—"

"Yes, yes," put in James. "But tell me about your barracks. And your bathhouse. Can you draw me a map? A friend of mine is digging there, and I'd like to be able to—" He turned to Hilary, who had just removed her pelisse and bonnet. "Take some notes, Lady Hilary, there's a good girl. You'll find paper and pens on the desk over there."

Hilary bristled.

"Do you not have a secretary?" she asked sweetly, settling herself in a comfortable chair.

"Of course, I have," replied James, a touch of irritation in his tone. "However, he is engaged in other duties. I rarely ask him to involve himself in my work with antiquities. I usually perform those tasks myself."

"Well, do not let me stop you from performing them now." Hilary poured a cup of coffee and helped herself to one of the scones that had been set out on the tray.

James drew a deep breath. "Lady Hilary," he said with a growl, "perhaps we had better get a few things straight."

Hilary bent a direct stare on him. "Yes, I very much think we should, Mr. Wincanon."

As he gazed into Lady Hilary's golden eyes, James experienced the oddest sensation that he was falling into a forest pool spackled by filtered sunlight. He had never known such a feeling before and it left him as shaken as though he were indeed in danger of drowning.

"If," she continued in a voice of purest silk, "your purpose in inviting me here today was to act as your employee, I think it would be best if I were to leave. It will be my pleasure to assist you, but I will not be dictated to as though I were a hireling paid to scurry at your bidding."

James blinked. This was exactly how he had expected their relationship to progress.

"Ah, no, of course not. That is"—he strove to regain his normal composure—"I do not consider you in any way my, er, hireling. However, I did not think you would mind a simple request. If you feel that taking a few notes is beyond your capability, why—"

"Mr. Wincanon, are you being deliberately insulting, or is this simply your natural unpleasantness manifesting itself?"

James paused as an unaccustomed and wholly unexpected twinge of shame snaked through him. However, he smiled perfunctorily. "You may interpret my words as you choose, Lady Hilary. What you call unpleasant and/or insulting is to me, simple honesty."

"And your honesty, of course, compels you to give voice to the male view that all women are feather-witted ciphers who care nothing and know even less of any subject that does not concern fashion—or family—or how to snare a husband." Anger brimmed in her incredible eyes.

"Exactly," he replied dazedly. "Or—no," he amended hastily. "That is—"

Lady Hilary's lips curved in what might have been called a smile. "It's all right, Mr. Wincanon. I am quite used to such a reaction."

"Well, but you're a female!" blurted James, all but clapping his hand to his mouth the second the words were uttered.

Lady Hilary stiffened as though he had slapped her. Good God, James thought in unwonted confusion, how could he have uttered such a completely unguarded—to say nothing of incendiary—statement to this spitting volcano in skirts?

"I suppose I should not be surprised at your blatant prejudice," she snapped. "However, do you think that just for a moment you might strive for reason?"

At this point, Rufus, who had been amusing himself by dipping James's pen into an inkwell and drawing stick figures on the cover of *The Gentleman's Magazine,* spoke complainingly in his own tongue.

"Could you two continue your battle later? I am weary of listening to you and I wish to go to the tower. Now."

Not unnaturally, the combatants fell silent, until James spoke at last.

"I apologize," he said stiffly, "if I have offended you, my lady."

Hilary held up a weary hand. "Oh, never mind, Mr. Wincanon. I—"

"You requested once before," interposed James, "that I address you by your given name. I—that seems like a good idea, since we will be working together." He placed a slight emphasis on the last word. "May I ask that you call me James, as well?"

He smiled suddenly, and Hilary drew in a sharp breath. She rather wished he wouldn't do that, even though—or perhaps because—it created such a delicious sensation deep inside her.

"That will be acceptable," she said primly.

"Very well, then—Hilary. I did indeed tell Minimus Rufus that we would go with him to the tower once you arrived. He seems to think that if he returns there, he might discover something helpful—toward getting him back to his own time."

Hilary's brows lifted. "I suppose that's as good a theory as any. And perhaps on the way, we can question him about his own time period—although I suppose you have already started that process."

"Yes, our guest has already provided me with enough information to keep me busy for years."

"Ohh," breathed Hilary. "I can hardly wait to ply him with my own questions. Actually"—she continued with a grin that James found unexpectedly attractive—"I still cannot quite believe what has happened." She glanced at Rufus, at the moment pouring a healthy dollop of wine from the decanter that stood on James's desk. "To look at him, in his brogues and breeches, you would never believe he was born in the reign of Tiberis Caesar."

"No, you could set him down into any country alehouse and he would fit right in."

Hilary laughed. "I see what you mean. Yes, let us see what a visit to the tower will produce."

Chapter Nine

It became apparent sometime later, as the three—accompanied by Jasper—entered the broken doorway of the tower, that little was to be accomplished there. There was nothing about the scene to indicate that an event of cosmic magnitude had occurred there the day before.

Truth to tell, the edifice was not impressive. It was roofless, and about ten feet in diameter. Its walls rose to a height of about fifteen feet in some places, and only two or three in others. What had once been an entryway could be plainly discerned, but its wooden door had long since vanished. One or two gaps along the walls indicated the placement of windows. Along one side ran an outcropping of masonry that might have formed part of the flooring for an upper story.

Rufus confirmed this. As Jasper, nose to the ground, made his own exploration, the warrior gazed about him in stupefaction.

"Gods," he breathed. "When I came here yesterday—or whenever—this structure stood seven or eight stories tall. I was told the height was planned to reach some thirty *pedes* tall, to be divided into six levels.

"When the storm struck, I was on the ground floor—luckily. In fact, I was standing just about where that partial flooring still remains. Over here"—he gestured to a spot just to his left—"was a table, and over there some tools. Beside that was just a lot of rubbish. The place had been abandoned for a number of years, you see."

He paced the inside of the tower, poking hopefully at the rubble left by yesterday's lightning strike. At his heels, Jasper sniffed purposefully at the building stones thus overturned.

"Oh dear," said Hilary, "I don't see anything at all that looks like a device."

"A device?" queried James.

"Well, Rufus was not whisked through the centuries by his own volition. Something sent him here, and I thought there might be some sign of a—a mechanical—thing."

"Mm." James frowned. "I see what you mean. But who could have created such a—thing? Of course," he continued, "it might have been one of those accidental discoveries."

"Yes!" cried Hilary eagerly. "Like electricity. But who . . . ?"

James, pondering an answer to her unfinished question, found his reflections unexpectedly halted by the eagerness visible in her eyes. Her gaze was open and clear as a forest stream, and her pleasure in the situation in which she found herself just as inviting. It was as though she was lit from within by a wholly irresistible spirit of adventure, one that she seemed compelled to share.

James had, he realized with some surprise, enjoyed their conversation during the short journey from Goodhurst to the tower on the Whiteleaves property. Perhaps, he reflected with a rueful smile, because the main topic under discussion had been himself. Hilary displayed no interest in touting her own expertise in antiquities, but rather questioned him about his own.

James had taken for granted that her interest was feigned, assumed to flatter him, but to his further surprise, Hilary had listened to his answers, interjecting more queries and comments. He was, he thought with irrational irritation, being forced to the conclusion that her professed passion for the study of antiquities was quite genuine, and that she had acquired an astonishing fund of information on the subject.

To be sure, she was obviously not to be the assistant he had envisioned earlier, for she displayed a distressing independence of mind. The fact that he prized such a characteristic in a male colleague he thrust to the back of his thoughts. As much as he deplored the necessity of spending time in the company of a nubile female of marriageable age, he experienced an unwarranted stirring of anticipation.

As he moved toward Rufus and Hilary, something flickered at the edge of his vision. He turned his head, but caught only a glimpse of what seemed to be a black cloak, slipping among the trees and out of sight.

"Who is there?" he called sharply.

"What is it?" asked Hilary, only to fall silent as James gestured with his hand.

After a moment, James continued. "It was nothing, I guess. I saw a figure—or thought I did—garbed in black. But now . . ."

Hilary's expression cleared. "That must be Dorcas."

To James's expression of inquiry, she replied, "An old woman who lives in a cottage near here. She has been there ever since I can remember, and she's somewhat eccentric, though perfectly harmless. She's known simply as The Old One hereabouts and she likes to visit the tower and the stone dance."

"Ah," was James's only comment. To Rufus he queried, "Have you seen enough, *optima*?" Rufus glanced up in surprise at this designation of a foot soldier about to be elevated to the rank of centurion. If he appreciated the unwarranted courtesy, no sign showed in his countenance. "I must say," continued James, "I do not perceive anything here to provide the slightest clue as to your remarkable experience."

Rufus glanced about him, a frown on his face.

"I suppose," he remarked, "I almost expected to see the old priest here, waving his staff and cackling." He kicked aimlessly at a small stone. "But there is nothing—"

"Well," interposed Hilary, "perhaps if you were to apologize . . ." She glanced sheepishly at James who had snorted audibly. "I know, but since we have no other explanation of Rufus' presence here . . . That is, what could it hurt?"

Rufus drew himself up. "I? Apologize? What for? And to whom? The old goat obviously did not choose to make the journey through time with me. How——?" He glowered as Hilary continued to gaze at him expectantly. "Oh, all right."

He turned toward the stone altar and lifted his face to the sky. He raised his voice uncertainly. "Very well, priest. I am sorry if I disturbed you and your spirits. I——I meant no disrespect. Please, may I go home now?" he concluded plaintively.

The three stood motionless for several seconds, but nothing stirred in the clearing around the tower except the birds and the mice and the leaves of the trees.

Rufus sighed. "I knew it wouldn't work," he muttered. "I suppose I shall have to make a sacrifice."

"A what?" echoed James and Hilary in unison.

"I shall have to purchase a fine, fat ewe, or possibly even a young bullock," Rufus muttered. "Or——oh, gods, I wonder if . . ."

"Urk," breathed Hilary through bloodless lips. Had she not read that the Druids practiced human sacrifice? She glanced at James, and from his expression, the same thought had occurred to him. Was Rufus contemplating . . . ?

"Well!" she exclaimed brightly. "No sense in lingering here. Why don't we return to Goodhurst and——and make our way to the villa." She turned to James. "I'm sure Rufus could give us a fascinating insight as to its construction."

"I would rather go to Corinium," said Rufus firmly.

Hilary and James exchanged glances.

"I don't think——" began James, but he was interrupted by the sound of footsteps approaching softly through the fallen leaves. A moment later, an old woman entered the stone circle. She was small and frail and bent with age. Her face, which resembled the surface of an ancient tree trunk, featured a pair of black eyes that glittered as brightly as water on stones. Her garb was almost nunlike. She wore a dark, somber gown, covered with a voluminous black cloak. On her head, almost completely masking hair so white it shone silver in the morning sun, she wore a homespun shawl that hung almost to the hem of her garments.

"Why, Miss Dorcas," cried Hilary in a pleased voice. "Good morning to you. I have not seen you out and about for months."

"I have been resting." The woman's voice was, surprisingly, low and musical. "The harvest season is a busy time for me." She scrutinized Hilary's face. "And how do you fare, little one?"

"Very well, thank you, ma'am." She turned to gesture to James and Rufus. "Allow me to present two new friends to you, Mr. James Wincanon and, er, Rufus."

The hand extended by old Dorcas seemed made of cobwebs and twigs, but James bent over it courteously and murmured a conventional greeting. As she turned to Rufus, the old woman hesitated for a moment, eyeing him keenly. Then, she laughed quietly. "Ah, it is you," she said at last. "I am surprised to see you here."

Rufus, startled, mumbled, "*Ave*, old one. The blessings of Juno be on you."

Old Dorcas chuckled once more, and to Hilary's astonishment spoke in Latin. "Juno, indeed. You are sore put upon, Roman. I wish you luck." She turned to leave, but paused to address James. "It appears your destiny is upon you at last, young man. Try not to do something stupid."

She lifted her hand in what might have been a benediction on the group and in a moment, she had vanished into the trees, leaving James and Rufus gaping after her.

"What the devil . . . ?" rumbled James.

"How did she know I was from Rome?" asked Rufus simultaneously.

"And she speaks Latin!" James exclaimed.

Hilary smiled. "The Old One is full of surprises, and she knows many things. Some say she is a witch. Mostly, however, she is regarded as a healer. The women of the neighborhood seek her out for cures and advice on all subjects of interest to females."

"She seems to like you," remarked James casually.

"Yes, I used to see her often when I came to the tower. She taught me the names of plants and gave me good things to eat."

"Interesting," he murmured. "And we ready to proceed to the villa?" he asked.

"I want to go to Corinium," stated Rufus, returning to an earlier theme.

"I don't think that would be a good idea," James said again.

"Why not?" asked Rufus, with that pugnacious tilt to his chin that Hilary was beginning to recognize.

"Um," said James. "You will not know the place. You will not be able to speak with anyone. You can't—"

"I don't care," Rufus barked stubbornly. "I want to see it."

"Perhaps it would not be a bad idea," interposed Hilary in English. "If Rufus sees what Corinium looks like today, he will realize the profound difference between our age and his. Perhaps he will then be more agreeable to confining himself to the haven of Goodhurst."

"Very well," replied James curtly, "although I am very uneasy about this."

Rufus' demeanor, as the three bowled along the Fosse Way, gave no credence to these forebodings. He gaped with fascination at the houses along the way and asked questions about the different types of vehicles they encountered. He sat quietly but interestedly as James paused at a toll gate, and when the gatekeeper addressed an inconsequential remark to him, he merely smiled and lifted a hand in acknowledgment.

James relaxed somewhat.

From her corner in James's carriage, Hilary shifted under the weight of Jasper's bulk, curled on her feet. Covertly, she watched James as he endeavored to impress upon Rufus the necessity of keeping his mouth shut. She was hard put not to laugh out loud. Gracious, he was the personification of pedantic stolidity. Did the man not have any sense of fun? She recalled the smile that had escaped him yesterday. Perhaps, she mused, she could coax another one out of him today. Why this endeavor should suddenly assume importance in her mind, she could not say, except that she was of the strong belief that everyone owed himself a smile at least once a day.

"Mr. Win—" she began thoughtfully. "That is, James. Now that you have met some of your new neighbors, I know you will wish to get to know them better. To that end, I hope you will reconsider your decision not to attend Mrs. Strindham's musicale. She was quite disappointed when you declined her invitation."

James turned a frigid glance on her.

"I am, of course, devastated to have become a source of displeasure to Mrs. Strindham, but I have no intention of either attending her musicale or succumbing to the dubious charms of her daughter—Emmaline, is it?"

"Evangeline, and there's no need to strike such a toplofty attitude. No one is asking you to succumb to anything. For heaven's sake, don't you like music?"

"I do, when it is adequately performed. It has been my experience that country musicales usually consist of locals coaxing execrable sounds from badly crafted instruments."

"My good man," declared Hilary, growing rather red in the face, "Mrs. Strindham may be the wife of a squire, but she has as good an ear for music as any of your fine London hostesses. In fact, that's where she usually finds her performers—in London, that is. Her musicales are considered excellent, and invitations to them are much coveted."

James snorted. "That may be the case, but I have no desire to plunge myself into the local—"

A sound from Rufus interrupted him.

"Have we arrived?" asked the warrior interestedly, waving his hand at the cottages that had sprung up along the roadside and the hint of larger buildings ahead.

"Yes," replied Hilary, with a last, darkling glance at James that indicated she was by no means through with the subject of Mrs. Strindham's musicale. "You will find it much changed, for I think it is not nearly as large as it was in your time."

"Now, remember," cautioned James once more. "Stay close and stay quiet."

As they made their way through winding lanes and shop-lined streets, the warrior appeared to be taking James's words to heart, for as they reached the center of the town, he fell silent. Wide-eyed, he stared about him.

"Corinium?" he whispered.

"Yes," replied James. "Only now it is called Cirencester."

"At least," put in Hilary, "the people here remember that this used to be a Roman fort. That is why they included 'cester' in the name. There are a great many place names in Britain that end in 'cester,' " she added in a spirit of helpfulness.

"Can you describe any of the buildings that used to stand where these houses and shops are now?" asked James.

Trust the scholar, thought Hilary somewhat irritably, to ignore Rufus' frightened confusion in order to scour out the information that lay beneath it.

"No—no," replied Rufus. "I do not recognize anything. It is as though I have never been here."

They had been traveling along Tower Street, but now turned into The Avenue.

"See there?" James pointed. "We have discovered, there by that ironmonger's shop, the remains of what we think was the Roman basilica. Does that tell you anything?"

He drew the carriage to a halt and Rufus, his gaze on the shop, slowly descended to the ground. He walked closer to the edifice, then moved a few steps away, looking about him in puzzlement.

"Yes," he said slowly. "If this is where the basilica stood— do you know in which direction it lay?" He gestured with his hands.

"We think the entrance was over there." James pointed to the shop. "The main part of the building spread to that alehouse."

"Gods," breathed Rufus. "I cannot believe everything could be so changed. Let's see." He paced a few steps toward the market square. "The forum, then, would have lain in this direction."

He grasped James's arm and strode down the street. Reaching the corner, he turned abruptly to the left and walked past several shops before he halted suddenly.

"Here!" he cried. "Here is where my shop is to be. It must be the place. Here is where I will set up as a worker in metal. Maia will help me, as will our children—perhaps my son. Maia would like to purchase a villa someday, but for a while we will live above the shop. She has been selecting furnishings. We live just outside the fort at Isca now, and she says all our old stuff is completely unsuitable." He shook his head. "It seems all right to me. I don't understand women."

James grimaced. "Believe me, Rufus, things have not changed in seventeen hundred years. Nobody understands women."

Hilary smiled faintly.

"At any rate," continued Rufus, "the town seems to have shrunk considerably. Even in the time of the Dobunni, it was more populous than this." He swept an arm about to encompass the market square, the church, and the buildings that lay beyond. "What is that?" He pointed to a high wall in the distance that spread for some distance along the perimeter of the shopping district.

"It is the estate of the Earl of Bathurst," replied Hilary. She turned to James. "I suppose you have met him?"

"Yes. He is one of the few among the peerage to display an appreciation of the Roman remains that are still to be found about the country. He has been instrumental in the excavation of many remains here in Cirencester and the surrounding area."

"So I understand. I am acquainted with him, as well. He has been kind enough to show me his collection of artifacts."

James's brows lifted in surprise. Bathurst was known to be exceedingly loath to share his finds with anyone except those he felt would truly appreciate them. Hilary must have impressed him greatly in order for him to invite her to his private museum.

"It seems—" he began, and then looked around quickly. "Where is Rufus?"

"Oh, dear. He was right here. How could—" She broke off as the sounds of loud disturbance reached their ears. James raced toward the noise, with Hilary and Jasper on his heels. As they rounded the corner into the Market Square, James halted abruptly, causing Hilary to bump into him from behind.

"What—?" she gasped. "Oh, my!"

Rufus stood in the center of an angry group of citizens, the most vociferous of whom appeared to be a pie seller, waving his hands in the air as he berated an equally irate Rufus. The others gathered around seemed to be interested onlookers, who apparently viewed the altercation as an entertainment carried on expressly for their amusement.

"Thief!" screamed the pie seller. "Pay me for my wares or I shall call the magistrate!"

"Bandit!" roared Rufus in his own tongue. He waved a portion of meat pie underneath the merchant's nose. "I paid you good money for his inedible piece of dung. Unhand me or I'll tear your fingers off."

James surged forward and reached the small throng just as the pie seller, his hands thrown up in outraged fear, cried out for someone to fetch the magistrate. That personage appeared in a few moments from a nearby inn, wiping his fingers on a napkin tucked under his chin, a chicken wing still in his hand.

"Oh, dear," said Hilary again.

James muttered a barely suppressed curse. "Now we're in for it," he growled.

Grasping Hilary's hand, he thrust himself into the center of the melee.

Chapter Ten

"Here!" said James brusquely, reaching the crowd at the same time as the magistrate. "Perhaps I can be of some assistance," he said to the pie man.

"Assistance be damned!" screeched this personage, red-faced and belligerent. "This oaf tried to chouse me out of my money." He flung up his hands. "Ain't I an honest merchant?" He asked the onlookers. "Don't I make the best meat pies in the Cotswolds? And don't I charge an honest price?"

Not receiving the wholehearted support on these points that he had anticipated, the pie seller continued hastily. "But when I asked for my sixpence, this lout starts babbling in some heathen tongue and tries to palm off a false coin. And now—" Here, feeling himself on stronger ground, the pie man again addressed the crowd. "And now, the cutthroat is threatening me very life!"

To this, Rufus bellowed a response in Latin that Hilary could not even begin to comprehend.

"Is the *furis* saying I did not pay him?" he asked James indignantly. "I asked him how much he wanted for one of his pies, but of course, I couldn't understand his gibberish. So, I gave him an *as*. That should have been plenty to cover this pitiful excrescence." Again, he waved the half-eaten pie in the face of the pie man, splattering gravy over those close to him.

The pie man thrust the coin in the face of the magistrate, a portly gentleman, and obviously irate at having his luncheon interrupted.

With a sigh of resignation, James withdrew a purse from his waistcoat and counted out a few coins. This action obtained the pie man's immediate attention, and when James selected a guinea from the little hoard, his eyes brightened. The next moment, he clutched his chest and gasped weakly.

"It's me old ticker," he explained in a pitiful voice. "The thought of an honest gent like me being cheated by his fellow man . . ." He trailed off, his gaze never leaving the golden coin.

"Yes, yes," said James soothingly, as the magistrate "What, what?"ed in bafflement.

"It was all a misunderstanding," James remarked to this gentleman. "My friend here"—he indicated a still-simmering Rufus—"is a stranger to our country. He speaks no English and has no knowledge of our currency. He was merely offering one of his own coins—perfectly legal tender in, er, Southern Andalusia, but, of course, unacceptable here." He proferred the guinea to the pie man. "I'm sure this will clear up the matter to your satisfaction?"

The pie man, his hand a blur of speed, twitched the guinea away from James.

"O' course it is, yer worship. No offense intended, I'm sure, and none taken."

To the magistrate, he remarked brusquely, "Here, now, what are you doin' here? No cause for you t'be harassin' honest folk."

With that, he gathered up the remainder of his wares and hurried from the square, leaving the magistrate, his mouth still full of chicken wing, gabbling after him.

Clutching Rufus firmly by the arm, James strode to where Hilary awaited them. Clutching tightly to Jasper's collar, she was convulsed with laughter.

"I am pleased to have afforded you a morning's amusement," he commented acidly.

To this, Hilary only laughed harder. "If you could have seen yourself," she gasped at last. "Brangling in the most undignified manner with a pie seller. And—and Rufus looking as though he might explode. Oh, my." She was again suffused in gales of merriment, and after a moment, a reluctant grin creased James's features.

"I suppose it was a memorable scene. I should imagine our little contretemps will provide the town with conversation for several days." He glanced about the square. "I suggest we take ourselves off."

Rufus smiled sunnily and licked his fingers, having dispatched the last of the maligned pie.

"I suppose he isn't hungry anymore," continued James, "but I must confess, I am feeling a bit peckish. Where do you recommend we stop for lunch?"

Over a meal at the Pelican, Rufus gave the lie to James's assessment of his appetite. While James and Hilary made a very good meal from a potato potage and some lamb cutlets with peas, the soldier consumed a steak and kidney pie, a sizable beefsteak, prawns in a basket, and an astonishing assortment of sweetmeats. When he at last declared himself replete, the little group, after one final circuit of Cirencester, made their way back to Goodhurst.

It must have been the Pelican's excellent comestibles, thought James, as they traveled through meadows and leafy lanes. For, despite the earlier confrontation, he was in an expansive mood. Rufus had already contributed immeasurably to his fund of knowledge about Roman Britain, and the promise of what else the old warrior might tell him burned hopefully in his mind.

Not that Rufus had contributed anything to the conversation for some time. In fact, that gentleman was snoring gently against the carriage squabs.

No, it must be admitted that his satisfaction centered around his other companion. How pleasant it was to converse with someone who not only shared his interests but could discuss them with intelligence. He assured himself that her sprightly charm, filling his senses like a perfect spring day, had nothing to do with his enjoyment of her company. He was as appreciative of feminine beguilement as the next man, but it was Hilary's mind, of course, that afforded him the greatest pleasure. He must admit he rather fancied himself as a mentor and looked forward to expanding the girl's knowledge of the antiquarian world.

If this project loomed in his thoughts as a vision of days spent in close quarters with his pupil, examining pottery shards and coins, and evenings with their heads bent close over dusty tomes studying Latin inscriptions in a pool of candlelight, he very properly banished this concept from his mind.

However, as he contemplated Lady Hilary Merton, he knew a moment of uneasiness. What in God's name was he doing, becoming involved with a female who bore the aspect of a street urchin and the mind of a scholar? One who, in addition, seemed determined to interfere in his comfortable way of life. He felt, for a startled moment, that his destiny had been whisked out of his control. It was not a feeling with which he was familiar, and he did not like it above half.

In her corner of the carriage, Hilary reflected on the events of the morning and smiled. Really, James Wincanon had revealed an unexpectedly human side of his nature that morning. And in the end, he had laughed at himself—a little, at any rate. Perhaps there was hope for him yet.

He was an unusual man, she thought, for though he was possessed of an astonishing intellect there was that about him that spoke of more physical pursuits. In addition, there was the air of authority she had noted before, that sat so oddly on the scholar's countenance.

A man of many parts, forsooth. Which was why, she told herself, she found him so interesting. He was different from most of the men of her acquaintance and therefore to be studied with some curiosity. And his path made straight. She did not understand why he had never taken a wife, but this must surely be a lack in his life. Perhaps she could help him fill this gap. She would consider the list of eligible women in the neighborhood and help him make a selection.

In addition, she would continue her efforts to widen his social life. His decision to live as a virtual recluse while he remained at Goodhurst was nothing short of ludicrous. Such a course would be detrimental not only to James but to the neighborhood at large, for it was the duty of a landowner to mingle with his fellow estate holders and to engage in activities of benefit to the tenantry and the villagers.

As for young Evangeline—She considered for a moment. What in the world had caused him to get the dust up over Evangeline? She was a bit set up in her own estimation, and a bit too eager for a splendid parti. And, of course, she possessed the intelligence of a garden flower, but that was no reason to react as though she carried the plague. The same way, in fact, that he had reacted to herself on their first meeting.

Was the eminent James Wincanon afraid of women, then? She

rather thought so, but she had detected something beyond fear. Contempt. That was it. She had been under the impression that James had taken a personal aversion to her own perfectly amiable self, but now . . . For heaven's sake, the man simply disliked women.

She turned over this interesting bit of supposition in her mind. What was there in James's past that had so turned him against the entire female sex? A disappointment in love, most likely. She nodded sagely to herself. Well, whatever the reason, he must not be allowed to hide himself away from the world, moldering in his own bitterness. Evangeline, it appeared, would not do as a mate for him, for she would bore him to tears inside a fortnight. But how about Amanda Ffrench? Mm, no. Amanda was reasonably learned, but she had that irritating habit of clicking her teeth. Well, there was Charlotte Ponsonby. No, all she ever thought about was clothes.

Now, that was odd, she concluded after running down a fairly extensive list of local damsels. Not one of them was suitable. They were either too flighty or too serious, too worldly or too naive, too—Hmm. Well, she would keep thinking. James Wincanon must not be allowed to wallow in his self-imposed slough of inertia.

She started, aware that James was speaking.

"If we are to stop at the villa, it will be late when you return home. Perhaps you would join me for dinner. Your father is included in the invitation, of course," he added hastily. "The thing is, I wish to interrogate Rufus again this evening, and he seems to be more amenable in your company. I know I shan't be able to speak to him in Lord Clarendon's presence, but"—his lips curved in his surprisingly engaging grin—"I thought you could perhaps turn him up sweet before you leave."

Hilary knew she should be affronted at this clear expression of disinterest in her company except to further Mr. Wincanon's ends. Unaccountably, however, a sudden warmth filled her spirit. She nodded in acquiescence, then drew a deep breath.

"You know," she said confidingly, "you have arrived in Gloucestershire at a most opportune time."

James merely raised his eyebrows.

"Our Halloween ball is approaching, but you still have time to contrive a costume."

"Ball? Costume?" James did not actually curl his lip, but his expression was far from encouraging.

"Yes, it is one of the major events of the year hereabouts. It is held on the day itself, but the costumes do not have to be related to All Hallow's Eve, of course. Last year, Lady Buffington was quite a sensation in her harem outfit. Lord B. came as a Red Indian."

"Very amusing, I'm sure, but as I believe I told you, I do not wish to participate in local festivities, giddy and brilliant as they sound."

Hilary pursed her mouth. "Really, James, this air of condescension is not at all becoming. Just because we are removed from London does not mean that we— Oh, who is that?"

The carriage had crossed onto Goodhurst land and, by previous agreement, James had driven directly to the villa site. As he followed the direction of Hilary's pointing finger, he stiffened.

"Oh, my God," he muttered. "What is *he* doing here?"

Hilary and James were still some distance from the site, but two figures could be seen there, one of which was seated on a broken stone wall. The other, arms waving, appeared to be expostulating.

Abruptly, James ordered the carriage to slow. "The slender gentleman is my secretary," he said tersely in answer to Hilary's question. "The fat one is called Mordecai Cheeke."

"Oh, my goodness!" she exclaimed. "I know that name! I've read—"

"Never mind that. I'm sorry to be so abrupt, but I don't have much time. Please be aware that I have good reason for wishing him to the very devil right now. He must not know about Rufus or be made aware of his, er, background." He grasped Hilary's hands in his. "Please trust me on this. Cheeke will try to weasel information from you, which you must not give him."

He turned to confront Rufus and said rapidly, "*Optima,* listen to me carefully. The man you see there—the one examining the stone wall—is my enemy. I feel about him as you do about your brother-in-law, Felix. I must act cordially to him, but I do not trust him. It is imperative that he not discover your identity. I'll explain later. I will tell him you are a visitor from a far-off country and I'll get rid of him as soon as I can. In the meantime—he speaks your tongue, so you must take care to say nothing in Latin, or—or anything at all. *Nothing.* Do you understand?"

Rufus nodded. "Do you want me to dispatch him for you, James? It would be the work of a moment."

"No!" cried James and Hilary in unison.

"That is," continued James, "I appreciate the gesture, but it—it would not serve. Just remain silent."

The carriage halted and the two people already on the scene turned as the little party disembarked. Jasper leaped from the vehicle and loped over to perform his duties as chief inspector of potential threats to his human's well-being. Mordecai fluttered his hands distastefully at the dog's enthusiastic investigation.

"James!" he cried when he had at last succeeded in pushing Jasper away. Today he sported what he must have imagined to be an ensemble suitable for country wear. A coat of dark brown velvet clung lovingly to his plump person, set off by a pair of fawn pantaloons. His waistcoat was a miracle of creamy, silken perfection from which only two fobs depended. "I have caught you out at last. You said the villa was of no importance, but, 'pon rep, it looks to be quite impressive. I knew you would not mind my coming to have a look. One of your servants was kind enough to give me directions."

James sent a fierce glare to Robert, who flung up his hands and shook his head. "Mr. Cheeke," he said tersely, "arrived at the house when I was momentarily away. A footman directed him to your diggings."

"I see," continued Mordecai expansively, "you have made a good start here." He gestured toward the strings with which Hilary had begun her grid. "The area looks to be quite large indeed. Do you think that section over there might reveal craft buildings? I understand that many of the villas hereabouts were supported by weaving." His gaze shifted to Hilary and Rufus, who were staring at him in some curiosity. "I did not know you were entertaining visitors, old man."

Unwillingly, James moved forward. "Lady Hilary Merton, may I present Mr. Mordecai Cheeke. Mr. Cheeke is interested in the study of antiquities." He gestured to Rufus. "And this is my friend, Mr., ah, Rufio. He speaks no English, I'm afraid."

Rufus inclined his head and extended his arm, lifting his forearm into a Roman salute. Mordecai blinked, but said only, "My gracious! If he speaks no English, how do you communicate? Perhaps he speaks French? Or one of the other languages in which you are so fluent?"

James shook his head. Mordecai's expression was one of simple, benign interest, but James was convinced that he had grasped instantly the fact that James was trying to hide something from him. "We usually speak through an interpreter, but the man is ill today. Now, then, what can I do for you, Cheeke? Have you come for a purpose?"

Mordecai smiled engagingly. "I suppose I should do the pretty and simply say that I wished to visit further with an esteemed colleague, but I may as well be completely honest." He flung his arms out in a gesture of simple, open sincerity. "I am intensely curious about your villa. I don't think one of this evident size has been discovered in quite some time, and I'm sure it holds secrets to delight the heart of an old antiquary like myself."

James's voice bore only the slightest edge as he replied. "One hates to disappoint an old antiquary's heart, Cheeke, but any delight taken in the secrets of this particular villa will remain at present solely for the edification of its owner. That would be me."

Mordecai's smile remained undiminished. He merely shrugged and allowed his glance to stray to Hilary. His eyes widened.

"Bless my soul!" he exclaimed. "Can this be the lady upon whom your heart has settled at last, James?" He made a sweeping bow and hastened forward to grasp Hilary's hand in his own. He ignored James's startled grunt and Hilary's gasp of affront. "Mordecai Cheeke at your service, ma'am." He planted a hearty kiss on her nerveless fingers.

Hilary said nothing in reply, merely gaping at him in stunned silence. Had she heard the man aright? She glanced at James wildly, but the scholar's composure had momentarily deserted him. He stared back at her, in blank incomprehension.

A strangled gasp sounded from the young man identified as James's secretary.

"Oh, but—" he began.

"I must say," Mordecai burbled on, "you are a lucky man, old friend. She is a diamond of the first water. What a sly devil you are, trumpeting your undying intention to remain single, when all the time, this lovely maiden awaited you in the wilderness. Like Sleeping Beauty," he rhapsodized, "awaiting the kiss of her prince!"

James was fairly goggling at the man and Hilary felt as though she must be doing the same. She opened her mouth to confound his misinformed impertinence, but her glance was suddenly caught by James's secretary, who stood behind Mr. Cheeke, screwing his face into what looked like a plea.

After a moment of confused thought, she bobbed a slight curtsy and murmured, "So, um, p-pleased to meet you, sir."

"What the devil are you blathering about, Cheeke?" James snapped.

"Why, your young friend here—oh, dear, perhaps he was not to have said anything." Cheeke's eyes, black as currants, sparkled with mischief. "But, yes, he has told us your real reason for purchasing Goodhurst."

"Oh?" James's voice was winter ice. Hilary merely stared in bewilderment.

Mr. Cheeke rocked back and forth on his heels. "I see you are keeping your interest a secret, you sly devil. I shall say no more then." He turned to Hilary. "I understand you are interested in antiquities, my dear."

"W-why, yes," replied Hilary, a trifle breathlessly, aware of the young man's continued gestures in the background. What was his part in this ludicrous scene? To Mr. Cheeke, she said with a becoming blush, "Indeed, your name is known to me, sir. I have seen it often in my reading."

Mr. Cheeke swelled visibly. "I'm pleased that you are familiar with my efforts to uncover the glory that was Rome in our own country. Which of my works have you read?"

"Oh," replied Hilary, scrabbling furiously in her mind. "Why, just the other day, I read your article in *The Gentleman's Magazine* concerning your find in Kent. A temple to Ceres, is it not? I thought it curious that such an edifice would have been uncovered in an area that supposedly remained dedicated to local gods."

Mordecai turned a startled gaze on her.

James smiled, oddly proud of his protégé's display of expertise. He shook himself. Never mind that now. His immediate priority was to get rid of Cheeke with all possible speed. Which would be no easy task. Perhaps—

"Jasper!" Hilary was burning with embarrassment as she moved toward the animal. Doglike, he was subjecting Mordecai to a thorough investigation, concentrating on certain intimate portions of the gentleman's anatomy concealed by his pantaloons.

"Leave Mr. Cheeke alone, you dreadful creature."

Obediently, Jasper moved away, but chose this moment to mark the villa site as his own. Unfortunately, he took little account of his aim. Thus, Mordecai found himself liberally sprinkled with the residue that splashed from the stones.

His immediate reaction to this outrage was to hurl a curse at the dog and to strike at him with his walking stick. Jasper's immediate reaction to what he considered an entirely unprovoked attack was to sink his teeth into the fleshy part of Mordecai's calf.

Chapter Eleven

Mordecai's howls of anguish and outrage echoed over the ruined walls and pavements of the ancient remains. Shaking with suppressed laughter, Hilary moved forward to restrain Jasper.

"I am so *very* sorry, Mr. Cheeke," she said, schooling her features into an apologetic expression. "Jasper seems to have taken an unaccountable dislike to you." She made a great show of pulling the dog away from his victim. "I'm very much afraid I won't be able to hold him much longer. He is such a large animal, you see. Perhaps you'd better—"

But Mordecai needed no further urging. With one hand clapped to his abused calf, he hobbled toward the curricle he had left standing nearby.

"Wretched beast!" he screamed from a safe distance. "Damned creature's a menace—ought to be shot!"

With these and other maledictions, he mounted his vehicle and clattered off. In a few moments he was out of sight, leaving Hilary to give way, for the second time that day, to the gales of laughter that convulsed her.

"Good dog, Jasper!" exclaimed James, rumpling the dog's ears vigorously. Jasper grinned malevolently and thumped his tail.

"Good God, that *is* a dog, isn't it?" remarked Robert, who had remained silent during the altercation. "I was wondering, rather."

"And *I* was wondering—" began James with some asperity, only to break off his sentence as Rufus sank suddenly onto a stone wall. James moved to him. "What is it, *optima*?"

For Rufus was looking decidedly unwell. A grayish pallor had spread over his face and a cold perspiration misted his forehead.

"N-nothing," replied the warrior. "I just came over strange for a minute. I'm all right now."

Indeed, the color had already begun to return to his cheeks, and he straightened his shoulders. James, assuring himself that Rufus was in no serious distress, turned again to Robert. "I was wondering just how it came about that Cheeke was able to make his way to the site unimpeded. And what the devil is this about a supposed, er, attachment between myself and Lady Hilary?" he asked, flushing. "Oh," he said, turning back to Hilary. "Lady Hilary Merton, may I present Robert Newhouse, my secretary, who has apparently taken leave of his senses."

Robert bowed to Hilary and shrugged sheepishly. "I'm sorry, sir. I had gone into the village to fetch those cigarillos you ordered. I did not expect Cheeke would appear so soon, but I had left orders to everyone in the house—or so I had thought—not to admit Cheeke or to allow him onto the estate grounds. It must be supposed that young Binks didn't get the word. At any rate, as soon as I arrived home and discovered that Cheeke was on his way to the villa, I hurried to intercept him. To no avail, as you saw."

"Mph," James grunted. "But, what about—"

"Yes," interrupted Hilary. "What was that, pray, about the awakening of my maiden's heart and all that other drivel?"

Robert reddened and shuffled his feet. "Almost as soon as I caught up with him, Cheeke started in." He turned to James. "He asked questions about your purchase of the estate and what you expected to find at the villa and so on. I told him, of course, that yes, I believed your primary purpose in buying the estate was to gain access to the villa and that you hoped to uncover some unusual artifacts and, perhaps, a center for some sort of craft industry—and so on.

"He seemed to accept that, but then he started prosing on about what else you were looking for! The man simply would not let up. I had to say something that would account for your wishing to be left alone—for I know you don't want him finding out about the soldier." He gestured toward Rufus, who was poking aimlessly about the crumbling stones.

"Then an idea struck me. I know it was outrageous, and completely buffleheaded, but it just sort of blossomed full-blown in my brain. And, at that point, I was desperate. I put on a sort of hang-dog expression as though he'd finally broken me, and said that you had come to Gloucestershire with a view to marriage and that you had settled on Lady Hilary Merton."

"What?" gasped Hilary.

"You—told—him—*what*?" James felt the hair lifting on his scalp.

"I'm truly sorry, ma'am," Robert said to Hilary, "but you are the only female in these parts with whose name I'm familiar. In any event," he continued, turning again to James, "I told him that your relatives have been after you to marry, and—"

"Well, that's true enough," muttered James, earning him a hard look from Hilary.

"And I said that you and Lord Clarendon were old friends and that his daughter was an amateur antiquary. I mentioned your estates marching together. I told him you did not want to mingle with friends and acquaintances while you were pressing your suit and I told him the arrangements were all but final, but you were keeping it quiet for the time being because of illness in Lady Hilary's family. At last, he appeared to be convinced."

Robert threw up his hands. "I'm truly sorry, sir, but he was like a burr. I had to tell him something, or he would have known I was hiding something."

To Hilary's astonishment, James chuckled.

"Well, I must say I always knew you were an inventive fellow, but I had no idea of the extent of your talent. It was a near thing, young Robert, but I should imagine no harm was done."

Robert blew out his cheeks. "Thank you, sir. You will not mind then, if I return to my duties?"

James acquiesced with a wave of his hand, pausing only to give instructions to Robert to send a note of invitation to the Earl of Clarendon. In what was obviously a rush to escape, Robert mounted his horse and cantered rapidly out of sight.

"No harm?" said Hilary in a gritty voice from where she still stood, frozen in outrage.

"Why, no," replied James in surprise. "Certainly, it would have been better if Robert had not been forced to such a ludicrous subterfuge, but with Rufus on the premises—" He lifted his brows. "It would not have done at all for Cheeke to become apprised of Rufus' identity, you know."

"Well, how in the world could he? At any rate, the man is a renowned antiquary. Could we not trust him with our secret? Would that not be better than having him think we are on the verge of a betrothal?"

"But it does not matter to me what he thinks about you. That is," he amended hastily as Hilary's fists clenched and her eyes shot sparks, "such an absurd notion is not liable to spread any farther. In the unlikely event that Cheeke were to repeat Robert's faradiddle, who would believe him?"

A wave of mortification swept over Hilary. "Indeed?" she queried with great precision.

There was a moment's awkward silence before James spoke again, his voice low and husky. "I only meant that every one of my acquaintance knows me for a confirmed bachelor—and you, I believe have also declared your intention to remain unmarried."

To Hilary's astonishment, James took her hand and gazed into her eyes with a sudden intensity. "Please do not misunderstand me. I meant you no insult."

She managed a light, humorless, laugh. "None taken, James. However, I believe you mistake the matter. That man believes we are to be married. Do you not know how quickly a tidbit of this magnitude will be swept into the rumor mill? By tomorrow afternoon the vicar's wife will have called to wish me happy."

James stared at her. "Nonsense," he said shortly. "Mordecai Cheeke is not a resident of these parts. The only person he knows here beside us, of course, is the man at whose home he is visiting, Sir Harvey Winslow."

"Who lives less than twenty miles from here."

"Y-yes. But—"

"Do you realize that he trades in the same village as we do? His servants are acquainted with those in nearly every other household in the neighborhood."

By now, James had partially recovered his equilibrium. "Come, come now, Hilary. You are making too much of this. Surely, you cannot be concerned over a parcel of country gossips. Please believe me, I have been the object of that sort of tittle-tattle all my life. I have learned to ignore it, and you should, too."

Really! The arrogance of the man. Hilary drew herself up. "Those country gossips are my friends, Mr. Wincanon. Being from the city you would not, of course, understands the bond among country folk. We rely on each other and we are interested in each other's lives."

"I did not mean to disparage your friends, Hilary. I'm sure they are all of sterling character and good intent. I'm merely saying that you should not allow the rumor mill to guide your life. In any event, a simple denial if anyone brings up the matter to you ought to suffice to stem the flow, and when the general populace realizes there is no truth to the rumor, some other juicy bit of news will soon occur to turn the stream into another direction altogether."

Hilary sniffed. "All well and good for you to say." She sighed. "I suppose there is nothing else to do. Except . . ."

"What?"

"Now, it will not do for me to spend as much time here as I had hoped. Particularly unchaperoned. For example, I believe it would be unwise for me to join you for dinner tonight."

At this, James knew an unexpected pang of disappointment. "But," he replied, listening with surprise to the crestfallen note in his voice, "Lord Clarendon will be here, as well."

"Even more so. Everyone will assume our supposed union already has his blessing."

Not, thought Hilary, that her father would not leap with open arms at an offer from James Wincanon.

There was a long pause as James digested this theory. "I don't know," he said at last. "It seems to me that, on the contrary, you should become a frequent visitor to my site and my home. From our demeanor, it will become perfectly obvious to anyone else on the premises—meaning those ubiquitous servants that concern you so—that our relationship is one of strict scholarship."

Hilary contemplated his words. She was ashamed to admit how badly she wanted to accept his arguments. She was uneasily aware that it was not just James Wincanon's Roman villa that intrigued her, nor the presence of Marcus Minimus Rufus in his house. No, it was the antiquary himself whose company she had begun to enjoy. He was infuriating, to be sure, and arrogant and at times downright obnoxious. And yet . . .

And yet, there was his humor, his intelligence, and the basic decency she was sure lurked beneath the forbidding exterior. Yes, she would like to get to know James Wincanon better—on a purely platonic basis, of course. She would like to bring him out of his shell and make him a part of the neighborhood. In short, she would like to make him happy—or at least happier than he seemed to be now.

Not that it would be at all wise to let him suspect her intentions.

"Mm," she replied coolly at length. "You may be right. Very well, Father and I will be among those present tonight at your home for dinner."

How the devil, wondered James, had the situation changed so drastically? His invitation to her had been unwilling, and now, a scant half hour later, he knew an urge to grin idiotically and dance a small jig at her acceptance.

"Very good," he said stiffly.

James gestured Hilary to the stone wall near where Rufus sat, gazing about him in boredom. Hilary, however, remained standing. "You don't seem to like Mr. Cheeke," she said, her voice rising in a question.

"Um, no I don't. Frankly, I think him little more than a charlatan." To his surprise, Hilary chuckled.

"I must say, my own impression of him was not favorable, but he seems as harmless as the veriest infant. Do you really believe he has come to winkle secrets from you about your new toy?" She gestured toward the villa.

"There is not the slightest doubt in my mind," replied James promptly. "However, the villa has taken second place in my list of items to be kept secret from Mordecai Cheeke. If he were to get wind of Rufus' true identity—"

"But surely he would not believe that Rufus is a traveler through time!"

"I did not believe it, either, if you will recall, but it did not take long to convince me."

"Yes, but I was trying to make you believe what had happened. If—"

James lifted his hand in an impatient gesture. "In all probability you are right, but if, for example, Rufus inadvertently spoke to him in Latin, he would become immediately suspicious. I don't think it would take much after that for Cheeke to put two and two together, incredible as the possibility might seem to him. Once he realized what he had discovered, there would be no stopping him. It's my belief he wouldn't rest until he'd got Rufus into his own hands, and then he'd put the old fellow on exhibition like a two-headed pig at Bartholomew Fair."

"Oh, dear." Hilary frowned in thought. "I suppose he would attempt to thwart our efforts to get Rufus back to his own time, as well."

"Precisely."

Hilary shook her head distastefully. "I must say, if what you suppose is true, Mordecai Cheeke is a perfectly dreadful man—and must be kept out of our plans at all costs. Your plans, that is," she amended hastily as he sent her a minatory glance.

James paused a moment before saying quietly, "No, Hilary. You were right the first time. Rufus was your discovery, and you have more right than I to plan his future in this time period—inasmuch as he will let you."

Hilary's breath caught. She knew it must have cost him a great deal to utter those words. Did this mean that he had come to accept her as an equal? Or at least one who could make a meaningful contribution to the burgeoning science of archaeology?

"Thank you," she said simply.

Lord, James thought, observing the glow that sprang to her eyes like the fire from a roomful of candles, you'd think he'd just gifted her with the crown jewels. He knew an urge to warm himself with that glow, and it was only the presence of Rufus, scuffing at one of the ruined walls of the villa, that prevented him from brushing his fingers along her cheek.

"You have never told me," he said rather huskily, "how it was that you came to be interested in the ancient Romans."

She laughed softly. "Oddly enough, it was the tower that snared me. I made up stories about it, picturing the troops who must have built it, and tended it, and their families who lived nearby. What a sight the soldiers must have been, with their polished helmets and their flashing swords."

"I see your fascination springs from the romantic," James said austerely. "My interest is purely academic. I have always been motivated by a desire to learn more of the history of the invaders and the effect their presence had on our own civilization."

"Pooh," responded Hilary. "You make the Romans sound as though they belonged in the pages of some dusty old tome. To me, they were living, breathing souls, with aspirations and problems— just like you and me. Many of them—like Rufus—came here and fell in love with British women. They married and raised families and died here."

James snorted. "They were the same as any other conquering race. They looted and pillaged and impressed their culture on the Britons with studded boot heels."

"Yes, but—"

They had continued their conversation in Latin, and now Rufus interrupted. "The devil you say! Studded boot heels, indeed. The imperial policy has always been one of assimilation. We demand obedience to our laws and our regulations, of course, but we have always encouraged conquered subjects to retain their own customs—their native religions. Perhaps you are unaware," he continued somewhat pontifically, "that the new temple to Minerva at Aquae Sulis is dedicated to Minerva Sulis, in honor of the spring's local deity."

"By Jove!" exclaimed James. "Is that right? The marble head of a deity thought to be Minerva was recently unearthed in Bath— that is, Aquae Sulis, but we did not know the whole spring was dedicated to her." His face fell. "It would be impossible to dig there, of course. The whole area is a clutter of pavement and buildings—mainly the abbey and the pump room, which rest atop the probable complex."

Rufus, whose interest in the matter seemed minimal, at best, shrugged. He glanced at the sun, which had begun its descent toward the western horizon. "Did you say something about dinner?" he asked hopefully.

"Oh!" exclaimed Hilary. "I should return home to change and accompany Father back to your home."

James glanced at her abstractedly. "Robert will have sent a note to Lord Clarendon on his arrival at the house, and there is no need for you to change. You look perfectly acceptable in your present ensemble."

Hilary knew a twinge of irritation. She had chosen her gown carefully this morning, knowing she would be spending most of the day in James's company. Why it seemed necessary to her to appear in her most becoming outfit, she preferred not to ponder, but she had tried on a number of gowns before she was satisfied she looked her best. Apparently, to no avail, she thought dispiritedly. She merely nodded in acquiescence, however, and allowed herself to be handed into the carriage.

Chapter Twelve

Dinner was a pleasant affair. Lord Clarendon professed himself pleased to meet Mr. Wincanon's somewhat unorthodox guest and the conversation around the table was general. Rufus had been warned again not to speak in Latin, for the earl, though not fluent in that tongue, possessed the usual gentleman's knowledge of it, gained in his school days. Rufus startled his host, instead, with a brief but impressive display of English. His primary acquisition appeared to be the word, "more."

"More wine," he instructed the footman, with an expansive gesture. "More meat. More cakes." And later, when Hilary had taken herself off to the music room, leaving the gentlemen to their postprandial decanters, "More brandy."

Not long before bedtime, however, the soldier's indulgence appeared to take its toll. Lord Clarendon and Hilary had just taken their departure, when, as he had earlier in the day, Rufus grew exceedingly pale. He swayed where he stood, near the fireplace in the music room, and James grasped his arm.

"No, no," declared Rufus at James's expression of concern. "I am fine." But his words were spoken weakly and he was obliged to sit down rather suddenly. "Too much wine, perhaps. I feel a bit queasy. I think maybe I'll just go to bed."

James assisted him to his feet, noting the perspiration that once more dampened Rufus' brow and the palms of his hands. By the time they had reached the top of the stairs, however, the warrior had regained a little color and seemed to feel better.

"Until tomorrow, *optima*," said James courteously. Rufus returned his wish for a good night and waved a genial hand as he disappeared inside his chamber. James turned toward his own suite, an expression of concern on his features.

On the path between Goodhurst and Whiteleaves, Lord Clarendon spoke in his most paternal manner.

"James Wincanon seems a very nice young man."

"Mm, yes."

"You and he seem to share the same interests."

"Indeed, he is one of the most knowledgeable gentlemen I have ever met on the subject of Roman Britain," Hilary said brightly.

"Do you think, my dear, that perhaps—"

"No, Papa," said Hilary patiently.

Lord Clarendon sighed.

Later, in her bedchamber, having been divested of the becoming ensemble and her hair brushed for the night, Hilary stared into her mirror. Contemplatively, she twisted one carroty lock of hair around her finger. What was it, she wondered, that James Wincanon looked for in a woman? Certainly more than her own meager attributes. Why, she wondered again, could she not have been born with dark hair? And eyes that were dark, liquid pools? A high forehead and a classical nose would have been nice, too. To say nothing of a few feminine curves.

She jumped up suddenly in irritation. Really, what possible need had she to make herself over, figuratively speaking, for the benefit of a single-minded scholar, for whose opinion she did not care a button?

Climbing into bed, she snuffed out her candle and addressed

herself firmly to her own repose. Which was a long time in coming.

The next several days passed uneventfully. Hilary spent much of her time at the Roman villa in unspoken companionship with James, the hours slipping by like pearls counted on a cord. The highlight of the week was the discovery of a mosaic flooring in one of the larger rooms toward the front of the building.

"Look!" cried Hilary, whose trowel had uncovered the first stone pieces of the floor. "It looks like a woodland scene. Is this not a nymph, dancing?"

"Yes," replied James, leaving his own excavation in another part of the building. "Perhaps it is a representation of spring." He glanced around. "I wonder what this room was used for. No doubt part of the living quarters, wouldn't you say, Rufus?" he asked, turning. Rufus had busied himself in yet another corner of the dwelling, digging out what appeared to be a smithy.

"Mmph," he grunted. "I'd say it was the triclinium. The dining room, after all, is the most important room in the house. We offer our guests couches instead of shuffling them off to a back room somewhere and making them sit in chairs. Meals last for hours, with conversation and entertainment. So, that's where people usually install a nice mosaic." He glanced around. "You know, this is just the sort of place Maia has in mind—for later on. She's always wanted her own home, and she hankers after a nice villa in the country. She says, if we have a son, he'll need a place to run. When she gets her villa, you can bet the first thing she's going to do is hire a crafter of mosaics. I don't know why women set such store by things like that." He shrugged.

James and Hilary exchanged a smiling glance. Hilary noted, not for the first time, that James was a sight to behold in his work clothes. He had discarded his coat, and toiled in shirt sleeves, a plain nankeen waistcoat, and leather breeches. An impressive set of muscles was observable beneath the skin of his tanned forearms and the worn breeches that covered his thighs. She turned away hastily to examine a small indentation she had discovered in the triclinium wall. She straightened abruptly.

"James! Look here. I believe I have found—yes, it's some sort of utensil."

James, hurrying to her side, bent over the object she held cupped in her hand.

"See?" she continued excitedly. "It's a beaker—perhaps a serving pitcher, for it is incised with a decoration."

"I believe you're right. And I'll wager the artisan who made it was local. A pottery shop was unearthed in Gloucester not long ago, and the wares turned up were very similar to this."

Rufus, who had come to look over their shoulders, grunted. "Aye, that's from the shop of young Terentius, in Glevum. I bought some of his stuff to take home to Maia when I came through there several weeks ago. To my mind, the merchandise is overpriced, but he's made a name for himself among the housewives hereabouts, so of course, she had to have a few bowls and plates with his mark."

James and Hilary gazed at each other in awe. This was the first time that Rufus had made a direct, physical connection between their own time and the ancient past.

"I can just picture it!" exclaimed Hilary. "The lady of the house traveling to Gloucester—or, rather, Glevum, on an errand—perhaps with her husband, and on the way home they stop at the shop of Terentius. 'Oh, Quintus!' she cries. 'Why—?' "

"Quintus?" asked James.

"Or possibly Gaius, or Lucius. 'Dearest, see that beaker there . . . No, the one on the next shelf. I must have one. Helena Drusus has a complete set, and, while we certainly don't need more dishes, I *would* like some little thing, for the wares of Terentius are all the rage, you know.' "

"You are being completely absurd." James tried to infuse his voice with austerity, but could not suppress a smile. "The beaker indicates merely that pottery making was a thriving industry in the Cotswolds and that there was trade among the cities of the area."

"Oh, for heaven's sake, James." Hilary's curls bobbed against her cheeks as she shook her head vigorously. "You have the soul of a pedant. You must let your imagination out for a run once in awhile. It would do you no end of good."

"Imagination plays no part in what is becoming known as the science of archaeology," James replied in his dryest tone. "That way lies supposition and exaggeration and all sorts of investigative sins."

"Pooh. It's what makes scientific investigation such a joy."

Hilary fell silent, contemplating the beaker, and James became immediately aware of her proximity. For one who gave such an appearance of boyishness, the outline of her body was soft and supple where it pressed against his. And her hair. Though it might put one in mind of an exploding sunset, her curls were silky where they brushed his chin. The scent of her, fresh and sweet with a hint of spice, filled his senses.

In another moment, Hilary seemed to realize the impropriety of their positions. Sliding the beaker into James's hand she withdrew her fingers and moved away abruptly, a gesture that left him feeling oddly bereft.

He took the beaker to the little shed to record the position where it had been found. Rufus moved to a rock outcropping and sat down heavily, mopping his brow.

"Rufus? Are you all right?" Hilary hastened to his side. This was the third or fourth time this week the soldier had been obliged to give in to a moment's weakness.

"Don't know what's the matter with me, lately. I feel like an old woman."

Hilary shot a glance at James, who had reemerged from the shed. Observing Rufus, he hurried to sit next to him.

"You do not look at all well, *optima*. Perhaps a doctor—"

"No!" Rufus said adamantly. "I can't abide quacks and their nostrums. Spare me their attentions. I wish to live to return to Maia."

"But—"

"No!"

"Rufus," interposed Hilary. "The science of medicine has improved vastly since your time. Our doctors don't dose people with frog's toes and bat's eyebrows anymore."

"I don't care," said Rufus explosively. "No doctors. Haven't we spent long enough here today?" he asked, in an obvious effort to turn the conversation. "I'd like to return to the tower."

"But *optima*, we've examined almost every stone of the place, and we've found nothing that—"

"I don't care," said Rufus again, standing abruptly. "I must keep looking for some clue that will tell me how to get home."

Moved by the forlorn crack in Rufus' voice, James assisted the warrior to his feet. The three, with Jasper, piled into the carriage.

Some minutes later, they entered the environs of the ancient tower. James noted once again the curious juxtaposition of the structure within the even more ancient stone dance.

He glanced at the altar stone. It seemed to wait for worshippers of—what? Or, perhaps he should say, whom? The stone lay atop its monolithic supports, polished and smoothed over by the centuries until it could have graced any cathedral in Europe. To his surprise, he observed old Dorcas standing at the far side of the circle. She did not speak, but lifted a hand in greeting. Jasper galloped up to investigate her presence, but at a quiet gesture from her, he stopped abruptly and sank obediently to his haunches, tongue lolling in uncharacteristic submission. Dorcas waved once more and disappeared into the trees.

James frowned. A most curious old character, he mused. Dorcas, the old one. He would very much like a few words with her. At their first meeting, she had called Rufus "Roman." How could she have known his origin? One would not think her capable of recognizing the language, let alone able to speak it. Even so, how could she have seemingly divined the fact that he was a visitor from an ancient time? In addition, she had actually seemed to recognize the old soldier!

Once again, an investigation of the tower proved fruitless. Scorch marks could be seen on some of the stones, indicating the recent lightning strike.

"And, could these black streaks not be from where it struck in Rufus' time?" asked Hilary, her fingers splaying over shadowy scars that lay along the same area.

"They could be," said James dubiously. He sighed. "I just don't know. Nor do I detect anything that could have led to Rufus' remarkable transference."

Rufus, stirring dejectedly about in a pile of stones, turned to Hilary. James watched as she struggled with one of the blocks. Rufus bent to help her and Hilary thanked him pleasantly but without coquetry. Most women of his acquaintance, he mused, would have fluttered her lashes instinctively and simpered a pretty thank-you. Hilary, however, merely nodded her head in acknowledgment of Rufus' ponderous gallantry. He had never known a female so lacking in artifice. Perhaps it came from being raised without a mother to teach her such useful wiles.

Odd, he had thought her awkward at their first meeting, but he perceived now that her movements were delicate and as graceful as those of a young deer. He also noted in passing that the eager movements of her compact body as she attempted to upend stones as large as her head, was provocative in the extreme.

"Are we through here?" he asked irritably. "I cannot see that we are accomplishing anything."

He turned without waiting to see if Rufus and Hilary followed and walked toward the carriage.

Now what was the matter with him? thought Hilary. How could the man be so companionable one moment and so prickly the next? She accepted his hand with what she hoped was a gracious dignity and climbed into the carriage.

Actually, she mused, she was enjoying the company of James Wincanon far more than she had anticipated. Over the past week, they had discussed James's discoveries in such far-flung locations as Cappadocia and Smyrna and his tales of adventuring in those regions had fascinated her. Apparently, James did not confine his investigations to the remote and dusty stones of antiquity, but pursued an interest in the varied lives of those who now inhabited the areas.

She marveled that she had ever considered him stuffy. To be sure, he seemed to have retreated from the joys of life into the ascetic world of the intellect, and he seemed to be a trifle acerbic by nature, but he was so much more. Or, at least he could be if he could be persuaded to emerge from his self-imposed exile from the human race.

Which brought her to another point.

"I heard an interesting piece of gossip this morning," she began, smoothing down the muslin of her gown where it fell over her knees.

"Oh?" replied James unencouragingly.

"Yes. I ran into Mrs. Strindham in the village this morning, and she told me that she has hired Frederick Selwyn, the pianist, to play at her musicale. It is quite a coup for her."

"Oh?" repeated James, even more disinterestedly than before.

"Why, surely you must have heard of him. He has performed be-

fore the Regent and other members of the royal family. I attended
one of his concerts at Covent Garden two years ago. He performed
a Mozart concerto and I thought him wonderful."

She smiled at him with such transparent innocence that James
was forced to smile. "I am sure he has the touch of Herr Mozart
himself, but I am not going to Mrs. Strindham's musicale, Lady
Hilary."

"Oh, but I am sure you would enjoy it prodigiously. Miss
Sophronia Gibbs has agreed to sing. She lives in Gloucester, but I
assure you the quality of her performance equals anything you are
liable to hear in the metropolis."

"No," said James firmly.

Chapter Thirteen

Mrs. Horace Strindham was quite beside herself. She had hosted a
musicale in her home annually for the past fifteen years and could
always be assured of seeing her rooms pleasantly full. This year's
crowd, however, exceeded her most hopeful estimations. Every
personage of distinction from miles around was here tonight.

She gazed fondly at a gentleman standing near the hearth in her
drawing room, for she well knew whom she must thank for this
sudden cultural interest on the part of the best county families.
What a coup that James Wincanon had been prevailed upon to
grace her musicale! With smug satisfaction, she recalled that he
had refused invitations to no less than three dinner parties and a
soiree, and now to have him appear in her home . . . She sighed be-
atifically.

In his corner of the chamber, ineffectively barricaded by two
small tables and a settee, James glowered at the guests who surrounded him. How the devil had he let himself be persuaded to
come here? Mrs. Strindham's musicale was precisely the sort of
social claptrap he usually avoided at all costs. Even in London, he
rarely let himself be inveigled into such an appearance. He glared
across the room at Hilary, laughing with a group of young people.

It was she, of course, with her fiery hair and her gold-flecked amber eyes, who was responsible for his unwilling presence here. How she had accomplished this feat, he did not know, for she had not coaxed prettily, or worn him down with argument. She had merely cocked her head and suggested that he would be missing an evening's prime entertainment if he stayed home. At least, he thought that's what she'd done. He snorted. Meddlesome chit. Just look at her. How, he wondered, could someone of her intellectual gifts display such amusement at the bucolic bons mots being purveyed by the gentleman at her side? The man had been introduced to him earlier as a Squire Pendleton, a bachelor of some forty summers. His property, though modest, was, according to Mrs. Strindham, pretty and productive. Look at the fellow, braying at his own wit—and actually laying his hand on Hilary's arm.

"Why, Mr. Wincanon, you did come!"

The words were spoken in the husky, slightly breathless, and ominously familiar tones of Evangeline Strindham, daughter of his hostess.

"I was sure you would be here," continued Miss Strindham, peeking provocatively up at him through a feathery curtain of lashes, "for I particularly wanted you to come."

James grimaced. What a very tiresome young woman, to be sure. Well, by God, he was not going to pick up the hint being proffered so obviously. He glanced across the room at Hilary, who, as though he had touched her, looked up to intercept his unspoken plea. She excused herself from the group with whom she had been speaking and moved toward him.

Following his gaze, Miss Strindham frowned.

"I understand you and Lady Hilary have become great friends," she said in a voice ever so lightly tinged with malice.

James's insides tightened. Miss Strindham's comment was the third or fourth veiled inquiry he had received so far this evening. Apparently, rumors of his imminent betrothal to Hilary had, indeed, begun making their way around the neighborhood circuit. It was time to plunge into the stratagem he and Hilary had crafted a few days previously. Assuming a bored tone, he said casually, "Oh, I think 'great friends' overstates the matter. Lady Hilary and I share an interest in antiquities and I am well acquainted with her father. She has spent some time investigating the Roman remains that lie on my property and has been kind enough to divulge to me the information she has discovered there."

There, he thought, glancing at Miss Stringham, that ought to satisfy the chit.

"I thought it must be something like that," the chit said, preening visibly. "You know"—she continued with the air of one producing a momentous piece of information—"I, too, am interested in antiquities. No—more than interested, I have an absolute passion for the subject."

She paused, gazing expectantly at James. By now, Hilary had made her way to his side and James turned to greet her in what he hoped was a suitably avuncular fashion.

"Ah, Lady Hilary, I am glad you happened by. Miss Strindham was just telling me of her fascination with the ancient past."

Hilary turned to stare in some astonishment at Miss Strindham, whose cheeks had stained a light pink, but who stared back somewhat belligerently.

"Yes," she said prettily to James. "For example, did you know there is a wall—somewhere north of here, I think. It was built by the Romans and stretches for miles."

Hilary choked, but James merely nodded and said with a creditable assumption of surprised enthusiasm, "Why, I believe I *have* heard of it. I think it was constructed by the Emperor Hadrian, in fact. I must see it sometime."

Hilary, who was aware of the fact that James had spent the better part of a summer some years ago examining Hadrian's Wall and had subsequently written a paper on the methods used in its construction, placed her fingertips on her lips to stifle an unladylike guffaw.

Miss Strindham, as though vaguely aware of an undercurrent, looked from James to Hilary. A crease appeared in her smooth, ivory forehead and her lower lip slid between pearly teeth.

"Yes," she said uncertainly. "I would like to see it, too. Oh," she concluded suddenly. "There is Maude Brindlesham. I have not seen her for this age. Please, do excuse me."

Tossing a brilliant smile to James, she scurried away.

"That was not kind of you, James," said Hilary, suppressing a smile.

"I thought I was being extraordinarily merciful," he returned tartly. "Really, one would think the little twit could come up with something a little less widely known than Hadrian's Wall with which to display her spurious expertise."

"All for the purpose of snaring you, of course," said Hilary, her brows quirked. Really, the man was impossibly conceited. Not that he lacked good reason. If she had thought him compelling in his rugged work garb, he was magnificent in evening dress. Buff knee britches clung to his muscled thighs and his coat of dark blue silk fit to perfection over well-formed shoulders. An amethyst stickpin winked from the folds of a precisely tied cravat, and the candle-light created warm, russet glints in the mahogany waves of his hair. Judging from the behavior of Mrs. Strindham's female guests this evening, his assumption that every female on the planet was plotting to become Mrs. James Wincanon seemed to be proving all too true, but that did not make it any more becoming.

James stiffened. "I did not say that Miss Strindham is trying to snare me," he said austerely. "In any case, I assure you I am aware that my physical or mental attractions are not sufficient to ensnare the female heart. However, I think I can say without contradiction that there are few men in the realm with my material appeal."

Hilary gasped. "Are you saying that all the women you have met in your whole life are grasping harpies?"

"No, of course not." His mouth curled in a wry grin. "I can think of, oh, two or three of them who do not fall into that category."

Hilary simply gaped at him. She did not know whether to be in-sulted or to feel sorry for James. As though reading her thoughts, he continued, "I am merely speaking an obvious truth, you know."

"I cannot believe—" began Hilary, but closed her mouth almost immediately, as Miss Cassandra Bunch, a maiden lady of uncertain years, bustled up to lay a hand on James's sleeve. "Ah, Mr. Win-canon," she said roguishly, "I perceive it is my duty to save you and Hilary from social disaster." She simpered at his expression of startlement and continued. "You must know it is not at all the thing to so monopolize our little Hilary. Whispers are already going around and now here you stand with your heads together, smelling of April and May."

Hilary wished she could simply dissolve into invisibility. She knew her cheeks must be burning with an intensity that matched her hair, and she could sense that James was virtually swelling with a retort that would melt poor Miss Bunch into the carpet. To her surprise, however, he merely smiled thinly. "I must thank you for your efforts, Miss Bunch. And, I shall take your advice. Now, if you will excuse me . . ." Bowing to both ladies, he turned on his heel and moved off into the milling crowd.

It was some moments before James regained his composure sufficiently to join another group of guests. He hoped Hilary was satisfied. Keeping in mind her admonitions on courtesy to his neighbors, he had refrained from giving Miss Bunch the set-down of her life. Lord, he hated being put in a position of obligatory conciliation. He simply wasn't constructed for it.

He did not find himself in proximity with Hilary until after dinner. The meal had been excellent and the recital following, pure pleasure, for Mr. Selwyn, the pianist, more than lived up to Hilary's encomiums. Even the offerings of the locals, consisting of a harp solo by the vicar's eldest daughter and two or three soprano selections by another lady whose name now escaped him, had been above approach.

Thus, his mood was decidedly benign when he escorted Hilary outside to the terrace. Several other couples had elected to take the night air, and they paced sedately outside the long windows that gave off from Mrs. Strindham's largest salon.

"How was Rufus when you left him this evening?" asked Hilary.

James frowned. "He was not feeling at all the thing. He insists there's nothing wrong with him, but he seems very ill to me. His appetite is decreasing, and he is lethargic."

"I wish he would allow us to bring a doctor for him." Hilary paused for a moment. "I have been thinking—do you believe his condition has anything to do with his traveling through time?"

"I must admit I have been wondering the same thing. Perhaps he needs some sort of conditioning period to acclimate himself to our century. At least, I hope that's the problem."

Hilary nodded, and gathered her shawl of gossamer closer about her. She should have worn something a little heavier she realized. The early October night was chilly. She shivered.

"Are you cold?" James asked instantly. "Would you like to go inside?"

"No, it is so stuffy there. I think Mrs. Strindham has a roaring fire in every hearth in the house. She cannot abide the slightest draft. And it is such a lovely night."

Indeed, Hilary could not remember so enjoying the beauty of an autumn evening. The air was clear and so sharp as to be intoxicating. A sliver of moon sliced through the star-crusted sky. She and her companion had by now left the terrace and strolled over a graveled path bordered by leafy shrubs.

"Besides," she continued with a sigh, "I am so tired of verbally fencing with every other lady in the county. I've been through a virtual gauntlet all evening. Everyone in that room"—she indicated the Strindham music chamber with a sweep of her arm—"apparently believes me to be on the verge of betrothal to you. I have never heard anything so ludicrous," she concluded with a sniff.

Feeling oddly affronted, James paused and reached to snap off the head of a withered rose. "I am sorry my secretary created such a problem for you—us," he said stiffly.

Hilary's laugh sounded softly in the crisp night air. "I guess I cannot blame him too severely. In fact, I suppose he must be commended for his quickness of wit."

Self-consciously, she bent to examine a Michaelmas daisy. "Tell me," she said, a moment later, "is it your intention never to marry at all?"

Instantly, all James's protective instincts sprang to attention. "I have not decided that," he said colorlessly. "Why? Are you applying for the position?"

Immediately, he could have bitten his tongue at his maladroitness. Her question had been personal to the point of rudeness, but that was no excuse for his own discourtesy. "Do you think you could forget I said that?" he asked awkwardly.

"No, but never mind," Hilary replied tartly. "I have come to accept your general unpleasantness. And, no, I am not interested in marrying you—or anyone else at the moment. I was merely thinking that you would be much better off with a good wife, and as it happens, I have one or two young women in mind who might be suitable for you."

"What?" gasped James.

"Yes," she replied placidly. "Catherine Silcombe is a widow—just two or three years your junior, I think. She has two delightful children and needs a husband and a father. She is living now with her parents, but I believe she is heartily sick of that arrangement. She is quite lovely and biddable, with a good mind and a—"

"Good God!" James all but shouted. "I cannot believe— Are you actually suggesting that I allow you to select a wife for me?"

"Well," Hilary replied in her most reasonable tone, "you don't seem to be doing so yourself. Yes, I know," she added quickly. "I do have a tendency to meddle, but this is for your own good, James. You would be much better off married—to someone who will pull you out of the ancient world once in awhile and see to it that you mingle with your fellow man on a regular basis."

Unthinking, James grasped her by the shoulders. "My good woman," he grated, "I am perfectly happy with my life the way it is. I do not need a wife to arrange my social life, nor do I feel the need to mingle. And, even if I did, I believe I could manage such a task on my own. I most assuredly do *not* require your interference in my affairs. I have allowed you to participate in my excavations and in my dealings with Rufus, but if you think—"

Hilary was intensely aware of the warmth of James's fingers on her bare flesh, but her voice, when she spoke, betrayed only the merest quaver. "But you are not, James. Happy, this is. I must tell you that, despite your personality flaws, I have come to like you very much. I cannot bear to see those I like made unhappy by their own buffle-headedness, when they need only a push in the right direction to improve the quality of their lives immeasurably."

"My God!"

Hilary noted interestedly that James's breathing was becoming noticeably erratic. Why, the man was actually sputtering.

"My God!" James exclaimed again. "You infuriating little twit, will you listen to me? I *am* happy. I have been happy for a number of years. I just want to be left alone. Why can't females understand that term? Left alone. A-L-O-N-E. Is that so difficult to comprehend? In addition, what gives you the right to play God with my existence? Who appointed you the arbiter of the universe?"

James halted abruptly and drew a deep breath. He heard the muted voices of the couples on the terrace and realized that he and Hilary had walked a good distance away from them. He felt assaulted by the scents of the night air. The fragrance of open earth drifting in from the distant fields and the essence of the late garden blossoms closer to hand were almost intoxicating. It was the scent of Hilary, however—that unidentifiable blend of flowers and spice and forest pungency that filled his senses and made them swim. The fire of her hair was silvered in the moonlight and, gazing into her eyes, he felt as though he were being drawn into a golden vortex.

He seemed about to explode with the maelstrom of emotions that seethed within him, and without volition—almost as though he were being compelled, he bent his head. When his mouth met hers in a crushing kiss, he felt her stiffen against him in resistance. The next moment, however, she seemed to melt into his embrace. Her body was warm and soft and pliant against him and his hands moved from her shoulders to enfold her tightly in his arms. His fingers brushed the curls at the back of her neck and the velvety flesh beneath them. He almost cried aloud at the wave of wanting that surged through him.

The next instant, Hilary pulled away from him, and it was as though someone had peeled away part of his soul. She stood staring at him for a moment, her eyes wide and stricken. Then she whirled and ran into the house, leaving him shaken, and wondering if he were going mad.

Chapter Fourteen

Entering Mrs. Strindham's music room from the dark witchery of the night, Hilary felt as though she had been thrust into an alien world. The chamber seemed bathed in a confusing glare of light, and peopled by strangers who spoke loudly and wore clothing altogether too bright.

Hilary blinked and moved unsteadily to the ladies' withdrawing room. It was mercifully empty, and she waved aside the maid who approached to offer her services. She sank into a chair and contemplated the events that had just taken place. What had possessed James Wincanon to behave in such a fashion? And what had possessed her to respond so wantonly? She had been kissed before—not often, to be sure—but she had never experienced the breathless surge of emotion that James's kiss had produced. Sensations had been created in her that she had never known existed. When his lips had met hers, she wanted nothing more than to lose herself in him.

Lord, what was the matter with her? It was only the voices of the guests on the terrace and the terrifying weakness of her own knees that had made her wrench herself from his embrace. It had taken all the strength she possessed to step away from him.

What must he think of her? It had been he who bent his mouth to hers, but instead of delivering a stinging slap, or at least a freezing, "Sir, you forget yourself!" she had participated with a most unbecoming enthusiasm in her own imminent ruination.

And why? She certainly had not formed a *tendre* for James Wincanon. She respected his intellect and enjoyed his company, but . . .

Oh, very well. If truth be told, it was the man himself who attracted her. That was no reason, however, for her completely unexpected response to his kiss.

And what of James? He had heretofore displayed not the slightest interest in her of a carnal nature. Which was not surprising, of course. He had been courted by some of the most desirable women in the country. Why would he suddenly become smitten with a skinny dab of a woman with carroty, fly-away hair and eyes like pennies? Yes, he had come to display a certain respect for her intellect, and, yes, despite his autocratic demeanor toward her, she believed he was beginning to feel a certain friendship for her. But— There had been nothing of friendship in the passion of his kiss or the fever of his embrace.

Ah, well. She sighed. She had undoubtedly angered him with her offer to find him a wife. And gentlemen often displayed their anger most unaccountably. She supposed she must simply—

"Hilary! There you are!"

Hilary jerked her head up to observe Mrs. Thomlinson bearing down on her.

"You disappeared with Mr. Wincanon right after Mary Bellamy's performance, and I was wondering if you were ill." The vicar's wife gazed anxiously at Hilary. "Are you all right?"

Hilary pinned a smile to her lips. "Of course, Mrs. T. I was just resting for a moment."

"Resting?" asked Mrs. Thomlinson dubiously. "But it's almost time to leave. Actually, some of the guests have already departed."

"Oh!" Hilary jumped to her feet. "I must have been air dreaming. Goodness, Father will be looking for me."

Mrs. Thomlinson glanced oddly at her young friend, but said nothing further, merely leading the way out of the room.

Hilary looked about her as unobtrusively as she could, but could not find James among the throng of guests who still drifted aimlessly in the corridors and salons of the Strindham home. She discovered her father in the card room, just finishing up a final hand of whist.

"Ah, there you are, my dear," he said, smiling. "Are you ready to depart?"

Hilary was more than ready, and a few moments later they bade their host and hostess farewell. In the carriage, Lord Clarendon dozed lightly, leaving Hilary ample time for further reflection on the astonishing confrontation that had taken place in the garden just off the Strindham's south terrace.

Why had she not seen James upon her emergence from the ladies' withdrawing room? she wondered. Had he fled the scene immediately after that soul-searing kiss, or had he returned to the house to mingle with the guests as though nothing had happened there in the magic of an autumn night?

Hilary was correct in both her assumptions—and very wrong. For some minutes James had simply stared in the direction she had taken to the house. He had not felt so angry, so confused, so baffled, so shaken—or, for that matter, so aroused—in a very long time, and he could not recall ever having experienced any of these emotions so sharply or all at once.

When he had placed his hands on Hilary's shoulders, his intention had been to shake her until her teeth rattled. He had been suffused with outrage at her temerity in trying to dictate his life. This action, unfortunately, had involved touching her. It was this, and her nearness in the shadowed garden, with the scents of night all about him, that had compelled him to draw her to him. Still, he had experienced a sense of shock and astonishment when he found himself actually bending to kiss her. He did not *want* to kiss her, after all. Lady Hilary Merton was an irritating little chit whose presence in his life he tolerated only because of her knowledge of the subject that was his primary interest in life. That, and her ability to handle Rufus.

True, he had come to enjoy her company. He had come to cherish her intelligence, her humor, and her sparkling wit. In addition, he found that he simply liked to look at her. He liked the way her fiery hair danced in elfin splendor about her cheeks, and her amber eyes with their dancing, golden flecks seemed magical in their ability to mesmerize him.

But, devil take it, he *liked* a lot of women. He wasn't too keen on their single-minded determination to marry well, but he could not dispute their need to be practical in such matters—as he had learned to his cost a long time ago. No, he had nothing personal against women, and he had from time to time availed himself of the pleasures of the body. Nothing he had ever experienced, however, had prepared him for the shattering wonder of kissing Hilary.

He drew a deep breath. This must not happen again. He did not wish to raise any unwarranted expectations.

Squirming, he reflected on this concept. Damn! If he were plain James Dash, without his blasted string of noble relatives and his damned money, he would not be indulging in such ridiculous puffery.

He could, of course, be rid of the problem if he were to marry. But he didn't want to. Marriage meant confinement, an obligatory consideration of the wishes and needs of another, and the unending, petty frictions that grew inevitably between two people thrown together for a lifetime of discontent. He had only to look at his parents' marriage. He turned from that thought, sickened, only to find Serena's lovely face dancing before him. He closed his eyes tightly. He had not thought of the seductive Serena Cheatham for years, and he had no desire to contemplate her image now.

Of course, there was his good friend, Ashindon and his wife. Married three years, with a fine, stout son and another child on the way, the two obviously doted on each other. Their relationship was lively, and the genuine passion they felt for one another was displayed every time they so much as exchanged glances. Moreover, James recalled, Amanda had been ready to sacrifice her own opportunity to marry a nobleman for the sake of Ash's happiness. Altogether, she was most unusual, with the most free-ranging mind he had ever encountered in a woman—except for one, perhaps.

Still, Lord and Lady Ashindon were an exception and the thought of Hilary's machinations on his behalf sent a cold shiver down his spine. The second half of that corollary, that she might envision him in her own, personal future, he found even more disturbing. She had given no indication of any hopes in this direction, of course, and in fact, had—

He became aware that the carriage had stopped. Looking up, he discovered that he was home and was surprised at the brief pang that skittered through him at the thought of entering his empty house. He snorted. Empty, indeed. The place was full of servants, to say nothing of Robert and, of course, Rufus. Somehow, though—the thought tickled irritatingly at the back of his mind— that wasn't the same.

The same as what? he wondered, as he hurried up the steps.

Hilary awoke at an early hour after a restless night. The sun's rays, sliding through a crack in the curtains of her bedchamber, seemed stabbing in their intensity and she rolled over, groaning.

At length, chiding herself for her unwillingness to face the day, she flung away her covers and forced herself from their nested comfort.

She was interrupted in the act of drawing back her curtains by Emma, entering with chocolate and biscuits, and she ate slowly before rousing herself to begin dressing. It was almost two hours later that she joined her father for breakfast, only to be interrupted once again, this time by Dunston, informing his lordship that Mr. Wincanon had come to call. The butler betrayed by only the slightest lift of his eyebrows that he was aware of the solecism being committed by their closest neighbor in calling at what was virtually the crack of dawn.

Puzzled but affable, the earl greeted his guest and offered eggs and toast. Declining both, but accepting a cup of coffee, James took a seat at the table and the three chatted inconsequentially for some minutes before the earl, as though sensing something in the air, excused himself.

There was a moment's awkward silence before James spoke.

"We have a matter of unfinished business between us."

"Oh?" Hilary retreated into a protective air of offended dignity.

"I owe you an apology for my behavior last night. I have no excuse for what I did."

Hilary said nothing, merely staring at him expectantly.

James rushed on. "I was extremely angry—understandably so, I think. Or no," he amended hastily. "Forget that, please. No matter what the provocation, I had no reason to—to—"

"To maul me like a tavern maid?" finished Hilary waspishly.

James flushed to the tips of his ears. "Well—well, yes, although that is not precisely the phrase I would have chosen."

Hilary found that, ignobly, she was beginning to enjoy herself. Never had she seen the eminent James Wincanon so discomfited.

"You have a strange way of displaying your anger, James," she said, an errant twinkle appearing in her eye. "I suppose I am fortunate you were not truly enraged. You might have proposed marriage."

James flushed even more hotly. Devil take the woman! he thought, sure that steam must be rising from his collar. Had she no sense of propriety?

"That eventuality," he grated, "is the farthest thing from my mind. I hope, therefore, that in the future you will refrain from attempting to arrange my affairs to suit your own deluded ideas of how a man should live his life."

Hilary said nothing, but looked provocatively through her lashes at him. Lord, James thought, startled. This was the first time he had seen her use that age-old trick of enticement. With Hilary, however, there was no trickery involved—it was as innocently accomplished as though she had giggled. He had seen the gesture employed by any number of beautiful, elegant women, but none with the unknowingly erotic effect displayed by Hilary.

It was odd, he mused yet again, when they had first met, he thought her coltish and plain—except for her hair, of course—and those eyes. When had he come to see her as absolutely enchanting? Or at least, he amended hastily, uniquely attractive. Her slender body, which he had thought awkward, he now perceived, moved with the grace of a young animal. Her eyes, which he had at first considered too large for her face, were, he realized, pure magic, set in the face of an elfin enchantress with wide, delicate cheekbones and pointed chin.

He shook himself. Good God, was he taking leave of his senses? She might be possessed of a certain, gamine charm, but it was her brains, of course, that he found attractive.

And he really did not want to pursue this line of thought any farther.

"Were you planning to come to Goodhurst today—to dig in the villa?" he asked impersonally. At her nod, he said stiffly, "Then, perhaps we should be on our way."

Since James had ridden over on horseback, it was decided that Hilary should accompany him on the return trip in the same fashion. Excusing herself, she hurried upstairs to change.

"You want the Devonshire brown just for a ride in the country?" asked Emma, startled. "You haven't worn that since you were in London last. What's the occasion?"

The occasion was, of course, thought Hilary, her chin lifted defiantly, the fact that it was her most becoming habit. The rich chocolate made her hair look almost auburn, and the jaunty feather in the matching hat lent her a look of elegance notably lacking in anything else she owned. There was absolutely no reason she should wish to appear at her best before James, but on this particular morning, for some reason she preferred not to dwell on, she wanted to impress upon him her more worldly aspect. And she really didn't want to pursue this line of thought any further.

She was, however, inordinately pleased at the expression on James's face when she returned to the breakfast room.

Conversation on the way to Goodhurst was at best desultory. Jasper galloped at their side, romping through ditches and into the fields, and taunting the horses as much as he dared. The day had inexplicably become overcast and the air was chilly. The only warmth, it seemed to James, emanated from the flaming mass of curls peeping from beneath Hilary's bonnet. He felt that there was much he had left unsaid during his more than somewhat graceless apology earlier, but he kept his remarks confined to innocuous comments about the possibility of rain later in the day, and when they were likely to receive the first snow of the season.

He was relieved, and at the same time disappointed when they arrived at Goodhurst. As they entered the house, he was even more dismayed at the unpleasant intelligence conveyed by Burnside, that Mordecai Cheeke had come to pay a call and was even now awaiting the master in the library.

Chapter Fifteen

Hilary and James exchanged startled glances. James, muttering under his breath, seized Hilary's hand and hurried her from the room. Entering the library, they were greeted by the horrifying sight of Mordecai and Rufus seated cozily together near the fire, chatting together like old friends—in Latin.

"Cheeke!" James exclaimed, pushing into the room. The word sounded like a curse.

Mordecai, on hearing his name, swung about easily in his chair. He rose, hand outstretched. "Ah, James, you are returned to hearth and home. And the Lady Hilary." He executed a polished bow. "I was devastated to find you away from home, dear boy, but your friend has been entertaining me—most satisfactorily." He smiled widely. "I was, of course, surprised to discover him here—reading Latin, but then, I should have realized that it would not be surprising that a guest of yours would be fluent in that ancient tongue."

"How fortuitous," said James, with an aplomb that Hilary could only admire, "that you found a common language in which you could converse."

Rufus chuckled and sent James a look of veiled triumph. "I've already told Mr. Cheeke," he said before Mordecai could reply, "that I'm a teacher in—what is it? Spain."

"Did you?" asked James in startled fascination. He had by now led Hilary to a chair, and taken one for himself. He crossed his legs and brushed an invisible speck of lint from his sleeve. "Did he," he said to Mordecai, "tell you that we met in Seville about ten years ago when I was there to examine the ruins that were found in the area by Sir Cooper Walgrave?"

Mordecai looked oddly discomfited at this piece of information. "No, he did not, but that was to be my next question to him. I was wondering why you were keeping his presence a secret."

James raised his brows languidly. "A secret?"

"Yes. My dear boy, your servants seemed unwilling to so much as let me in the house, and when your secretary walked in and found me in conversation with the good Mr.—ah, Rufio, his eyes fairly started from his head. His efforts to separate us were laughably obvious, and I was left with the distinct impression that he did not want me speaking with your guest."

James opened his mouth, but Rufus forestalled him. "That's nonsensical, but now, if you do not mind, I will be moving along." He bowed to Mordecai. "Nice to have met you, Mr. Cheeke. You're almost as knowledgeable on matters of Roman antiquity as my friend, James." He smiled faintly as Mordecai flushed angrily and, bowing once more, he left the room.

James gazed after him dazedly and turned to Mordecai once again. "And where is Robert?" he asked, wondering why his secretary had elected to leave Cheeke and Rufus alone together. Damn, he added under his breath, wondering why God had seen fit to inflict Mordecai Cheeke on him just when he was on the threshold of what might be the historical discovery of the century. By rights, Cheeke should be away in Kent, investigating his damned temple to Ceres, or whatever. Instead, here he was, busily inserting himself into James's business. Well, by God, that nonsense wasn't going to fadge.

"He was called away by your butler," explained Mordecai, still obviously smarting from Rufus' slur on his expertise. "Something about a housemaid spilling ink on some of your papers in the study. Said he'd be right back."

James was forced to smile, picturing the dilemma Robert must have faced in deciding whether to attend to the minor crisis in the study or the major one taking place in the library. Even as he pondered this situation, however, the door to the library swung open to admit Robert, breathless and perspiring.

"Oh!" he exclaimed on catching sight of James. He murmured a courteous greeting to Hilary. "I'm sorry, sir," he continued in anguished accents. "I had to leave for a moment. There was a slight accident in the study—nothing serious, I'm happy to report, but it was something that had to be dealt with promptly." He glanced around the room. "I don't see—"

"Rufus has retired for the moment," said James in some amusement.

"Oh. Good," Robert declared. "Well, then—"

"And Mr. Cheeke was just leaving, as well."

"But I came to see you," said Mordecai rather plaintively.

Hilary stepped forward, feeling it was time she lent some assistance to James in his hour of need.

"How unfortunate, Mr. Cheeke that James—Mr. Wincanon and I are leaving again almost immediately."

"For the villa?" asked Mordecai eagerly.

James cast Hilary a look of gratitude. "No," he said tersely. "I have an errand to run and Lady Hilary is to accompany me."

"But still, you will be visiting the villa sometime today. I would like to join you, if I may." Mordecai's expression was open and ingenuous.

Really, thought Hilary, he was like a schoolboy, begging for a treat.

"I think not," replied James quietly, but with a certain note in his voice that Hilary had not heard before. "I prefer to work with as few people present as possible. A single assistant will do nicely for the present. In addition, I'm sure you have work of your own in progress."

His tone was so dismissive that even Mordecai could not fail to discern its meaning. He flushed once more and rose from his chair.

"I have no intention of interfering in your investigation—or of making a nuisance of myself. It is merely that, since I am visiting here—away from my own excavations in Kent, I am finding myself rather at loose ends. You must know Harvey Winslow is not worth conversing with."

"Then I suggest you return to Kent and your digs," remarked James. "There is obviously nothing for you here."

Mordecai's pale eyes glittered angrily, but he said nothing, merely turning to move toward the door. Before exiting the room, however, he said over his shoulder, "I can certainly understand your desire to work alone with your new—assistant." A sly smile curved his soft mouth. It was quickly erased at the sight of James's clenched fists. "Now, now, dear boy. No need to take snuff. You know, James," he continued meditatively, "the more I see of you in your charming new home, with your charming bride-to-be, and, of course, your fascinating guest, the more I am convinced that you are hiding something from me. I begin to wonder if your guest is not somewhat involved in your, er, project."

It seemed to Hilary that James stiffened slightly, but his face remained impassive. On the other hand, she thought ruefully, she supposed Mr. Cheeke must hear the thumping of her heart at his words.

James sighed. "Get out, Cheeke. Get out and take your smarmy implications with you. I don't know whether I have ever mentioned this, but I do not like you. I take leave to inform you that you have worn out your already slim welcome in my abode, and I do not wish to behold you here again. You will excuse me if I do not see you out."

Rigid with offended dignity, Mordecai chose not to reply. Instead, he stalked from the library through the door held open for him by Richard. The secretary exited behind Cheeke, dropping a wink at his employer as he left.

James sank into a chair. "At last," he murmured. "I thought the fellow would never leave."

"At least not without the use of blasting powder," agreed Hilary, breathing a sigh of relief. She seated herself nearby, curling her legs under her. "Do you think we've really seen the last of him?"

"Who knows?" James chuckled and expelled another gusty sigh. "I don't know why I didn't do that long ago. It feels marvelous after all these years to be rid of the necessity of being polite to him."

Hilary lifted delicate brows. "Were you ever? Polite to him?"

"You wound me, my dear. I'm always the soul of courtesy."

Hilary grinned and uttered a rude sound. James grinned back, struck anew by her gamine charm. This morning she wore her hair clustered atop her head in a flaming bundle of curls that fell about her cheeks in reckless disarray. The riding habit that she had donned that morning clung delightfully to her slight curves. Tucked in her chair, comfortable as a cat, she looked the complete hoyden. And she was wholly enchanting. He was struck by a sudden, appalling urge to go to her, to draw her to her feet and bury his face in the blaze of her hair and to kiss her until she was breathless.

Instead, he rose, and moved to the window.

"I believe the day will continue fine, and Rufus seems in good health. Perhaps we should indeed spend the morning at the villa."

Hilary expressed her agreement with this plan, as did Jasper when they left the house. He loped behind the little party in great good humor as they set out for the remains. Rufus, mounted on one of James's favorite geldings, spoke little. To Hilary's surprise, he rode awkwardly and seemed to have some difficulty managing his spirited steed.

"I'm not used to the thrice-damned beasts," he explained testily. "I'm not in the cavalry, after all. In fact, I don't trust horses—never like to be around them in battle—never know what they're going to do. If the gods had intended men to ride horses, they wouldn't have given us two good feet of our own. Marching's the only way to get where you want to go."

Finally, having reached a certain amity with his mount, the warrior contented himself with side excursions to examine such features of the estate as the dry-stone fencing and an abandoned cottage that sat at the edge of a meadow.

Upon reaching the remains, James and Hilary spent a companionable if largely silent two hours uncovering the mosaic in the triclinium. Rufus searched without success for the spring James had thought might exist to the north of the villa, while Jasper lent his somewhat dubious assistance to all three. To James, the time spent in such pleasurable company passed swiftly.

At length, Rufus declared himself weary of pottering among the villa's skeletal remains. James and Hilary exchanged glances. Rufus did not look well. As before, his skin was pale and his hands shook with a sudden weakness.

"Right," said James. "It's time to call it a day."

He assisted Hilary into her saddle, and as unobtrusively as possible, assisted the old soldier in clambering aboard his own mount.

Oddly, the conversation between James and Hilary on the way home dealt little either with Rufus and his troubles or with the subject of Roman Britain. They chatted on a wide range of subjects, among which were the poetry of Byron, which they agreed was highly dramatic, if somewhat silly, the Corn Laws, which they agreed were iniquitous, and the philosophy of Mary Wollstonecraft, after a spirited debate over which they agreed to disagree.

The state of amity thus engendered lasted until shortly before they turned into the gates of Goodhurst.

"Have you thought about a costume for the Halloween Ball?" she asked suddenly, determined to gain his acquiescence in this matter while he seemed in a receptive mood.

The amiable smile vanished like the last swallow of summer, to be replaced with a forbidding stare.

"I told you, Lady Hilary, I will not be attending your ball."

"Well, yes." She smiled winsomely. "I know you said that. You also said you wouldn't come to Mrs. Strindham's musicale, but you changed your mind, and I know you thoroughly enjoyed—" She stopped abruptly, pressing her fingers to her mouth. Lord, how could she have committed such a gaucherie? Recalling the Strindham musicale was sure to bring about a recollection of the kiss on the Strindham lawn.

James drew in a startled breath and Hilary rushed on. "I was thinking—the ball is only a little over two weeks away. Perhaps Rufus would let you wear his uniform."

James glanced back at Rufus, who had stopped momentarily to avail himself of the ripe fruit of an apple tree that stood by the side of the lane. "There is some disparity in our sizes. In addition, I think you have no understanding of the mind of a military man," James said dryly. "If someone had asked me, when I was in the army, to borrow my uniform to wear to a fancy-dress ball, I should have been insulted. At any rate, if you think I'm going to appear before the world in armor and a short kirtle, you are much mistaken."

Hilary blinked, struck by yet another instance of the illogic of masculine pride. "You're quite right," she replied in a conciliatory tone. "My experience with military men is limited, of course. However, perhaps if you explain the circumstances to Rufus—and you could wear some sort of leggings."

"Perhaps, but I shan't have to worry about it, for I won't be attending the bl—the ball."

"Mm," said Hilary, willing to leave the subject for the moment. "By the by, my father said to tell you that he's planning to go to Little Merrydean next week. It's a village about two hours' drive from here, and Squire Sainsbury, who lives there, is holding a horse sale. He's known for the quality of his stock and Father thought you might like to accompany him."

"That's very kind of him. Indeed, I've been on the lookout for a hunter. I'll send over a note to thank him. Will you ride with Lord Clarendon, as well?"

"Oh, no. The squire is a bachelor and the sale will be a wholly masculine affair, but I hope you will stay for dinner at Whiteleaves when you return."

"I'd like that," replied James, realizing somewhat to his surprise that he had spoken the truth. He was much averse to meaningless social concourse, but he liked the earl. In addition, he had discovered long since that he very much liked the earl's daughter, despite her tendency to try to run his life.

A companionable silence fell for a few moments before Hilary spoke again. "Tell me, James. How long will you be staying at Goodhurst? I received the impression when we first met that you do not plan to make the estate your permanent residence."

"No," he said promptly. "I moved here intending to stay only as long as it would take to excavate the villa."

"I see."

"However," he added almost despite himself, "I hope we shall see more of each other, even when I have removed to London. Perhaps—" He stopped abruptly, aware that his features had frozen into an expression of dismay. Good God, he had come dangerously close to making some sort of a commitment. To his annoyance, he was forced to suppress an eager hope that she would agree to maintain their acquaintance.

However, Hilary merely replied prosaically, "I very rarely travel to London."

She apparently had nothing further to say. They rode in silence until they reached the house. James dismounted, but when he would have assisted Hilary from the saddle, she demurred.

"I have been gone from home for quite awhile," she said coolly. "I really must be getting home."

Nonplussed, he stared at her, but Hilary, allowing him the merest brush of his lips over her gloved fingers, wheeled about with a nod. The next moment, she had called Jasper to her and galloped off in a spray of gravel, leaving James to stare after her in puzzled dismay.

For the love of heaven, he wondered in exasperation, what had he said to make her hare off in such a pelter? He entered the house, shaking his head over the unplumbable depths of feminine vagary.

Hilary maintained her pace along the path to Whiteleaves, muttering unladylike epithets under her breath all the way. What an infuriatingly toplofty man! Her heart had fallen at his avowal to return to London as soon as possible, but she had been pleasantly surprised by his expressed wish that they continue their friendship after he had removed from Goodhurst. Not so much as a second later, an expression of blatant horror had crossed his face, as though he had inadvertently invited Lucrezia Borgia to dinner.

Was it so very difficult for James Wincanon to accept a female as a friend? Did he see every member of her sex as a threat to his precious bachelorhood? He must truly think himself God's gift to the women of the world that he viewed himself as a target for their uniform machinations. To be sure, if the behavior of the ladies of the neighborhood were any criteria, there might very well be grounds for his fears. But how could he think that she considered herself as anything but his friend? Or that she would stoop to such tactics? Really, he was simply the outside of enough. She should have rescinded her invitation to dinner. She should have—

She paused abruptly, aware of the sadness that lay beneath her simmering anger. She was forced to admit that she was hurt more than she would have dreamed possible that he thought her like "all the others," and that he suspected her of trying to ensnare him.

Observing that she had reached the portals of her home, she thrust her shoulders back. She must not give in to such profitless maunderings. If James chose to regard her as a conniving witch, it was his problem. She was not going to try to change his mind, for she was blameless in the matter.

With these salutary thoughts clasped to her bosom, she handed her reins to the waiting groom and mounted the front stairs to her home.

Chapter Sixteen

At Goodhurst, James had repaired to his library, where, with a snifter of brandy at his side, he perused a recent tract on excavations currently underway in Northumberland. Robert and Rufus were engaged in a sanguinary game of cards.

"Yes, everything went well today," replied Robert in response to James's query, but he shifted uneasily.

Rufus grinned widely and spoke in a mixture of Latin and English. "I like this game," he said, gesturing with the pasteboards. "It is similar to one we play in the barracks, only we use small clay tablets. I have to say," he continued expansively, "I think your number system is more sensible than ours, once you get used to it."

A smile curved James's lips. "Yes, that's one thing we declined to borrow from your culture. We went instead to the kingdoms of Araby. Have you been gambling away your sustenance all day?" he asked Robert.

"Ah," replied Robert, an apologetic frown forming on his brow. "N-no. No, we did not. Actually—"

"We've been shooting!" exclaimed Rufus, and James felt the hair lift on his scalp.

"Shooting?" he asked faintly.

"Yes, sir," replied Robert, his shoulders shrugging apologetically. "It seemed like a good idea at the time. That wretched dog was all but tearing the house apart and I thought it a good idea to get him out and away. And Rufus, too. I never stopped to think that Rufus was probably unfamiliar with gunpowder."

"Probably!" snorted James. "Of course, he's never so much as considered that anything like gunpowder might exist. I suppose—"

"What wonderful stuff!" continued Rufus enthusiastically. "I'm going to take some back, if I can, along with—what d'you call 'ems?" He swung to Robert. "Guns! Gods, we could wipe out whole cohorts with one or two. My commander would fall on my neck if I could present him with a dozen or so."

James groaned, visions looming before him of the course of history changed beyond recognition. "Absolutely not," he growled. "How have you been feeling today?" he asked, more to change the subject than because he was seriously concerned, for Rufus was at the moment the picture of health.

"Very well," replied Rufus. "I think I must have had a touch of the gripe. I've been eating things I'm not used to, you know."

James breathed a sigh of relief. He would not contact his friend in Gloucester quite yet. No sense in letting Rufus slip from his grasp until absolutely necessary. "That must have been it," he said easily. "I'm glad you seem to be recovering."

He smiled as a thought struck him. "Tell me more about Italica, your birthplace, and your old friend, Hadrian."

"Ah, well then, he's not really my friend. More like boyhood playmates." He glanced reproachfully at James. "You didn't tell me he will be Caesar one day."

"Oh?" asked James, startled. "And where did you come by that information?"

Rufus waved toward one of the bookshelves. "I found a book by somebody called Spartianus. He wrote a life of Hadrian." He rubbed his chin thoughtfully. "I am wondering if Hadrian's good fortune might not be of use to me."

"I shouldn't wonder," contributed Robert, "if you actually know the fellow."

"Perhaps," said James, groping for another change of topic, "we might have a chat about the fort at Caerleon—that is, Isca."

Rufus seemed amenable to this program, and, sweeping aside the cards, he gestured James to another chair at the table. Pausing only to scoop up paper and pen from his desk, James seated himself while Robert bowed his way out to return to his duties.

"Now," said Rufus, dipping into the ink bottle, "the fort is shaped like one of those playing cards, with a gate in the middle, more or less, of each of the sides. See? In the center is the principia."

"Yes," murmured James, "the headquarters."

When Rufus finished his drawing, James gazed in fascination as the fully drawn plan of Isca, whose faint, all-but-indecipherable outlines he had studied so many times, began to take shape. He poured over the sketches until Robert reappeared to call them for dinner.

The evening was spent in similar pursuits until at last Rufus yawned broadly and declared it was time to call it a night.

He paused at the door, already unwinding his cravat, about which he continued to complain bitterly on a daily basis. "I'd like to go back to the tower tomorrow," he said.

James lifted his brows. "Again? I thought we had decided there was nothing—"

"No," replied Rufus brusquely. "You decided—and the Lady Hilary—that there was nothing there that could be of any help. I feel differently. There is something peculiar about the place—and I mean to find out what it is."

James shrugged. "Very well. When Lady Hilary arrives tomorrow, we'll jaunter over there. Then, perhaps we can return to Cirencester—that is, Corinuim. I believe there is much you can show me there."

Rufus merely grunted, running a finger around his shirt collar. "Damned instrument of torture." He stripped himself of his cravat and left the room. He could be heard mumbling to himself until he was out of earshot.

James remained in the library for some time, pouring over the maps Rufus had created. He could hardly wait to show them to Hilary in the morning. He recalled the coldness with which she had bid him farewell earlier in the day. Hopefully, she would have come out of her sulks by tomorrow morning.

He retired to his own bedchamber then, but thoughts of Hilary remained with him long after he had extinguished his bedside candle. He recalled uneasily the spurt of pleasure that had shot through him at the thought of sharing Rufus' drawings with her on the morrow.

This was not good.

In the past, he had, from time to time, mused on the charms of certain women who had taken his fancy. They had all been certified beauties, not known for their intellects, although he required a certain degree of intelligence in his inamoratas. None of them, certainly, had possessed gamine features and the awkward grace of a colt. To say nothing of hair like a bursting rocket.

It must be her eyes that so distinguished Hilary physically. At times they seemed as unreadable as golden disks, and at others were clear and fathomable as a running stream. And then there were those dancing flecks that drew a man into their swirling depths like a drowning swimmer falling into an irresistible vortex.

He thumped his pillow, snorting. What fanciful nonsense! Aside from her interest in and knowledge of ancient history, and her spirited conversation, and, of course, her engaging warmth, she was, he was sure, much like any other female—out for the main chance. Once again, a beautiful face floated before him. He smiled a little sadly. This was the second time in a few weeks she had come to mind. At least, he could think of her without bitterness now. He shook himself a little and continued his musings. To give Hilary credit, she did not seem interested in marriage herself, but her practical instincts had apparently found an outlet in arranging satisfactory partis for all her friends. In fact, if he were not careful, she'd have him irrevocably bound to some god-awful female of her acquaintance before the cat could lick her ear.

In short, he'd best put a leash on this distressing tendency to want to share significant moments in his life with her. She had made it plain at the outside that she wanted to maintain their relationship on a businesslike basis. He'd better not forget that that was precisely what he wanted, as well.

Still, it was many moments before sleep overtook him, and his last thoughts were of Hilary, her head bent close to his desk as they examined Rufus re-creations of a Britain long since gone.

The next morning, breakfast came and went and so did Hilary's usual time for arrival at Goodhurst. The lady herself, however, did not put in an appearance. James shrugged.

"Apparently," he said to Rufus, "she has more pressing matters to which to attend today." He laughed lightly. "However, I do not suppose we need concern ourselves. We'll go to the tower without her."

Rufus looked at him rather oddly, but merely nodded.

James refused to admit to himself the depth of his disappointment at her defection. He had, he told himself, grown accustomed to her presence at Goodhurst. If he missed her, it was only because he was used to making plans with her and discussing Rufus' firsthand view of the ancient world. If the house seemed strangely empty this morning, it was merely because . . . because, he concluded dismally, her laughter had become an integral part of his day.

"Actually," he said to Rufus, "I believe I'll just ride over to

Whiteleaves. If she is under the weather, it would be remiss not to ask after her."

"But what about the tower?" asked Rufus.

"Oh. Well, you could come with me to Whiteleaves and we could visit the tower later. Or," he continued hastily as Rufus frowned unhappily, "we can ride to the tower now. I'll drop you off there and pick you up later."

To this, Rufus agreed, remarking that it was about time his host trusted him to be on his own for a few hours instead of hovering over him like a mother with a dim-witted child. He continued in this vein during the short journey to the tower, but James paid little attention, his thoughts being wholly centered on his likely reception at Whiteleaves.

Hilary was in the conservatory when Dunston approached to inform her that Mr. Wincanon had come to call. She jumped slightly, nearly dropping the sweet william she had been transplanting, for Mr. Wincanon had been in her thoughts all morning, as well as a good part of the night before.

She still smarted painfully from the blatant rejection James's features had displayed on their parting last evening. He had virtually withdrawn his offer of a continuing friendship with her the moment it had been spoken. She supposed it was her own fault for believing that she could ever be anything to him beyond a barely tolerated nuisance.

Her reflections continued in a like vein through the dark hours of midnight and beyond and concluded with the decision that, though she would maintain a connection with Rufus, she would break off her friendship with James. This resolution had caused her a great deal of heartache, for the rapport that had grown between them, thorny as it was, had come to mean a great deal to her. Too much, she had concluded, or she would not feel such a deep emptiness at its demise.

In the end, she decided she felt not so much anger at his obvious distrust of her as a deep regret. She would have liked to call James Wincanon friend, even though she had an uncomfortable feeling that she might eventually want more from him. However, she could not face the prospect of continuing as the recipient of his years of inexplicable, unreasoning animosity toward the female sex. James stood in dire need of a female friend—or, for that matter a good wife—and for a while she had seen herself as the former and imagined she could provide the latter.

But it was obviously not to be.

That her opportunity to give him his congé would come so much sooner than she planned, she found slightly unnerving, but she nodded coolly at Dunston and instructed the butler to inform Mr. Wincanon that she would join him shortly in the morning room.

She paused to review her appearance in a mirror, vaguely pleased that today she wore one of her most becoming ensembles, a round gown of ivory linen trimmed with embroidered wildflowers. Running nervous fingers over her hair, Hilary hurried to greet her guest.

The sight of him created an unhappy stirring within her. He may have epitomized masculine elegance in the evening garb he had worn to the Strindham musicale, but she would always remember him as he was now, his lean frame clothed in his usual working attire of boots, breeches, and worn coat.

James turned at her entrance to the morning room. He moved somewhat diffidently toward her.

"Good morning, Hilary. Are you well?"

Feeling remarkably foolish, she assumed an expression of faint surprise. "Why, yes, thank you. Quite well."

He bent over her hand and Hilary was intensely aware of the warmth of his lips on her fingers.

"I thought perhaps, since you did not appear at Goodhurst, that you were indisposed."

"No." She felt that the air in the room was pressing down on her. "I'm—quite well."

James said nothing, but looked at her quizzically.

"I must assume, then, that I offended you in some way."

He listened to himself in some astonishment, for he had resolved on his drive to Whiteleaves that he would make no mention of the coolness with which she had departed his home yesterday. Now, however, having spoken the words, he found himself awaiting her reply with an almost painful intensity. If he expected a laughing dismissal of his fears, he was doomed to disappointment. Instead, she drew herself up, and her gaze held a militant sparkle.

"You don't even realize what you did, do you?" she said, vexation plain in her voice.

His only response was a blank stare.

"You mentioned," she began patiently, "that you would like to continue our friendship after your return to London."

"Good God!" James expostulated. "Was that so repugnant to you?"

"No," Hilary continued. "It was the obvious dismay you felt immediately after you spoke that offended me. An expression of the utmost horror sprang to your face, as though you could not believe you had so forgotten yourself as to make friendly overtures to the enemy."

"Oh, but—" James halted abruptly. It was no good denying that Hilary had accurately described his emotions. Lord knew, the moment the words were out of his mouth, he had regretted them. Now, he knew a sudden shame. Hilary was not just any female. She would not use his friendship to further her own devices—except for her annoying tendency to arrange his life to her own specifications.

He exhaled gustily and seated himself on a settee, drawing Hilary down beside him.

"You are quite right, my dear. I have become, perhaps, overcautious in my dealings with the gentler sex—"

Hilary uttered a delicate snort.

"And," continued James, "I was momentarily taken aback by my own lapse in—"

He halted abruptly and took her hand in his. "Lord, Hilary, I'm making a frightful mull of this. I must sound the most appalling, pompous ass. Please—will you let me try to explain?"

Hilary said nothing, but she made no demur. She wondered if he could hear the pulse that thundered in her ears.

James sat silent for a moment, keeping her hand in his grasp. Finally, he looked up, an expression—almost of diffidence—in his velvet-brown eyes that she had never seen before.

"My experience with women," he began hesitantly, "has been extremely limited. I have no sisters, and my mother—well, she was a good mother, I think, but she had no natural instinct for the position. I always rather had the impression that I was one more duty in her life, like visiting the vicar and giving baskets to the poor. Her parents, my grandparents, visited often, and they always chided me when my behavior slid into something that was, 'unbefitting my station.' Grandfather was the son of a country curate. He was an academic, rising to the position of headmaster of an obscure college in Northumberland. He was ambitious, however, and in hopes of securing a place at Oxford. He believed a son-in-law from a noble family might be useful in reaching that goal. In short, my mother had made a marriage of convenience, and did her best to uphold her part of the bargain. My father was a typical second son. He toiled not, neither did he spin, yet his raiment certainly outshone the lilies of the field. His life was one of wine, women, and song—notably the first two. Mother, as I learned later, accepted his infidelities as part of the price of her splendid parti. She was faithful, dutiful, and fruitful, bearing her husband four healthy sons."

"Dear Lord," breathed Hilary, thinking of her own mother, taken from her years too soon—contentious and domineering, but brimming with good humor and love for her slightly bemused husband and children.

James drew another long breath and stared at her carpet for a few minutes. "I—I did manage to become betrothed—when I was a young man. That is, almost betrothed."

His voice was so low that Hilary could barely hear him. Her heart thumped uncomfortably.

"She was beautiful, and charming and I thought she loved me as I did her. Perhaps she did, but that did not stop Serena from ending our association when an even more eligible parti than my own impeccable self came along. To be sure, her entire family was depending on her to make an advantageous marriage, but—as I said—I was very young, and the whole episode was painful in the extreme."

Beholding her gaze, wide and dark with pity, James shrugged and laughed awkwardly. "I overstate my case, perhaps. In any event, in latter years I have been somewhat, er, wary of the gentle sex. Particularly, since—" He halted, uncertain as to how to proceed.

Hilary felt her fingers curl into rakes. She was well able to picture the pain and humiliation the young James must have suffered at the hands of a mercenary female, and she would very much like to have five minutes alone with said female. From somewhere she produced a shaky laugh. "Particularly since you have been pursued unmercifully since the time you were out of leading strings. I have observed the behavior of the ladies in my own neighborhood."

James flushed. "Yes. Well, in any event, I decided long ago that to throw one's heart to a female was to court disaster, and I became pickled in my own cynicism. I'm ashamed to say that I grew to take a certain pride in my own sour philosophy. No woman was going to pull the wool over *my* eyes, by God, and she'd better not try. Frankly, when I invited your continued friendship after my return to London, I was immediately terrified that you would regard it as a prelude to a proposal of marriage."

James paused, but encouraged by the twinkle in her eye, he plowed on. "I—I have come to truly enjoy your company, but I have been so conditioned to wariness that I could not simply take pleasure in your presence. Now, I have come to the realization that not every woman has designs on my precious person, and that to refuse so determinedly the opportunity to acquire a new friend is the height of foolishness."

He stopped abruptly. He had not at all meant to expose quite so much of himself. He searched Hilary's face for a response.

Hilary's lips curved into a smile and she heard herself say, "Very well, James, but in the future, I trust you will choose your words with more care. Heaven forfend that a poor female might read a marriage proposal into a mere suggestion of future correspondence and an invitation to drop by one's London residence from time to time. I have no interest in marriage, James," she said with some asperity. "Although heaven knows my family have been after me to marry since my come-out. They believe that a woman's life is wasted unless she is under the thumb of some man, producing hordes of children for him."

Merciful heavens! That was not at all what she meant to say, and she straightened primly.

"Ah, it is the concept of marriage in general that you abhor," returned James. "I am relieved it is not merely the thought of marriage to me that you wished to avoid."

"No, of course not," Hilary snapped. "If I were to encounter a man to whom I could give my heart and my respect, I would marry him. If he were to ask, of course," she finished in a flustered rush.

"Of course—if he were to ask," replied James gravely, with the merest spark of amusement in his chocolate gaze.

"Needless to say, I have not met such a man, so far," she hastened to add, at which the spark only grew more pronounced.

"Needless to say," he murmured, and Hilary noted, to her discomfiture, the faint note of relief under the amusement.

Nonetheless, little sizzles of happiness fizzed inside her at the thought of continued days with James at the Roman villa, or sitting across the table from Rufus, taking notes. In the future, she might regret her lack of decision, but now . . . For the present, she would simply enjoy the status quo.

James rose and, smiling, held out a hand.

"Shall we join Rufus at his tower?"

Hilary knew a twinge of irritation that he had apparently been so certain of her capitulation, but she rose and, inclining her head, moved with him toward the door. She acknowledged the chill of uneasiness that lay beneath her anticipation, but she found it difficult to suppress a strong urge to grasp James by the hand and skip with him out into the sunshine.

Chapter Seventeen

At the tower, they found Rufus, not in the ruined structure, but seated on one of the fallen stones in the circle surrounding it. He was deep in conversation with Old Dorcas. They turned at the approach of the newcomers.

Jasper, who had, of course, accompanied them, romped forward with the confidence of a dog who knows itself assured of a welcome. He flung himself to the ground before Dorcas and rolled over, his legs waving in the air. The old woman stretched forth her fingers and scratched his belly, reducing him to grinning idiocy.

"I have been telling the lady Dorcas of the old Druid priest," said Rufus, assisting Hilary to a seat beside him.

James raised his brows, but Rufus continued unnoticing. "Actually, I think the old lady must be short a few grains of a bushel. She acts as though she knew the priest."

Dorcas merely smiled benignly.

"Good God, Rufus," put in James. "I hope you haven't been spilling—that is, you haven't been filling this good lady's ear with your nonsense, have you?"

Rufus grimaced sullenly. "I haven't told her anything. I just mentioned that I used to know an old codger who lived hereabouts, claiming to be a Druid. Gods, do you think I can't be trusted to keep my own counsel?"

This was precisely what James did think, and he shook his head in exasperation.

"Are you through here? If so, perhaps we could repair to the villa. Lady Hilary and I have not accomplished much there so far. I would like to finish uncovering the mosaic in the triclinium and get some sort of protective covering over it."

"Yes," concurred Hilary. "And I'd like to start in on that little structure to the north. I think it may be a shrine."

"Mm," said James. "I shouldn't wonder—and I still think there's a spring there. The two very often go together."

Hilary turned to bid farewell to Dorcas, but the old woman was nowhere to be seen. Jasper whimpered softly, his nose into the breeze that trembled through the clearing.

"What an odd creature," remarked James. "I never knew a person with the ability to fade into the scenery with such rapidity."

"Yes, I've always thought it would be a handy trait to acquire."

"Never mind," James said with a smile. "You have enough unsettling traits as it is."

Startled, Hilary raised a questioning eyebrow, but James, reddening slightly, merely turned away. Rufus smiled benignly at the two as they mounted James's carriage, which today, he drove himself. Jasper took up his position behind the vehicle and Rufus, sprawled in the backseat, commented lazily. "I don't know why you persist in mucking about in that crumbling old villa. It's only someone's farmhouse."

"Yes," replied James, "but a perusal of what is left of it will tell us a great deal about the people who lived there—how they lived—what they did to earn their bread—perhaps even the gods they worshipped."

Rufus snorted. "I can tell you that. They were farmers, apparently fairly well-to-do. A retired officer and his family, perhaps, and they made their living on the soil. They probably kept sheep and manufactured wool, which they sold or traded in Corinium. From the looks of the place, they probably maintained a pottery, as well. As for the gods they worshipped, they no doubt made sacrifice to the same deities as everyone else—Jupiter, Juno, Fortuna, and the rest. And the *lares,* and *penates* of course. If the owner was a retired military man, he maybe worshipped Mithras, as well."

"Do you, Rufus? Worship Mithras, that is?" asked Hilary interestedly.

Rufus shifted and his face reddened, presenting the picture of a bluff warrior unused to discussing his personal views on spiritual matters. "Well, I'm all for the discipline and sacrifice practiced by the Mithraics, and I attend rites in the shrine at the fort, but—"

"There is a shrine to Mithras at Caerleon?" interposed James eagerly. "I knew there were such features in many military installations, particularly in Germany and France, but I have not heard of one being found in Britain. Perhaps you could show it to me one day."

Rufus grunted, running a beefy hand over his thinning hair. "I don't plan on being around here much longer, you know. You told me earlier you have some sort of scheme for getting me back home. Have you done anything about that?"

James exchanged a glance with Hilary.

"Um," he said. "In the press of all our activity in the last few days . . . And there have been other, personal matters to which—"

"Have you or haven't you contacted that friend you were talking about?" snapped Rufus.

"No."

"Mars Victrix! Why not?"

James opened his mouth, but Hilary forestalled him. "Because he doesn't want you to leave, Rufus. And neither do I. I fear I, too, am at fault for not doing something about your predicament, for I have not encouraged James to contrive a means for your return. Please don't be angry," she said earnestly, as Rufus swelled in indignation. "It means so very much to us to have you here—to be able to talk to a real Roman soldier—one, moreover, who lives— lived—in the time of the occupation of Britain. You must know by now what an unequaled opportunity you provide for someone like James—and me."

Rufus seemed very little mollified by this speech. "And you

must know," he growled, "how much it means to me to try to get home. I do not belong in your time and I don't like it here. By the gods, if I did not need your protection in this ludicrous situation, I would leave and chance my fate in the world of this century. In fact," he added, a crafty expression crossing his features, "perhaps I should go to your associate, Mr. Cheeke. I'm sure he would be willing to help me, in return for a few scraps of my famous information."

Hilary gasped, but James said levelly, "I'm sure he would. He'd help put you on exhibit like a two-headed rooster—assuming, of course, you were able to convince him of your credentials. I seriously doubt, Rufus, that you would ever get home, once Mordecai Cheeke gets his hands on you. However, you are free to leave anytime you choose."

He felt Hilary's accusing stare, but continued to hold Rufus' gaze. Rufus made no response, but turned his face to the distant horizon and sat in glum silence for some five minutes. When the carriage pulled up before the manor house at Goodhurst, Rufus at last heaved himself to attention.

"You haven't left me with much choice, have you? Very well, I'll cooperate with you. I'll answer your question as best I can." He brought his chin up abruptly. "For two weeks." He grinned mirthlessly as James's eyes narrowed. "At the end of that time, if you haven't used some of your modern wizardry to get me back home, not another word will you get from me. I'll close up like a Cretan clam."

He clambered down from the carriage. "I will promise to stay away from that Cheeke fellow," he said sardonically. "Can't say as I care for him much, anyway. And now, if you will excuse me, I think I won't accompany you and Lady Hilary to the villa."

With a curt wave of his hand, he disappeared into the house. Jasper, taking advantage of his exit, scrambled into the warrior's place.

"Whew," said James. "Our friend grows testier by the day."

"Can you blame him? Just think how you would feel if your positions were reversed. Or no," Hilary amended with a chuckle, "if you found yourself suddenly transported to second-century Britain, you would probably take up permanent residence there."

"Not permanent, I think," responded James with a smile, "but I would certainly take an extended lease on a nice villa with all the modern conveniences."

They strolled to the back of the house and thence to the stables, where James chose a small gig in place of the carriage that had brought them to Goodhurst.

James assisted her into the vehicle with care, and, skillfully rebuffing Jasper's attempt to join them there, mounted the driver's seat.

"To return to the subject of Rufus," said Hilary, adjusting the skirts of her dimitiy round gown, "do you feel not the slightest bit guilty over keeping him here so long?"

Slapping the reins, James gazed at her in surprise. "Guilty? Why? I know he doesn't want to stay here, but I am providing him with a comfortable place to live and seeing to his every need. I don't think it's too much to ask to expect some cooperation from him."

"But what about his illness?"

"What illness? Ah, you mean the megrim he has been suffering off and on? I don't see that it is of any significance."

"But what if it is not simply a megrim?"

"Nonsense. You just saw him. He is the picture of health."

Hilary frowned unhappily. Rufus might seem recovered, but he had been quite ill, and James knew it. Furthermore, there was a real possibility that Rufus' indisposition was directly related to his precipitate journey through time. How could James be so uncaring of Rufus' well-being?

In a few more moments they reached the villa, and, while Hilary regretted that she had not taken the time to change from the ivory linen into something more practical, she wielded spade and pick to good advantage. Jasper provided his usual assistance by digging furiously in all the wrong places, spraying dirt to the four winds as he did so.

James continued to uncover the mosaic in the triclinium, while Hilary worked in another, smaller chamber. Progress was slow, and for some time nothing was heard in the sunny clearing save the sound of metal implements clinking against the occasional rock.

Despite his absorption in his work, James found his attention wandering to where a bright head bent over mud-encrusted walls. Unbidden, a smile curved his lips. The breeze blew her gown against her slight curves and he thought Hilary looked the veriest wood sprite, lingering from the time when mysterious, ancient deities ruled these glens and forests. Her flaming hair escaped its Clytie knot in gleaming tendrils, drifting over delicately curved cheeks of purest ivory. Her lovely, golden eyes narrowed in concentration and her small nose wrinkled determinedly. Altogether, he mused, beginning to perspire slightly, with her coltish grace and quick, neat movements, she was all lithe, pagan beauty.

He turned abruptly back to the mosaic, and toiled in silence for some minutes until the sound of clattering stones and a muted cry reached him. He stood immediately and ran to Hilary, to observe that she lay sprawled over the section of wall on which she had been working. As he approached, she struggled to rise, without success.

She lifted her face to him.

"Oh, bother!" she exclaimed. "I'm afraid I've got myself into a fix. I saw what I thought was the edge of a pottery shard tucked in the base of this wall, and when I began digging, the whole thing fell on me. Now, I seem to be stuck in this—this rubble."

James, gazing in the direction of Hilary's pointed finger, saw that her left foot was twisted behind her and firmly wedged in the fall of stones. He squatted for a closer examination of the problem, and rested his hand lightly on her leg.

"Yes, 'stuck' is the mot juste. Luckily the wall wasn't very high at this point, otherwise—you're not hurt, are you? I mean your foot is turned, so that—"

"No," she answered irritably, aware of the warmth of James's hand through the fabric of her gown. "I didn't break anything. I'm simply—stuck, and I can't reach around to extricate myself."

James began removing the rubble on top of and surrounding Hilary's abused appendage and in a few minutes, with James's assistance, she stood upright. She faced him, breathless and flushed. She was much more disturbed by his nearness than by her contretemps with the wall and she was made profoundly uneasy by this knowledge. She moved away hastily.

"It looks as though—" James said, and at the harshness in his tone, Hilary glanced at him, startled. He cleared his throat and bent to pick up a small, curved piece of clay. "—as though you were correct," he continued in a milder tone. "See? This is more than a shard, it is a small pot—almost whole. Look at the incising along the side."

Hilary's eyes grew dreamy. "The family must have dropped it in their flight," she murmured. "I can just see them, snatching up their most precious possessions, calling to one another through the rooms, hurrying to—"

James's brows lifted. "What flight?" he interposed.

"Why, it's obvious they left in a hurry," said Hilary impatiently. "Look at the things they left behind—coins, a shoe, a comb." She counted off the items on her fingers that she had discovered on her earlier, solitary investigations.

James uttered a snort of exasperation. "Those artifacts don't mean a thing, except to give us an idea of how the family lived. They cannot tell us their state of mind when they abandoned the villa. Really, Hilary, you'll never be a true antiquary until you leave off these fanciful imaginings."

Hilary's jaw jutted stubbornly. "It seems to me that it is you who are missing the whole point of the—the essentials of the antiquarian effort. It is with our imaginations that we fill out the bare bones of our findings. For example, if the last persons who lived here left in an orderly fashion, they surely would not have left a store of coins."

She drew closer to him as she spoke and by the time she had finished her rather indignant little diatribe, she and James were almost nose to nose. James found that he had suddenly lost track of the conversation. He was wholly absorbed in her unexpected closeness. He discovered that, no, her cheeks were not like purest ivory, but were sprinkled with freckles. This fact seemed of intense significance to him, as did the way the freckles drifted over the enchanting curve of her nose.

Hilary stopped talking and gazed at him, so wide-eyed that once again he felt as though he were falling into two golden pools. He lifted a hand, and, as he'd been wanting to do all afternoon, he gently brushed back one of the fiery tendrils falling over her forehead, and allowed his fingers to drift over her jawline.

He moved hesitantly, as though he were approaching a young wild creature, but she did not, as he half expected, whirl to run away. Instead, she remained so still that he could discern the beating of her heart in the quivering of the lace that framed her throat.

Without conscious will he bent to her and covered her mouth with his in a kiss that held nothing of the violence of the encounter on the Strindham's lawn. Instead, his lips moved slowly over hers tenderly, savoring the sweetness of her.

His hands spread over the exquisite curve of her spine as she pressed herself against him, seeming to fit into all his hollow places. Her arms went around his neck and her fingers moved delicately through the hair at the back of his neck. The feeling thus produced was like nothing else he had ever experienced in his life, and he almost groaned aloud at the maelstrom of wanting that surged through him.

Slowly, his lips left her mouth to trail kisses over her delicate jawline and along her throat until he came to the pulse that beat so wildly there. The scent of her filled him, and his fingers fumbled at the buttons holding the fringe of lace in place. A small sound from deep in her throat nearly destroyed what was left of his control, but when she repeated it, he was abruptly brought to his senses.

Good God, what was he about? He dropped his hands from the delicious swell of her firm little derriere and stepped backward so suddenly he almost stumbled over Jasper, who had elected to nap at James's feet.

Chapter Eighteen

Bereft so suddenly of James's support, Hilary swayed for an instant. The next moment, she gasped, horrified at what had just taken place. Dear Lord, she had simply stood like a pea-goose while a man whom she knew felt nothing for her but the mildest friendship made the most intimate, indelicate overtures on her person.

But no, she had not simply stood there, had she? She had participated with the utmost willingness in his advances. Of course, she certainly had not encouraged his overtures.

Had she? From the moment he had grasped her ankle to remove

it from its little stone prison, she had sensed something between them. An electricity that was almost palpable. When he lifted her to her feet she had welcomed the minor dispute in which they had found themselves engaged. Then he had drawn his fingers across her cheek and she had been wholly undone.

Now, she stood, simply gaping at him. What must he think? She attempted to arrange her distracted thoughts in some sort of order and became aware that he was speaking.

"I—I'm sorry," he said in a strangled voice. "I don't know what happened, but—I'm sorry."

"Y-yes," murmured Hilary, cursing herself for her inanity. She groped in her mind for a response, but seemed unable to locate so much as a single coherent thought. It was with some relief that she noted someone was approaching them on horseback. And traveling at a great rate of speed.

Hilary and James whirled to greet the newcomer. In a spray of dirt, Robert Newhouse drew his mount to a halt and leaped from the saddle. He ignored Jasper's excited leaps of welcome.

"It's Rufus, sir," he said to James, panting from his exertions. "He's very ill."

"What!" exclaimed James.

"Yes, the same sort of thing that happened before. We were playing cards—I was showing him how to play piquet, when he came all over queer. He turned that sort of fish-belly white and said he was very tired and that he thought he would lie down. He went up to his chamber, and when I went to look in on him a half hour or so later, he was stretched out on his bed, still fully clothed but out like a snuffed candle, and I couldn't rouse him."

"Did you send for the doctor?"

"No, sir, Rufus having expressed himself pretty firmly on that point. I didn't like to take it upon myself to—"

"Yes, very well. We'll have him fetched immediately."

Exchanging a glance with Hilary, he assisted her into the gig and climbed into the driver's seat. In anxious silence, the three completed the short journey to Goodhurst, and if either Hilary or James felt any residual constraint over their recent encounter, it remained unspoken.

Inside, they were greeted by a distraught Burnside.

"I'm glad you're here, sir," the butler said. "We've been that concerned."

Unconsciously, James grasped Hilary's hand. "Will you wait in the library?"

"Of course." She flashed him a smile of encouragement, and despite himself, James felt his tension somewhat dissipated.

Pausing only to order that the doctor be fetched immediately, James hurried to the stairs, taking them two at a time.

"Can I order some tea for you, Lady Hilary?" asked Robert, ushering her into the library and thence to a comfortable chair near one of the long windows that led to a small terrace outside.

"That would be lovely, if you will join me, Mr. Newhouse."

A few moments later, the two sat in a rather abstracted silence, sipping from cups of steaming bohea. Hilary's thoughts were on the scene taking place upstairs and she rather thought the same must be true of young Mr. Newhouse. She was surprised at the depth of concern she felt for Rufus. She hardly knew the man, after all, but even after such a short acquaintance, she felt an undeniable affection for him. Was it possible that the transference that had proved such a boon to James and herself was making Rufus ill?

"I do hope he'll be all right," she whispered. She was startled to hear the sound of her words, for she was not aware that she had spoken aloud.

"Oh, I'm sure he will be," replied Robert reassuringly. "After all, he's been through these spells before and popped back with no ill effect."

"But I don't believe he has been taken so ill before."

"That's true, but the doctor should be here soon, and he'll have the old trout up and about in no time."

Hilary smiled perfunctorily at Robert's hearty tone, which she knew to be assumed.

"Yes, I'm sure you're right. Tell me," she continued in an effort to turn the conversation to an easier topic, "have you been with Mr. Wincanon long?"

"For about two years. Actually, we're distantly related. My father, Lord Newhouse, and Mr. Wincanon are some sort of cousins, though I never met him until five years or so ago. I'm the third son in my family, and I've always had a hankering for politics. I am just employed here in training, so to speak, until a position opens up as secretary to a member of parliament."

"And is James an easy man to work for?" she asked, more to keep the conversation going, she told herself, than through any real interest in his answer.

Robert grinned. "Well, yes and no. He pays me a handsome salary to do very little. He's what you might call extremely particular about his papers and books and projects, and likes to handle most of that himself. He doesn't correspond with very many people outside his circle of antiquarian friends, and his social engagements are practically nonexistent."

"Yes." Hilary smiled wryly. "I know about his aversion to social functions."

"Actually, the dinner party at your home and Mrs. Strindham's musicale are the only times he's dipped into the social swim all year, to my knowledge."

Hilary's brows lifted. "Really? Is he that terrified of women?"

Too late, she bit her tongue to stifle the words she knew to be inexcusably forward, but Robert merely laughed.

"I think terrified is too strong a word, but—really, Lady Hilary, if you could see the tricks that have been used to snare him."

Hilary knew she should bring the subject to a close. She had no business encouraging James's employee to gossip about him.

"Oh?" she asked interestedly.

Nothing loathe, Robert continued, describing the unending efforts and the devious methods employed by what seemed like half the female population of England to entrap the eligible James Wincanon.

"My goodness!" exclaimed Hilary. Dear Lord, in addition to being convinced his own mother had sold herself in a marriage of convenience, to discover himself the target of every grasping female in the *ton* . . . No wonder he held such a jaundiced view of her sex.

"It's all his connections, of course. That is"—Richard amended hastily—"he's one of the finest men of my acquaintance, and he's certainly well-looking enough, but if he weren't related to most of the contents of Debrett's and worth umpty-thousand pounds a year, I doubt he would cause so much as a flutter among the dovecotes of the *ton*."

Hilary sighed. "What a sad reflection on the members of my sex."

Richard stared anxiously at Hilary. "Of course, present company is most decidedly excepted. No one could accuse you of being on the—" He halted abruptly, his face crimson.

Hilary broke into a peal of laughter. "On the hunt for a rich husband? No, I think not. Or any kind of husband at all, for that matter. Mr. James Wincanon is safe from my wiles, Mr. Newhouse." She grew serious. "Still, he seems a lonely man, and I think he would be the better for a good wife."

Her heart gave an odd little lurch at these words and she wondered why the thought of James's possible nuptials to some worthy female of her acquaintance seemed to have lost some of its appeal.

"As to that, ma'am," replied Richard in a startled tone, "I don't think—"

He was interrupted by the entrance of Burnside, who bore the intelligence that the doctor had arrived and was now closeted with Mr. Wincanon and, "the patient."

When James had pushed into the warrior's chamber some minutes earlier, he had found him in bed, his eyes closed and the footman, Josiah Briggs, who had been assigned as his valet hovering over him in obvious anxiety.

"I removed his coat and breeches—and his breathing seems easier now, sir, but he still won't be roused."

James nodded and Briggs, with an air of one relieved to be rid of an onerous responsibility, scurried from the room. James sat down beside Rufus' bed.

He scrutinized the warrior's face. Briggs was right, he was pale as death. His breathing, however, seemed normal to James's untutored ear. James experienced an unnamed sadness. The man on the bed had seen the face of Trajan—and Hadrian, his future emperor. He had strolled in the ancient forum of Rome when it was whole and gleaming with marble. His eyes had squinted against the sun of Boudicca's Britain and watched the construction of the baths that now lay in ruins beneath the streets of England's most famous spa.

How must he feel to be a stranger in the land he had decided to make his home? James felt a twinge of shame. He had been so busy plundering Rufus' mind for his own selfish purposes that he had failed to see him as a man, with wants and aspirations of his own. He had done nothing to put forward a plan to get Rufus back to his Maia.

As though he had spoken his thoughts aloud, Rufus stirred and opened his eyes. He seemed startled to behold James at his bedside.

"Ah, you're home then, James." He spoke with some difficulty and his words were slightly slurred.

"Indeed, and I return to find you knocked into horse nails."

Rufus' brows lifted and, shaking his head as though clearing the cobwebs from his brain, he struggled to a sitting position. "Me? No such of a thing. I was a little tired—and that fool man you assigned to me has been fluttering over me like a crazed bat, but there's nothing wrong with me."

"Nonetheless, I've sent for a doctor."

"What?" Rufus threw back his covers and swung his feet over the side of his bed. "I told you—"

"I know what you told me, and I'm sorry to go against your wishes, but there *is* something wrong with you and it's time we discovered what it is."

"Bah!" Rufus reached for the dressing gown tossed on the foot of the bed.

Indeed, James was forced to admit that at the moment Rufus seemed in perfect health. His speech had cleared as the conversation progressed, and his eyes sparked in indignation. His gray hair stood up in spikes about his head where he had rubbed it in his perturbation. After stamping about the room for a few moments, nightshirt flapping about his ankles, he returned to seat himself in a chair near the window.

"I don't like doctors," he grumbled.

"Yes, I had grasped that fact," James replied placidly. "However, it won't hurt to have him examine you."

Rufus subsided at last, with an air of martyred weariness.

Dr. Meadowes, on his arrival, displayed some displeasure at being summoned so arbitrarily to attend a seemingly robust patient, but made a thorough examination. Later, as Rufus sat in frustrated impatience at being unable to understand the man's diagnosis, the doctor spoke in suitably grave accents to James.

"Well, I can't pinpoint a specific ailment. His heartbeat is slower than normal, and so is his breathing. His reflexes are not what they should be. There is some congestion in his lungs, but it does not seem serious. In fact, nothing about his condition seems serious," he concluded somewhat testily.

"That is good news," said James heartily. "I do appreciate your coming out on such short notice. I would not have asked, but he seemed in sad straits at the time."

"Mmpf," said the doctor, picking up his bag. "Call me if he experiences any more of those episodes you mentioned," he added grudgingly.

James hastened to the library to apprise Hilary and Richard of Rufus' seeming recovery. Hilary expressed her pleasure and relief at this news, but now that the crisis was past, James felt the immediate return of the constraint that had fallen over them after the kiss that he still felt burning his lips. He was intensely aware of the awkwardness that stood between him and Hilary like an unwanted guest.

He was unable to account for the impulse that had led him to kiss her. Yet, he knew from the moment he reached to touch the silk of her cheek he'd been helpless against the need to hold her and to press his mouth against the flower softness of hers, and to experience the feel of her against him.

He could not even work up an ounce of regret over his actions, and suspected that if he was not extremely circumspect in his future relationship with the lady, he would be strongly tempted to repeat them. But that was the trouble, wasn't it? It was becoming more and more difficult to be circumspect when it came to Hilary Merton. Good God, what was he going to do about that? He smiled tentatively at her.

She rose and brushed the skirt of her gown. "I must be going," she said abruptly.

"Of course." He hesitated. "The doctor seems to think there is nothing much wrong with Rufus," James continued, "but I am wondering if you were right in your belief that he may be suffering from some malady induced by his journey through time."

"Oh, dear!" exclaimed Hilary. "Perhaps—"

But James was plunging on.

"I spoke of a plan earlier—to create an artificial bolt of lightning—to get Rufus back to his own time, but I must confess I haven't a clear idea of what that plan might involve. I prattled about artificially created lightning, but I'm not particularly knowledgeable in this field of research. I know that such experiments have been performed, but I have no idea how to reproduce them. I—I told you of someone who might help, but"—James sighed—"I've made no attempt to contact him."

Hilary tried to fix him with an austere glance, but he appeared so crestfallen and unwontedly humble, that she forbore to express the disappointment in him she had experienced earlier.

"I have a friend—Cyrus Bender," continued James, "with whom I attended Oxford. He's a brilliant scholar, and I am in hopes that . . ."

He cocked his head and smiled quizzically.

"How would you like to accompany me on an excursion tomorrow morning?"

Hilary lifted her brows.

"I shall send a message to Cyrus Bender to expect us," he said as he ushered her from the library. "He rarely stirs from home and hearth, so I believe we shall find him in situ. It promises to be fine, so we may take an open carriage."

Hilary felt herself flush. James was telling her that Emma need not accompany them. She preferred not to consider why she should relish the thought of several hours spent with James unencumbered by her abigail. The fact remained that the idea caused her pulse to quicken.

"That would be very nice," she replied demurely.

Outside, James assisted Hilary once more into the gig, but when he began to mount the vehicle himself, she lifted her hand.

"No. That is—I think you should stay with Rufus."

He looked at her for a moment and nodded before gesturing to the groom waiting nearby.

As the gig rattled away down the drive, Jasper loping along behind, Hilary waved briskly in farewell, leaving James to stare after her.

Chapter Nineteen

As the gig made its way through the leafy lane that led to White-leaves, Hilary was wholly preoccupied with what had occurred earlier, both at the villa site and in James's home.

It was time, she concluded, that she embarked on a serious examination of her feelings for James Wincanon. For all her loudly professed aversion to marriage, she was carrying on like a smitten schoolgirl. She had allowed the man to kiss her—twice—without so much as a "How dare you, sir!" She reveled in his company and the thought of spending a day virtually alone with him sent her into a most unbecoming flutter of anticipation.

She had held to the notion for some time that he was her friend. It was an attractive picture, and she certainly wished to maintain their amity. However, she was forced to admit that a new, disturbing element had crept into their relationship.

And what about James? The first time he had kissed her, it was in a fit of pique. This seemed a strange way for a man to vent his irritation, but as she had reflected before, the ways of a man's mind were foreign to her. This morning though, his lips had been tender on hers, and she still felt their imprint. What had prompted his actions this time? Despite his prejudices, she might almost believe that James had formed a tendre for her. However, other than that shattering embrace, there had been nothing in his demeanor to so much as hint at any loverlike emotions on his part toward her.

She grimaced. It hardly seemed likely that her physical charms had swept him into a blinding *coup de foudre*.

The memory of her wanton response to his kiss swept over her. She squirmed in mortification. Had she fallen in his estimation to the level of the scheming damsels who sought to entrap him?

How was she to face him at their next meeting? What would be his demeanor when they saw each other again?

She spent that interval in like musings, and the next morning, when James appeared in her drawing room at precisely the time appointed for their journey to Gloucester, she searched his face for some sign that the encounter at the villa had left its mark on him.

She found nothing but an amused courtesy. She shrugged irritably and ushered James from the house.

As they rattled through the gates of Whiteleaves toward Gloucester, the weather was fine. It was one of those crisp, autumn days that tastes like fine wine on the tongue, and Hilary felt her crotchets dissolve.

James, too, despite—or perhaps because of—the memory of the interlude between himself and the Lady Hilary at the villa, felt especially lighthearted.

"Tell me, my dear," he said to Hilary, who sent a startled glance at this endearment, "how is it you were able to amass such an astounding amount of information on ancient Britain?"

"Particularly for a female?" she asked pertly, a militant sparkle in her eye.

"Did I say that? No, I did not. In fact, I will take leave to tell you that your knowledge is extraordinary, for a person of either sex."

Hilary felt the heat rise to her cheeks, pleased despite herself at this encomium.

"I am fortunate that my father supports my efforts. Or, at least, he has never put any obstructions in my path. He allowed me free access to his library, which is probably the most extensive in the county. Then there is Vicar Thomlinson, who taught me Latin. Unfortunately," she sighed, "whatever knowledge I have acquired has come solely through books. Other than brief trips to other remains discovered in the area, I have never had the opportunity to do any real delving into a Roman site. You, I know have been to Rome—more than once, I think."

"Yes, I've had that pleasure several times. I've dug with Il Professore Eugenio Battaglia in the Forum Romanum, as well as in Hadrian's forum. I was fortunate to have visited in a time when the government of the Eternal City had decided to investigate its deteriorating ruins, rather than let them continue crumbling into oblivion."

"Oh yes," said Hilary with a laugh. "I remember reading that you were one of a band of renegades apparently dedicated to 'disturbing those most picturesque remains of a vanished civilization.' "

"Mm," replied James dryly. "Perhaps it would not have vanished quite so rapidly if the citizens of the city had not profited from the countless artists and writers who came to sob over the glory that was Rome. Not to mention the aristocrats who pilfered what was left to build their famed palazzos."

"What about the discoveries of *insulae* at the foot of the Capitoline Hill?"

"No, those have taken place since my last visit. I plan to make another trip there next summer, however, and will try to participate in those excavations."

"Ah!" Hilary cried involuntarily. "How I envy you. I wonder if the time will ever come when a woman can simply leave her encumbrances behind—just for a while—to go a-traveling on her own."

James glanced at her, startled. He had never really considered the matter, but he had always assumed that the contribution of women to the world of science and letters was minimal because of an inherent inferiority in the female intellect. It had never occurred to him that women were often held back intellectually solely because of the obligations of family and rigid social dictates.

Observing the wistful sparkle in Hilary's eyes, he knew a desire as strong as it was startling, to sweep her off on a journey to distant lands, to watch her golden gaze widen at the sights he could show her. What would be her reaction to the splendor of the Parthenon, glowing palely in the moonlight? Or the rosy, earth-sprung pillars of the temple at Petra? And what wonders could they discover together? The fabled walls of Troy, perhaps, or the lair of King Minos on Crete. His pulse quickened at the prospect, and he found himself dwelling on the prospect of days spent on the heat-drenched summer isles of Greece—and of throbbing nights under star-strewn, Mediterranean skies. He pictured her garbed in the filmy draperies of the maidens portrayed on Grecian friezes. Remembering the feel of her mouth under his, he imagined his lips pressed against skin that was like scented satin.

He sat up with a jerk. Good God! What the devil was the matter with him, weaving prurient air dreams like a spotty-faced adolescent? He shot a glance at his companion. He had decided on their first meeting that she was not the type of female to inflame a man's passions. Why, then, were his thoughts so continually entangled with her physical attractions? Attractions that he had heretofore considered negligible. The whole thing seemed inexplicable, and to his relief, he observed that they were entering the outskirts of Gloucester.

Cyrus Bender occupied a house on the edge of the city, in a small lane just off Lower Southgate Street. It seemed too large for a single gentleman, but James observed cryptically that Cyrus required a great deal of room. For some moments, there was no response to their knock, but at last the door was opened by a rather untidy fellow garbed in the sober raiment of a gentleman's gentleman.

"Mr. Bender?" he replied vaguely to their query, as though he had never heard of the man. "Oh. Yes," he said at last. "Yes, he is home, I think, but I'm not sure . . ." He trailed off disconsolately, as if he were wishing himself elsewhere, absolved of all responsibility for his errant employer.

"Perhaps if we could come in . . ." said James, ushering Hilary through the door. The gentleman's gentleman gave way unhappily, and led the way through a dark corridor smelling of must and mouse droppings to a spacious and surprisingly well-furnished drawing room.

The gentleman's gentleman, perhaps recalled to a sense of his duty said stiffly, "Mr. Bender don't like t'be disturbed when he's workin'. If you could come back—"

"Nonsense," interrupted James impatiently. "He's always working. We must speak to him. Now, will you please search him out and tell him that James Wincanon is here to see him?"

The man sighed. "Well, it might take awhile, as I ain't sure exactly where he is. In fact, he might be out in—"

This time, the man was interrupted by a thunderous crash that came from directly overhead. Hilary jumped.

"Ah," said James. "It appears we have discovered his location."

He rose, and over the servant's faint mutterings of protest, led Hilary from the room. Following the sound of the thud and ensuing minor crashes and tinkles, they soon located the source of the uproar. Throwing open a door, they plunged into another large room. Hilary gasped. She had never beheld such a chamber, and rather fancied this was what Aladdin's cave must look like. The room was lined with shelves upon which rested rocks of every size from small pebbles to largish boulders. Some were polished to a glowing sheen, others sparkled with exposed crystals. Almost all of them were either oddly shaped or strangely colored, or both. More rocks lay on tables and even chairs scattered about the room. Also prominently featured were beakers of bubbling fluids, copper tubing that coiled like gleaming serpents around the beakers, and great glass jars filled with unidentified but somehow sinister-looking liquids.

Standing at one of the tables, engaged in pouring the contents of a large beaker into a small iron pot was one of the tallest men Hilary had ever seen. He was also one of the thinnest, and thus presented the aspect of a restless stork. As he moved, various papers, obviously notes, fluttered about him like molting feathers. He looked up as James and Hilary entered the room.

His expression was not welcoming, and it was only when he peered myopically for several seconds from behind a pair of large, thick spectacles that a smile appeared on his angular features.

"James!" he cried in pleased accents. "Welcome to my minerals room."

Cyrus placed the beaker on the table and moved toward James. "I do not believe we have seen each other for some time. Have we?"

"Indeed, no. However, I see you are still carrying on in great form." James turned to Hilary. "Lady Hilary Merton, allow me to present Cyrus Bender, friend and scientist extraordinaire."

Cyrus bent awkwardly over Hilary's hand before speaking to the gentleman's gentleman, who had entered behind the pair.

"Digweed, we have guests. Do be a good chap and bring us up some refreshments."

"We don't have any," replied the serving man in a surly tone. "Leastways, there's some of the cakes we had last night, but they were stale then. Prob'ly hard as them rocks by now." He swept an arm about the room.

"Ah," replied Cyrus, unfazed. "Just bring 'round a pot of tea, then. And some cups," he added, apparently as an afterthought.

With meticulous care, he removed the rocks from the only two comfortable chairs in the chamber and gestured to Hilary and James to be seated. He settled his own spindly frame on a three-legged stool. Evidently feeling he had discharged his duties as host, he gazed expectantly at his guests.

James cleared his throat and glanced at Hilary, who was eyeing him in some amusement. "What are you working on now, Cyrus?"

"Oh. Several things, actually. I'm experimenting with black powder at the moment, and a device for measuring static electricity, and—Oh, you mean in here?" He glanced around the "mineral room."

"Yes," said James patiently. To his surprise, Cyrus blushed.

"Um, well about a month ago, Septimus Hodge—a colleague of mine—wrote that he had been doing some experiments with base metals. He said that he believed he had come across a method for transforming a certain iron alloy into—well, a precious metal."

"You mean, gold?" asked Hilary incredulously. This time, Cyrus flushed to the tips of his prominent ears.

His voice sank to a whisper. "Well, actually silver."

"Good God!" exclaimed James. Once again, he felt Hilary's gaze on him, and he turned to intercept a warm look of shared mirth that he felt down to his toes. With an effort, he bent his attention again to his friend. "Are you actually dabbling in alchemy, Cyrus?"

Cyrus blinked. "No, of course not," he replied, his tone frosty. "I wrote immediately to Septimus, telling him his theories were ludicrous. I was merely repeating his procedures to prove him wrong."

"I see," said James.

"And is he?" asked Hilary. "Wrong, I mean."

"Well, I have yet to produce so much as a scrap of silver so far."

"Ah," said James again, following which a dispirited sort of silence fell over the little group.

"Perhaps," said Hilary at last to James, who appeared to be sinking into Cyrus's wooly cloud of abstraction, "we should tell Mr. Bender why we are here."

James jerked slightly. "Of course." He swung about to face his friend directly. "Tell me, Cyrus, is it possible to create an artificial bolt of lightning?"

Cyrus snapped to immediate attention. "Actually," he said pedantically, "lightning cannot be duplicated, as it is a unique phenomenon. However, sparks similar in form to lightning can be formed, and I have done this many times."

"Excellent! And are these—sparks—very, er, large?"

"It depends on what you call large," replied Cyrus thoughtfully. "They do not compare, of course, to the ordinary strikes that occur in a thundercloud. Those can produce up to several hundred million volts. I have achieved flashes of barely a hundred volts—although they transverse a distance of several centimeters. Real flashes, of course, we measure in meters."

"I see." James, who had straightened hopefully at the beginning of Cyrus's statement, now sank bank in his chair.

Hilary, too, knew a moment of discouragement, but she asked tentatively, "But do you think it would be possible to produce something larger—in a workshop—that would be comparable to a natural flash?"

"Well, now." Cyrus's face lit with interest and he launched into a very nearly incomprehensible monologue that featured phrases such as, "coalescence of droplets," "mass movement of charge by air flow," and "negative and positive charge centers."

Within a few moments, Hilary felt as though she were drowning under the deluge of Cyrus's information on the formation of lightning. James reached to touch her hand lightly, and she was instantly brought back to the moment at the villa when he had grasped her shoulders and brought his mouth to hers. She lifted dazed eyes to his.

"Wh—wha—?" she murmured.

"What, what?" asked Cyrus, interrupted mid-flow.

Hilary blushed hotly. Lord, she was behaving like a schoolgirl with a crush on her dancing master. Murmuring a disjointed apology, she was forced to remind herself firmly—realizing that she seemed to be doing this with increasing frequency—that she had no interest in James Wincanon beyond his formidable intellect and his interest in her own hobbyhorse, Roman Britain.

Cyrus droned on for several more minutes, before James finally interposed. "If I am correctly following the thread of your discourse, Cyrus, you are saying you can, indeed, reproduce a bolt of lightning equivalent to that of a natural flash."

"Um," replied Cyrus. "That is, yes. I think so."

"Do you think you could create this phenomenon outside a laboratory?"

"Yes. I think so," responded Cyrus again after a reflective pause. "That is, in what sort of environment will I be working?"

James and Hilary had previously decided to say nothing to Cyrus about Rufus and their efforts to transport him through time. There was no reason to believe Cyrus would treat their story with anything less than the contempt any true scientist would display toward such an obvious faradiddle. Thus, James merely described the interior of the Roman tower.

"Hmm," said Cyrus consideringly, his eyes narrowing behind his spectacles. At last, his head bobbed approvingly, making him resemble a stork drinking from a pond. "Yes, such an enclosed structure should serve admirably. When do you need to produce this phenomena?"

"The sooner the better," said James heartily. "How about next Tuesday?"

He glanced at Hilary, who nodded in agreement. She had grown fond of Rufus and she would hate to say good-bye to him. In addition, there was still much she wished to learn from him. However, it was obvious that the old warrior was not thriving in the nineteenth century. Whether it was an illness that would have come upon him in the natural course of his life, or whether traveling through time was detrimental to the human condition, could not be determined. However, they could not, in good conscience, keep him here any longer than necessary.

At this point, Digweed returned, shuffling under the weight of a tray containing an ancient, tarnished, and slightly dented teapot and the requisite accoutrements. Having been politely requested by Cyrus to do the honors, Hilary poured tea into mismatched cups and James watched with delight as she passed them around with the grace and aplomb of a duchess in a London drawing room. After they had refreshed themselves, Cyrus led his guests to another chamber at the top of the house. Here, he displayed with pardonable pride his "electrics room," in which could be seen an astonishing array of totally incomprehensible equipment. Wire lay in great coils on floor and shelving, and pieces of metal of assorted sizes were stacked haphazardly. A humming sound filled the air, coming, apparently, from a large metal object shaped a little like a small stove on wheels.

"Whew!" exclaimed James. "Does all this stuff actually do something?"

Cyrus smiled in a superior fashion. "I realize it does not look like much to the layman, but this"—he indicated the stove on wheels—"is a generator. It produces electricity, which can be stored in a Leyden jar." He gestured to a glass container lined with foil and capped with metal. After several seconds, Cyrus turned off the generator and struck the lid briskly with a metal mallet, which he held by a wooden handle.

Instantly, with a sizzling pop, a blinding spark flew upward from the glass jar, dissipating as it rose to the ceiling.

"Now, you see," said Cyrus, as though nothing out of the ordinary had taken place, "by applying the same principles, only using a much bigger jar, one produces lightning."

"My," said Hilary faintly. To tell the truth, she had been momentarily terrified at the unexpectedness and the blazing vehemence of the spark. James's fingers curled around hers and she grasped them gratefully.

"An impressive display, old friend," said James. "And you believe you can reproduce this effect in the tower I have described?"

"I should certainly think so." Cyrus spoke with a studied nonchalance but it seemed to Hilary that she detected a certain eagerness in his tone. "Of course, it will involve a much larger jar. Fortunately, I have such a one on hand. I had it blown specially for me some months ago for an experiment of a different sort. I will have other items to bring with me, as well, of course." He waved an arm vaguely to encompass the generator, several other pieces of unidentified equipment, and what seemed like several miles of the ubiquitous coiled wire.

"I will gladly provide the transportation," murmured James.

"Might one ask what all this is in aid of?" Cyrus asked.

"Oh," replied James vaguely, "just settling a wager, of sorts."

Cyrus sent him a glance of mild suspicion, but asked no further questions. An hour or so later, the logistics of the project settled, the scientist stood at the front door of his house, the lugubrious Digweed in attendance, to bid farewell to his guests. With arrangements for the forthcoming experiment made to the satisfaction of both parties, Hilary and James made their way to the phaeton.

Chapter Twenty

Hilary and James returned to Goodhurst to find Rufus still decidedly down pin.

"I feel fine," he grumbled, as they walked in the door to his bedchamber. He waved his hand irritably toward Briggs, who stood silently by his bed. "But this blasted old woman insists I stay in bed."

Despite his assertions, it was all too obvious that the old warrior had not recovered from his indisposition with the quickness he had displayed on previous occasions. He was pale, and his hands trembled slightly as he spoke. His eyes flashed, however, with a belligerent spark.

"I believe you may get up if you wish, *optima,*" said James soothingly, and to Hilary's shocked amusement, Rufus immediately flung back his covers and swung a pair of muscular, hirsute legs over the side of the bed. He rose unsteadily, and James moved hastily to his side. He eased Rufus gently back to a sitting position.

"Well," said the soldier in some surprise, "I seem to be more tired than I thought. Still, I'm not going to loll around in bed any longer."

He rose again and this time, with James's assistance, made his way to a chair by the window. Sinking into it, he raised a palsied hand to his head.

"Phew! I'm weak as a cat. I don't understand what's come over me."

Hilary and James exchanged a glance as James pulled up two chairs close to Rufus. He seated Hilary in one of them, and took the other himself.

"*Optima,*" he said, lightly grasping Rufus' wrist, "we have good news for you."

With insertions by Hilary, he related the events of the previous day.

"Tuesday next!" exclaimed Rufus, when he had finished. "Let me see, according to your system of days, Tuesday is Mercury's day, is it not? Right after Luna's, and—why, that's only five days!" His eyes lit, and a wide grin creased his already round face.

"Yes, it is," replied Hilary, "so you had best take care of yourself between now and then."

"Indeed," corroborated James. "You must rest."

"But I must make preparations!" expostulated Rufus. "There are many things I wish to take back to my own time," he continued in explanation, as Hilary and James turned puzzled faces to him.

"For example—?" asked Hilary, fascinated.

"Why, some pens and ink, a clock or two, a diagram for making a gaslight, and, of course guns—and powder, and—"

"Good God!" interposed James explosively. "Are you planning on taking the nineteenth century back to the first? Rufus, you cannot possibly haul all that gimcrackery with you."

Rufus' jaw thrust forward. "Why not?"

"For one thing, because you would change the course of history—perhaps of time itself. For another—" he added hastily, as Rufus opened his mouth, "you might very well jeopardize the whole experiment."

Rufus closed his mouth, but the jaw remained at attention.

"Don't you see?" James rose from his chair to pace the floor. "The operative word here is 'experiment.' We have no idea what will happen when Cyrus creates his lightning bolt. You arrived here with nothing, and if you load yourself down with extra clutter, who knows what might happen? Perhaps it would prohibit you from traveling back at all—or you might—"

"All right, all right," interposed Rufus testily. "You've made your point. Do you think," he asked with a hint of sarcasm in his tone, "I just might possibly leave my chamber between now and next Tuesday? Or am I too frail to step outside for a breath of fresh air and a ray or two of Lord Apollo's good sunshine?"

"Of course not. In fact, if you feel up to it, I see no reason why you cannot come down for dinner this evening."

Rufus grunted.

And he did, reported James to Hilary the next morning, go down to dinner.

"He is not his old, robust self," he said, "nor did he make much of a meal, but he was in better point than he was day before yesterday."

The two again spent the day at the villa, this time uneventfully. Rufus accompanied them, but participated little in the digging, contenting himself with idle comments, delivered from his perch on a sun-warmed rock.

Hilary had declared herself ready to assist James in gleaning what information they might from Rufus during the time left to them. Rufus seemed to appreciate their purpose, and answered their questions willingly. The hours slipped by uneventfully, as did the four days following. To Hilary's relief, Mordecai Cheeke was no more to be seen, and Rufus seemed to gain back a modicum of his well-being. One day, he took spade in hand and worked for some minutes on the supposed shrine a little to the north and east of the main house.

A whoop from his direction caused Hilary and James to hasten from their work in the kitchen area and the triclinium respectively. They found Rufus waving something in one, beefy hand.

"See!" he exclaimed. "See, what I have found."

His discovery proved to be a bronze statuette, badly corroded, but identifiable, declared James, as a water goddess.

James flung an arm about Hilary. "This *is* a shrine! Just as you thought, my dear. I shouldn't wonder if it was built to honor the deity of the spring. For, now I am certain we shall find one when we investigate that reedy area."

Turning to look down into her happy, flushed face, James felt his heart lurch. He had cursed himself at some length for giving in to the impulse to kiss Hilary the last time they had been in the villa together. His transgression on the night of the Strindham musicale was bad enough, but he had blamed that on temper. Try as he might, however, he could find no excuse for gathering her in his arms a second time and giving way to the longing that had surged through him as his fingers brushed her cheek. Even now, he wanted nothing more than to take that fiery mop in both hands and draw her to him, to cover her face with kisses, to move his lips down to the silken triangle of flesh so demurely displayed at the collar of her gown, and to invade the delights that lay hidden from his gaze beneath the ruffle that trimmed her bodice.

Drawing a deep breath, he turned once more to Rufus.

"You have done well, *optima*. If you're feeling up to it, perhaps you might continue digging here. There might be an altar, and perhaps some sign of whatever was customarily offered to the deity."

A pleased grin spread over Rufus' blunt features, only to be replaced by one of puzzlement.

"I still don't understand why all this means so much to you, James." He waved an arm to indicate the gaunt remains of what had once apparently been a flourishing homestead. "But I'm glad to be of help." He chuckled. "I suppose you are like those fellows who prowl about the pyramids in *Aegyptus.* I never could understand that, either. What is so fascinating about piles of old bricks?"

"You have a point," said James musingly. "But don't you see? An insight into the future can be gained from a study of history."

Rufus grunted. "That's too deep for me."

"At any rate," said James, laughing, "I appreciate—" He halted abruptly, suddenly alert. He cocked his head.

"Did you hear something?"

Hilary, who had also caught a sound, as though from a snapping twig, some distance off, also turned to listen. After a few moments, when nothing further was heard, James relaxed.

"A rabbit scurrying through the brush, most likely."

Thoughts of Mordecai Cheeke looming in her mind, Hilary nodded dubiously. Surely, the odious little man would not stoop to spying on them from behind the shrubbery, but her instincts concerning Cheeke lent no support to this assumption.

The little group resumed their tasks, Rufus remaining at the shrine. A layman might have perceived very little in the way of accomplishment among the remains, for the work was painstakingly slow, but Hilary and James declared themselves well satisfied when they put their equipment away to make the journey back to Goodhurst.

Rufus, from whom they had heard nothing since his stellar performance earlier in the day seemed oddly bemused as they mounted the gig. He was silent on the trip home and was still in a thoughtful mood as they ate a modest nuncheon in their favorite haunt, the library.

"Tell me, *optima,*" said James through a mouthful of salad, "what do you know about events taking place elsewhere in the Roman Empire of your time? For example, the Judaean revolt."

"It was an abortive affair, and too many good men lost their lives over there in that godforsaken desert," said Rufus dismissively. "And that's all I know about it."

"But what about—what about Masada?"

"Never heard of it." Rufus gulped at his wine. "I told you, I don't know anything about it."

"For God's sake!" uttered James explosively. "How could you have lived through one of the most important events in Western history, and not know anything about it?"

"Because it ain't my business to know about it." Rufus growled. "A man can get into trouble messing about in the affairs of his betters. I tend to my business, which is mainly marching and repairing armor and hurling a *pilium* when called upon. I look out for my comrades and my family, and I go to the baths and the games now and then, and that pretty much takes up most of my time."

James grimaced in exasperation.

"For heaven's sake, James," expostulated Hilary in English. "Rufus is a foot soldier. If you asked a man of equal rank in Wellington's army his opinion on the government's East India policy, what do you think he would say?"

James did not reply, but sighed heavily.

"The next time," added Rufus, his tone heavy with offended irony, "you winkle somebody from the past, try for a centurion, or better yet a praetor. I did not ask to come here, you know."

James smiled ashamedly. "Please accept my apologies, *optima*. I can only be pleased that you are not one of the cognoscenti of your time, for experience has taught me that that sort are a parcel of very dull dogs. I am much happier to have made your acquaintance."

Rufus snorted, but appeared mollified.

"Will you come back out to the villa with us this afternoon?" James asked.

"No, I'm still not feeling up to par. I believe I'll try reading some more of this Spartianus fellow. I want to hear more about Hadrian, and I'm still working on the clock I took apart yesterday. I want to know how it works. Perhaps I'll make one for Maia when I get home."

"To be sure," replied James, concealing the fervent hope that the workings of the clock he had donated for Rufus' inquisitive fingers would remain a closed book to the warrior.

"I shall not be returning with you, either," said Hilary. She smiled at James's crestfallen expression. "I promised our house-

keeper to run into the village this afternoon to pick up some
beeswax candles for the receiving rooms."

"She cannot do this by herself?"

"I suppose she could. However, I think she feels I've been ne-
glecting my household duties of late—and she is perfectly right, of
course. Since you arrived, I've spent most of my time here."

"That's because you have important work to do here," James
snapped.

Hilary was astonished at his dictatorial tone, and stared at him
in affront.

"I had hoped," he concluded, softening his words only slightly,
"to make a drawing of the area in which Rufus found the statuette
this morning, and to catalog it with its proper description."

Hilary knew a surge of irritation. So that was the reason for his
look of disappointment? The fact that she would be unavailable to
work at his direction this afternoon?

"I'm sorry, but you will have to catalog it yourself," she replied
frostily. "Good day to you, James." She nodded at Rufus and swept
from the room.

"My," remarked Rufus, as the sound of a firmly closing front
door reached their ears, "you certainly have a way with the ladies,
James."

James stiffened. "I beg your pardon?"

"Gods above, boy, why do you persist in treating the girl as
though she's nothing more to you than an educated slave? A pretty
young thing like that—you should have wedded and bedded her
and put a bun in her oven by now."

James flushed to the roots of his hair. "Good God, Rufus! What
a thing to say! Hilary is a lady!"

Rufus chuckled. "O' course, she is. That doesn't mean she isn't
a woman, too. And don't think I ain't noticed you noticing. Mars
Victrix, lad, I've seen how you watch her when she's not looking,
and I've seen her pink up like a rose when you and her laugh together over some silly thing. You'd do well to say more silly things
to her, if you ask me," he concluded.

"Well, I'm not. Asking you, that is," James informed him with
icy precision. "My only interest in the Lady Hilary is her intellectual attributes."

Rufus snorted. "Tell that to someone who'll believe you." He waved airily and exited the room, leaving James to stare after him in bemusement.

An hour or so later, Hilary made her way into the small village of Little Merrydean, located a scant five miles from Whiteleaves. She mused rather forlornly as her gig clattered along the road.

It had seemed as though James was beginning to look on her as a friend. She might have known better. Men like James Wincanon did not form friendships with females, even females of superior intelligence and learning. Perhaps, she thought for the thousandth time, if she were endowed with long, silky, dark tresses instead of hair like a stack of bricks . . . She sighed again. No, to give James his due, she didn't think he'd be impressed by dark hair—or willowy curves for that matter. Her reflections were halted as she entered the village and stopped before a small shop in the High Street. At the threshold of the little establishment, she paused abruptly. For, just rounding a corner down the street, headed away from the store, she beheld a plump figure on horseback. A figure garbed in a coat of a virulent mustard hue.

Chapter Twenty-one

Hilary bolted into the little shop, and when she had concluded her business, she looked about cautiously as she left. The street was empty save for a few passersby, mercifully devoid of mustard-colored coats. What in the world had Mordecai Cheeke been doing in the village? she wondered. Silly question, she thought, a moment later. He was snooping, of course. But what was it he was snooping into? He already knew that James was investigating the villa. Surely, he did not think that anyone in the village would have knowledge of any finds James might have made there.

Hmmm. He had evinced an interest in Rufus. While he could not possibly suspect the old soldier's identity, he obviously sensed a mystery in the presence of Rufus in James's home. That must be it. Cheeke was no doubt canvasing the residents of the village in hopes of uncovering some clues as to who Rufus was and what he was doing at Goodhurst.

She chuckled inwardly. Well, good luck to him. The villagers knew no more of Rufus than Cheeke himself. The servants had not been instructed to keep silent about him, for that, Hilary and James and Robert had agreed, would only arouse curiosity. However, the staff had apparently accepted James's story of an old friend from a far-off land come to visit. After all, the peculiar Mr. Wincanon maintained odd interests in all sorts of strange people and pursuits.

She would miss Rufus when he was gone, Hilary reflected, but she would be glad when they had sent him on his way. The sooner he was back in his own place in the cosmos and away from Mordecai Cheeke's prying eyes, the better off they'd all be. Thank goodness his send-off was set for day after tomorrow.

She turned to mount her carriage for the return to Whiteleaves.

James awoke on Tuesday morning with a sense of anticipation mixed with regret. He was pleased for Rufus that he would be on his way home at last. However, he had come to enjoy the old warrior's company, beyond the knowledge of ancient Rome he contained in his head, and would be sorry to see him leave.

He found Rufus before him at breakfast. To James's critical eye, he did not look at all well. He was noticeably thinner than when he had tumbled into their lives a scant two weeks ago, and his skin was an unhealthy clay color. The soldier insisted he felt "well enough," however, and as they chatted over the coffee cups, they were joined by Robert.

"When will Lady Hilary be arriving?" he asked.

James's pulse stirred at the sound of her name, but he waved a casual hand. "Oh, not much before noon, I should imagine. We cannot expect Cyrus before then, even if he starts out early from Gloucestershire, which, knowing him, I am sure he will not."

Rufus was in high good humor, making short work of a steak and a plateful of eggs. He had, he declared, been up since dawn, occupying himself with polishing his armor.

"It wouldn't do," he declared, "for the garrison's armorer to appear after such a lengthy absence in rusty armor."

"But will it be?" asked Robert after a moment. "A lengthy absence? Perhaps no time at all has elapsed at your end of the transference, and it's only been a moment or two since you disappeared from your companions in the tower."

Rufus stared blankly, then turned to James, a questioning expression on his face.

"I have been wondering the same thing myself," James admitted. "There is no way of telling how the transference affected the passage of time at your end of the spectrum."

"In addition," added Robert, "what if the thing doesn't work at all?" He darted a glance at Rufus. "I'd be dashed reluctant to expose myself to—"

"Robert!" said James sharply.

"Oh." Robert dropped his gaze, chastened. "Sorry."

To James's surprise, Rufus laughed. "—to expose myself to a lightning blast on the chance I might ride it to my own time?" He shook his head. "No, I'm not worried. I have every confidence that it will work. I'll be home for *cena* tonight—I hope the cook serves his salmon in caper sauce—and I'll live to be an old man."

James gazed at him in wonder. "I must say, I didn't want to bring up the possibility of failure, but it is something we should consider. The field of electrical experimentation is very new—and very tentative."

Rufus gestured dismissively. "It will work," he said simply. "I know it will."

"But—"

James was interrupted by the advent of a footman, who announced that Lady Hilary had arrived and awaited Mr. Wincanon in the library. James fairly leaped from his chair. He had been confident, of course, that Hilary would put in an appearance, for she would not want to miss Rufus' grand disappearance. In the normal course of events, she would have come early if nothing else to enjoy a final few hours with Rufus. However, such had been her demeanor when she left the day before that he doubted she would arrive any earlier than she felt necessary to see Rufus off.

Devil take it, he seemed unable to put a foot right lately in his dealings with Hilary. This would be the third or fourth time in a very short while that he felt obliged to apologize for some transgression or other. At least, this time he knew where he had erred. Rufus had brought to his attention in painful detail his tendency to treat Hilary like an unpaid and not-very-bright clerical assistant.

He could not, in all honesty, blame her for taking snuff at such behavior.

The trouble was, he had realized at some point in the cold, dark reaches of the night before, he was using this attitude as a barrier. There was no doubt that his feelings for Hilary were plunging far beyond what could be considered proper between a gentleman of scientific pursuits and his acolyte in matters archaeological. She possessed the ability to transform him in an instant from the cool, detached intellectual he had been for so many years, to an addled schoolboy, consumed with longing. Even now, his pulse was pounding like that of a child on Christmas morning, just at the prospect of seeing her.

When he entered the library, she was standing at the far end of the room, caught in a slanting beam of early sunlight. Her hair was a glowing salute to the glory of autumn and her slight form was outlined in a golden halo against the long window that overlooked a velvety lawn. She raised her head and smiled at the opening of the door, and James felt his heart turn over. As she lifted her hand in a shy greeting, he was swept by a stunning realization. Good God, he was in love with this woman!

He almost stumbled with the force of the knowledge. He halted, simply gazing at her. He knew, with a burst of clarity, that all his life he would remember this moment. He would carry in his heart forever the picture of an enchanting sprite, garbed in a simple gown of forest green, embellished with crisp, white frills of lace. How had this happened, he wondered dazedly, and what was he to do now? How was he to deal with the maelstrom of emotion sweeping through him?

His first impulse was to run to her and to gather her into his arms. To pour out his feelings. He drew a deep breath. He would not do this, of course. He must think this thing through—approach the situation from a logical perspective. Perhaps the shattering revelation that had just come upon him was the result of a momentary madness. He had been so careful for so many years. Surely, he was not about to abandon the precepts of a lifetime for an elf in a green gown.

Her brows lifted quizzically and he felt the blood warm in his veins. He moved toward her.

"Good day to you, Hilary," he said prosaically.

"Good morning, James," she responded in the same tone. Her irritation of the day before, he noted with some relief, had evidently subsided.

James had some difficulty in controlling his bemusement when Robert and Rufus joined them in the library a few minutes later. The tension in the room, generated by Rufus' imminent departure, was almost palpable, but the conversation remained light. James, despite his heightened awareness of every facet of Hilary's appearance and demeanor, managed to keep at least some of his attention on the matter at hand. He asked questions of Rufus pertaining to his everyday life with his military unit and his family. Rufus, remarkably expansive and genial, took up pen and paper to list potential sites in Gloucester and Cirencester that would likely prove productive for further endeavor on James's part.

Cyrus appeared shortly after luncheon. Almost everyone in the household gathered in the stable yard, where the weedy scientist had directed his wagon be pulled. It was a very large wagon, as needs must, for its cargo was the largest glass vessel any of them had ever seen. Fully the size of a man, it was anchored in the center of the wagon's bed by ropes wound about the jar's neck and tied to the sides, and it was cushioned all around by bales of straw. The glass was by no means a prime example of the glazier's art, for it was thicker in some spots than in others, and its surface was disfigured with cloudy patches and misshapen bubbles that appeared randomly, like warts. The bottle was capped by a flat, metal lid.

"But where is the generator?" asked James.

"We don't need that now," replied Cyrus with some irritation, pushing his spectacles up on his nose. "I've been filling the jar with an electrical charge ever since you left, and it's ready to go now. We need only to take it to the site where you wish to—"

"Yes, yes," interrupted James, mindful of the yard full of servants listening with palpable interest to this discourse. "Have you lunched?" The question was put out of absentminded courtesy, but here Rufus thrust his burly form forward.

He had donned his military uniform, the polished metal of his breastplate reflecting the sun in brilliant flashes with each movement. James was struck by the imposing figure he made. To be sure, he had conformed well to the image of a country squire in his breeches and brogues, but garbed in his armor and his cloak, now cleaned and pressed and fastened with the brooch Hilary had seen on that first day, he was every inch the soldier. His sword was in place, as was the dagger James had so admired, and an undeniable air of authority surrounded him. Now that the moment had at last arrived for his release from his temporal prison, he obviously would brook no delay.

"Lunch?" he snapped. Aha, thought James in some amusement, here was yet another word the warrior had absorbed from the English language. Rufus lapsed immediately into Latin. "You're not asking him to eat, are you, for the gods' sake? At a time like this? Mars Victrix!" he sputtered. "He can fill his gut later. Let's get on with it."

Cyrus, peering curiously at Rufus, opened his mouth. "What—?" he began, but he was forestalled by Hilary.

"Perhaps," she said brightly, "we should just go immediately to the tower." She repeated the words in Latin for Rufus' benefit, and the soldier, now fairly dancing in impatience, signified his emphatic approval of this plan.

Thus, in a few moments, Cyrus, who had driven the wagon himself, proceeded carefully from the stable yard, accompanied by Rufus, Hilary, James, and Robert, all on horseback. In some disappointment, the servants shuffled back to their duties.

To Hilary, the short journey to the tower seemed to take an eternity, although she was aware that the pace must necessarily be excruciatingly slow. At last, the wagon creaked ponderously up to the entrance of the tower, and the next phase of the experiment began—the placement of the jar inside the structure. Again, this was accomplished with painstaking caution, with all the gentlemen involved in the removal of the jar from the wagon, easing it through the aperture and into position near the spot of Rufus' transference. At last, all was in place.

"Now, then," said Cyrus to James, "you have not divulged to me just why you need this extraordinarily large charge of electricity, and I do not wish to pry, but I believe that I might be of more help to you if I knew the desired end result."

James and Hilary exchanged glances, and after a moment, Hilary nodded almost imperceptibly. Drawing a deep breath, James turned back to Cyrus.

"Well, my friend, it's like this—" he began, and as the scientist's mouth dropped open, and drooped further with each sentence, James told Rufus' story in succinct phrases.

For several long minutes, Cyrus said nothing, his jaws working soundlessly. At last, with a strangled croak, he spoke.

"Traveled? Through time? This man here? James, have you lost your mind?"

"I know how it must sound, and I experienced the same reaction—at first. And, of course, I may, as you say, have taken leave of my senses, but all the evidence points to a genuine leap through time by this gentleman." He gestured toward Rufus, who muttered a questioning expletive. Hilary, in an undertone, explained the nature of the delay.

"Gods!" Rufus fairly exploded. "What difference does it make if this scrawny lack-wit believes me or not? Can he or can't he give me a push back to my own time?"

Cyrus, who possessed enough Latin to understand the warrior, replied with offended dignity. "Of course, I can. Or, at least," he amended, "I believe I can provide you with the simulation of a lightning bolt—if, indeed, such a bolt caused a warp in the fabric of time, what did you say?—seventeen hundred years ago." He gazed at Rufus with all the skeptical disdain of an entymologist asked to examine a new and highly suspect species of beetle. "Tell me," he continued, "precisely what were you doing at the time of your, er, transference?"

Rufus stared back blankly. "Doing? Why—I was just about to pry a section of wall loose."

"Ah, and were you going to use your sword, perchance?"

"Hades, no. Do you think I would ruin my *gladium* by using it as a pick ax? No, I had a big iron bar handy for the job. The rain was coming down hard, and I was about to take shelter, but I wanted to get in one good lick at the wall—as an example to the men, I suppose—before I did. In fact, I was just reaching for it."

"Ah," said Cyrus again. "The conductor." He turned to James. "We will need a similar instrument. The sword would do well, or"—his glance strayed over the interior of the tower—"that iron-bladed shovel."

James hurried to retrieve the implement from where it leaned against the wall. Hilary recognized it as one she had purloined from one of Whiteleaves' barns one morning a year or so previously. He handed it to Rufus, who placed it, at Cyrus's direction, in approximately the spot occupied by his crowbar so many centuries before.

"Now, then," declared Cyrus, "the Roman will stand in roughly the same place and position in which he stood during the lightning storm. Then, you two gentlemen"—he gestured to James and Robert—"will take up the mallet I have brought and bring it down with all possible force on the jar lid. This will create a spark, which in turn will set off the electrical charge. Lady Hilary, of course, will take shelter at a safe distance from the tower."

"Um," interposed Robert dubiously. "It sounds as though we will have to approach the jar—that is, we'll be in close range to—"

Cyrus waved airily and drew their attention outside the tower to the wagon, in which, besides the jar, reposed a hop pole, some six feet long, to which was strapped a large metal mallet. "Using this, we should be perfectly safe."

Robert stared at the contrivance dubiously, and James spoke bracingly. "Come, come, my boy. I know this sort of thing was not in your position description, but surely you do not mind a little risk in the cause of science? Particularly since it is for Rufus?"

"N-no," replied Robert, his voice lacking certainty. "I suppose not."

With some effort, the gentlemen present, Rufus included, hefted the mallet into place, after which a thoughtful silence fell on the group. Suddenly, Hilary ran forward and threw her arms about Rufus in an impulsive hug.

"Oh, Rufus," she cried tearfully, "it's time to say good-bye, and I didn't know it would be so hard. We'll never see you again!"

Rufus returned the embrace, patting her back awkwardly.

"There now, lass, I'm going back to where I belong. It's been nice meeting you—all of you, but you'll forget old Rufus in no time."

"Indeed, we won't," interposed James. He drew near to stand at Hilary's side. He shook Rufus' hand. "It's been a pleasure knowing you, *optima,* and not just because you've provided this struggling antiquary with the opportunity of a lifetime. You're a good man, soldier, and a credit to the *Legio Secundum*."

"Tcha!" Rufus, red-faced, but beaming with gratification, clasped James's forearm in a salute. "I can't say this ain't been an interesting experience, even though I'll be glad to get home to Maia and the children. I'm glad to have been of help to you, James, and I wish you well—not just in your shoveling and scraping, but—" He glanced significantly at Hilary.

"Yes," said James hastily. "Thank you very much."

Rufus then shook hands with Robert, and even with Cyrus, who still apparently viewed the proceedings with skepticism.

"Righty ho, then," said that gentleman. "Are we ready?"

Gulping, Rufus nodded. He stepped into position near the interior wall of the tower and raised his arm as though preparing to lift the shovel that had been laid in place nearby.

"Ready?" Cyrus asked again, this time Robert and James nodded. Hilary, unwilling to miss viewing the results of this literally earth-shaking experiment, stepped back a few paces, but did not leave the tower.

"Now!" cried Robert. With Cyrus's help, the two men strained to lift the mallet and moved forward with it in unison. Raising it above their heads, they brought it down upon the metal jar lid with a clang that reverberated about the stone edifice like the crack of doom. The next moment, a brilliant spark shot from the lid. A blinding flash, accompanied by a thunderous roar, erupted from the jar, shattering it into a spray of glittering shards.

Then, all was still.

Chapter Twenty-two

Hilary lifted her head slowly and discovered that she was lying in a crumpled heap on the ground. She was dizzy, and realized she had been unconscious for several moments. A searing pain at her wrist drew her attention to an ugly burn that encircled it under the bracelet she had donned that morning. The bracelet itself had melted into a misshapen band.

"What have you done?" The voice came from nearby. It was feminine, though it rang with an almost supernatural timbre. "What have you done, you foolish men?"

The woman's words were echoed by a faint groan, and Hilary pulled herself to a sitting position. To her astonishment, she saw that it was Dorcas who had spoken. Good heavens, what was she doing there? Rufus was stretched out at the old woman's feet. To her horror, she observed that his face and arms were badly burned. Near him were James, Cyrus, and Robert, who like her were stirring from sprawled positions nearby. They, too, were marked by burns on hands and face, though not so severely as Rufus.

Dorcas bent to huddle over Rufus. Her remarks had been directed toward the three men, who stared back at her, dazed.

Hilary struggled to her feet, almost crying out in her disappointment. They had failed! They'd created a lightning bolt, but Rufus was still here. She glanced at her companions, who had risen and hastened to where Rufus writhed painfully in Dorcas' arms. Hilary ran to join them. As she approached, Dorcas glanced up, and her face hardened.

"Were you a part of this, too, daughter?" she asked sternly. Her garments floated restlessly about her gaunt frame, although there was no discernible breeze in the clearing.

"Y-yes," admitted Hilary, feeling like a murderer. "But we meant no harm, Old One. Indeed, we were trying to help."

"Help him to do what?" asked Dorcas, her anger undiminished. She reached into a capacious sack she carried slung over one bony shoulder and withdrew a small tin pot. It contained a salve, which Dorcas applied to Rufus' burns, seeming to bring the soldier some ease.

"Why, to help him return home," replied Hilary. She caught herself. "That is, Rufus is a—a traveler from a great way off—and— and this gentleman"—she pointed to Cyrus—"is a scientist."

"Yes, yes," said Dorcas impatiently. "Did you think frying the Roman like a sausage would help him?"

James, stirred from his place among the little group surrounding Dorcas and Rufus. "How did you know—?" he croaked.

Dorcas silenced him with an imperious wave of her hand. "He

will survive," she declared, her voice still carrying the odd resonance that Hilary had noticed earlier. Corking the pot, she returned it to her sack. "However, he is not well." Rummaging once more, she produced a glass vial, which she handed to Hilary. "Give him two drops of this daily in some hot wine."

She stepped away from Rufus and sent a glare about the group that left them feeling as scorched as had Cyrus's bolt. "You will not again try to mimic the gods. Do not forget, you are but puny mortals, who will only come to harm through such sacrilege."

The puny mortals gaped silently. At a groan from Rufus, however, they dropped to their knees as one to minister to him. When Hilary raised her head a few minutes later, Dorcas had disappeared. Nonetheless, Hilary had the uncomfortable feeling that they were being watched.

"What happened?" asked James of Cyrus. "Why is Rufus still here?"

"How should I know?" snapped Cyrus. "I gave you your damned lightning bolt. I'm not responsible for the failure of the rest of your project." He glanced disdainfully at Rufus, being helped to his feet by Robert and Hilary. "In addition"—he scuffed petulantly at the small shards of glass settling in drifts about his feet—"my jar has been destroyed—all to no good purpose."

James turned away from Cyrus to address Rufus. "I am so sorry, *optima*. I had so hoped this would work."

Rufus shook his massive head. "I don't understand it," he whispered. "I was so sure . . . What am I going to do now?" he said to James, his gaze anguished.

James stood silent for a moment, then said heavily, "I don't know."

Watching Rufus's face, gray with disappointment, Hilary interposed, "Oh, but we will think of something, Rufus. We'll get you home somehow."

Cyrus, as though ashamed of his earlier outburst, spoke. "Perhaps the spark from the jar was simply not strong enough. We could try it again with a bigger one. Although the man who made this one said that he thought he could go no bigger. He told me he had the devil's own time with it. Begging your pardon, ma'am," he added hastily to Hilary. "In any event, it would take days, perhaps weeks to complete it." He hesitated, then asked James, "You really do believe this fellow traveled here from Roman Britain?"

James frowned irritably but gazing sharply at Cyrus's open countenance, he relaxed. "Yes," he answered simply.

"And you're trying to get him back where he belongs?"

James nodded, then added, "He has become ill in our era, and he is declining rapidly. I'm very much afraid that if we don't do something soon, he will——"

"I see." Cyrus stood silent for several moments before speaking again. "Perhaps——"

Suddenly, Rufus swayed and Hilary, standing next to him, gripped his arm. The soldier's face was a mask of pain, and a sweaty sheen glistened on his forehead. James, coming to Hilary's assistance, led Rufus to a boulder and eased him into a sitting position.

Hilary looked around nervously. Once more, she had the feeling that beyond the perimeter of the stone dance, where the forest stood dark and waiting, someone watched.

"I think we should get Rufus home," she said abruptly, and James glanced up in surprise.

"Yes—yes, I suppose we should. Are you up to the journey, *optima*?" he asked gently. "We must get those burns seen to."

Rufus looked down in surprise, examining his hands and arms. "Actually, they do not hurt much now. I wonder what's in the old lady's salve."

The soldier was obviously much the worse for his ordeal, however, and he accepted James's support as he rose. From the tower, they moved to the wagon that had transported the glass jar. The group mounted the wagon and set off for Goodhurst.

Just as they reached the lane that led to James's estate, Hilary glimpsed a flash of color fluttering at the edge of her vision from some distance away. When she turned her head, it was gone.

The group was largely silent during the journey, and on their arrival, Burnside, displaying not the least curiosity, assisted the men in bringing Rufus inside the house and up to his bed. Unresisting, Rufus permitted himself to be disrobed and soon sank into a restless slumber.

Having sent for the doctor, James repaired with Robert to the library, where Hilary awaited them.

"What are we going to do now?" she asked, breathing a worried sigh. James's assurance that Rufus appeared to be in no immediate danger had not allayed her fears for the warrior.

Casting a look at Cyrus and receiving no encouragement there, James slumped in his chair. "I don't know. I suppose we can hustle Rufus to the tower every time a genuine thunderstorm blows up, and hope that nature will take a hand, but that hardly seems like a viable solution to the problem."

"Or," contributed Robert, "perhaps the old fellow will adjust to the nineteenth century eventually, and live here happily ever after."

"There is that possibility," said James, brightening.

"But he does not want to stay here!" exclaimed Hilary.

"I didn't want to go to Eton, either." Robert grinned. "But my parents bundled me off anyway, and I survived."

"Yes, but—"

Burnside appeared at that moment with the information that the doctor had arrived. Robert rose, declaring he must return to his clerical duties. Bowing, he left the room.

"No, I must not stay," replied Hilary in response to James's query. "I promised Mrs. Fimble I would help her with the menu for the Halloween Ball dinner. It's only a few days away, you know."

She raised her eyes to James and smiled. "Are you sure you would not like to join us? We will have a lovely time."

Lord, thought James dispiritedly. What would it take to convince his tedious little love that he would rather be tied by his ankles over a pit of crocodiles than participate in a country costume party?

"Why—why, yes." He listened to his words with appalled astonishment. "I'd like that."

He opened his mouth a moment later to refute his promise, but made the error of looking into her eyes. This morning, he decided, they were the color of fine brandy. He beheld the pleasure sparkling in their depths and closed his mouth again.

"That's wonderful, James! I shall, of course, send an invitation to Robert, and one to Rufus, as well, if you think he would enjoy it."

James smiled to think of the warrior at large in an assemblage of that most English of modern classes, the country gentry.

"We shall see how he is feeling."

Hilary picked up her bonnet and, drawing on her gloves, allowed James to escort her to the front door.

"Have you any thoughts on a costume for the ball?" she asked, as she drew on her gloves.

"Actually, yes. I think I could come as King Lear."

"King Lear! Goodness, how did you come to choose such a . . . such an unlikely personage?"

James grinned, and, as usual, the process turned Hilary's knees to soup.

"I played the part in a production at Oxford, and kept the costume in a trunk for years. When I bought Goodhurst, I took the opportunity to retrieve my life's clutter from various storage places and bring it here. I found the costume when I began the sorting-out process."

"I did not know you harbored a talent for acting, James." Hilary smiled mischievously. "So, the eminent antiquarian has a secret life."

"I beg you will not reveal my shameful vice," replied James solemnly. "I promise it was a onetime aberration."

"I shan't breathe a word of your wicked past," replied Hilary with equal gravity, belied by the twinkle in her eye.

What a darling she is. James was caught unawares by the thought, and he was forced to suppress yet another urge to move to her, to touch her, to warm himself at the spark of her vitality. It was as though, he thought in some irritation, she were a lodestone to which he must return at frequent intervals for sustenance. This was nonsense, of course. On the other hand, if he had any sense, he would abandon his excavations at the Roman villa, pack up the ailing Rufus, and scurry for London as fast as his curricle would carry him.

Dropping the hand he had unconsciously lifted to her, he asked casually, "And what will you be wearing?"

"Oh. I believe I shall appear as Diana."

"Ah, the goddess of the hunt."

"Yes. I'm afraid I have not started my preparations yet, but a few gauzy draperies and some arrows should suffice. And a pasteboard crescent moon covered with glitter on a band around my head."

James, who had stopped listening at the part about gauzy draperies, nodded, finding that his mouth had gone dry.

Pulling himself together, he managed to chat amiably and vacuously (although he suspected that he was babbling) as he bundled her into her gig and waved her off down the drive. However, watching her disappear into the distance, he leaned against the jamb, feeling as spent as though he had just run the distance between Goodhurst and Whiteleaves.

Was this what love did to a man? Destroyed his ability to reason, and churned his emotions so that eventually he abandoned all the carefully constructed precepts of his life? This could not be happening to him! The whole idea of his falling in love at all was ludicrous, let alone with someone like Lady Hilary Merton, a slender witch with flaming hair and the insidious determination of a flood tide.

He clenched his fists against the unaccustomed feeling of helplessness that seemed to permeate his soul.

Clattering along the lane, Hilary tried to immerse herself in plans for James's future. She was, of course, pleased that he had agreed to attend the ball. Now, she must consider how best to throw him together with the ladies on her list of prospective mates. It should not be difficult, she told herself. She would seat him next to Amanda Ffrench at dinner. Charlotte Ponsonby's name would be placed before him for the first set of country dances and, the Widow Silcombe later. After that . . .

She became aware of a distinct sense of dissatisfaction in her musings. The cause, unfortunately, was not difficult to discern. She had absolutely no desire to pair James with any of these highly eligible females. In fact, if she were to be honest with herself, the only female with whom she wished James to spend the evening was herself.

She slumped over the reins. For the last several days she had attempted to define her feelings for the antiquary, and now she knew the answer had been lying in her heart all along, waiting for acknowledgment. She could, she now realized dismally, no longer escape from the fact that she was in love with James Wincanon.

Really, she thought with some irritation, for a woman who professed herself reluctant to marry, she had allowed her emotions to tumble her into an impossible bumble broth. For there was no question she had made the worst possible choice in the matter. James was arrogant. James was dictatorial. He was self-centered and opinionated. He was also intelligent—and witty—and considerate at the oddest times—and wholly compelling—and . . .

And the whole question was academic in the extreme, she told herself in a not-quite-successful attempt at briskness. For, James Wincanon was not in the market for a wife. He had made it clear that he preferred to be left alone. To be sure, he had kissed her—twice—but she had already ascertained that those pleasurable but inexplicable encounters had meant nothing to him.

He had agreed to attend the Halloween Ball. Surely, he had done so merely to please her, for he obviously had no real desire to don a costume and point a toe with the local gentry. Unless, of course, he had decided, as he had indicated before, that he wished to be a good neighbor while he resided at Goodhurst.

She looked up to see that she had come abreast of the tower. Unwilling to go home just yet, she halted the gig. Making her way to the stone dance, she sat down on the polished altar and continued her dismal reflections.

She had made a decision only a few weeks before to expunge James Wincanon from her life. She should have remained steadfast in her resolve. Now, here she was, sitting by herself in the forest like a disheartened troll, bemoaning her fate. She realized that her cheeks were wet with tears.

"Hilary!"

Hilary jumped at the sound of Dorcas' voice and turned to see the old woman approaching from the edge of the clearing. Good heavens, did she not have a home of her own? Did she spend all her waking hours in the dance?

"Why do you sit, weeping?" continued Dorcas.

"I—I—"

Mercifully, Dorcas did not wait for an answer, but continued. "How fares the Roman?"

"He is still not well. But I'm sure your medicine will help," Hilary added hastily.

"Mm, yes, although perhaps not enough. But you"—Dorcas returned to the matter at hand—"you are unhappy, little one." She sat beside Hilary on the altar stone, her gaze penetrating but not unkind.

To her horror, Hilary felt more tears well in her eyes and spill down her cheeks. She raised a hand to wipe them away, but Dorcas lifted her own to intercept it.

"It is ever the way of a maid to weep for a man. And usually, quite uselessly, too."

"Y—yes," gulped Hilary in agreement. "I am being very silly, I know. But Old One!" she cried, to her astonishment abandoning all reserve. "I do love him."

"And yet you despair. This is not wise." The old woman sighed. "Young people always complicate their lives so. Love should not be an occasion for weeping."

"Perhaps," retorted Hilary, "but he considers me nothing more than a handy clerical assistant. That makes it a little difficult to rejoice."

Dorcas' lips twitched, but she said only, "Perhaps you're taking too dim a view. At any rate, how do you know that he sees you merely as an unpaid clerk?"

Hilary uttered an unladylike snort. "Why, I have no idea, unless it's because he orders me about like a serving wench and never says please or thank you."

"A damning indictment, to be sure," murmured Dorcas, the merest tremor in her voice. "And yet, he kisses you?"

Not pausing to wonder how the old lady had come by this information, Hilary tried for a casual insouciance in her reply. Waving an airy hand, she said, "Oh, but that meant nothing. Gentlemen, as you must know, are distressingly free with their kisses."

"Even such a one as Mr. Wincanon? He does not seem the sort to indulge in such frivolities."

"No, I don't suppose he does, but— You see, other than the kissing, he has not shown any indication that he regards me at best as anything more than a friend for whom he holds a slight affection."

"Do you think friendship cannot serve sometimes as a cloak for love?"

Hilary blinked back more tears. "Not in this case," she said firmly.

"Or that friendship has already bloomed into love without the gentleman's knowledge?"

Hilary could have laughed at the absurdity of Dorcas' statement, if she were not already crying. "No, I don't think so," she whispered at length.

"But did not the advent of the Roman accomplish your purpose?"

"Purpose?"

"You prayed for success in your meeting with James Wincanon. Have you not become close to him because of the Roman's presence in your lives?"

Hilary could no longer suppress her curiosity. "How is it that you know about—about the Roman?" she asked.

Dorcas brushed a few grains of—what was that? Wheat?—that clung to the dark fabric of her skirt. "I am old and I know many things. Was not the Roman the answer to your prayer?"

"Well—" replied Hilary doubtfully. "Yes, I suppose so—in a certain sense, but even my silly wish has turned to disaster."

"Oh?" Dorcas' silver brows rose.

"You see, Rufus does not thrive in our time. That is why we were trying to return him. Despite our efforts, he grows more ill every day, and if he doesn't get back to his own time, we fear he will die."

Dorcas grew thoughtful. "I see. I had not thought of that. Hmp. Do you plan to try again?"

Hilary sighed. "I don't know."

"I believe you should make another attempt, for next time you may well be more successful." Dorcas shook a bony finger. "But no more trying to create lightning, daughter. Now, about James Wincanon, you are so sure he does not return your feelings for him?"

"Quite sure." Hilary sniffed purposefully. "However, I'm sure I will survive."

"Ah, little one," breathed Dorcas. "You persist in surrounding yourself with darkness. You must look beyond the uncertainty of the present and into the sunlight of the future. For, there is light ahead for you. I know this."

Lifting her head, Hilary gazed into the distance, trying to absorb the old woman's words. They were sheer nonsense, of course, yet she found them oddly comforting. When she turned back to Dorcas, a few moments later, the old woman was gone.

Sighing, she moved to her gig and resumed her journey home.

Chapter Twenty-three

The remaining two days before the ball passed quickly. Robert professed himself delighted at his invitation, and even Rufus declared himself fit and ready for action.

Thus, on the evening of the event, James stood before the mirror in his chamber, donned in the royal, if somewhat moth-eaten robes of King Lear.

"Devil take it, Friske, what did you use on this beard? It feels like cement." He swung about from the mirror to confront his valet. "I can barely open my mouth."

"I'm terribly sorry, sir, but none of the shops in the village carries theatrical glue, so I was forced to rely on a concoction made up for you by Cook. I believe it contains bone marrow—and possibly flour."

"To say nothing of eye of newt and toe of frog, I suppose," muttered James. He patted his long, white mustaches into place and settled a battered crown on his head. "There, am I presentable?"

Friske stepped back to survey his handiwork. "The very image of the tragic monarch, sir, if I may say so." Pausing only to make a minor adjustment to his majesty's cloak, he turned to answer a peremptory knock at the door. A fearsome figure stood there, swathed in animal skins and an assortment of brass necklets and chains.

"Good God, what are you got up as, Robert?"

"Attila the Hun," was the terse answer. "Could you not tell?"

"I see merely an unidentified barbarian. You need a crown to give you that certain air of authority." He touched his own circlet.

"Mm. It looks as though it's been gnawed on by dogs."

"It probably has. Where is Rufus?"

"Polishing his sword, I think. He's rather keen on appearing in full military regalia for his first time in public. He's grumbling over his missing helmet, though."

"How is he feeling?"

"He seems quite chipper, actually. That potion the old lady gave him must be remarkably efficacious. He has his bad spells—and they're getting more frequent, but right now he's merry as a grig."

"I suppose that's good. I just hope this evening won't be too much for him. Well, let's be on our way, then." He glanced out the window. "I see it's clouding over. I shouldn't wonder if it didn't start sprinkling on the way to Whiteleaves."

Gathering up his scepter, James accompanied Robert from the room. They were joined in the hall by Rufus, resplendent in blindingly polished armor and accoutrements.

"I must say I'm looking forward to this, James. I've always enjoyed dancing, and it will give me a chance to practice my English."

"Dancing? I don't recall reading much about Roman dancing. Except for the nude damsels at the orgies, of course."

"I've never gone in for those things," replied Rufus primly. "They cost a lot of money, you know. No, I'm talking about dancing at festivals and sometimes dinner parties. The British have some jolly traditional steps, you know. Maia's family are hell on a barn floor at harvest."

"You must demonstrate for me sometime," said James as they mounted the carriage awaiting them in the drive. Tonight, though a full moon had been promised, the lane was rendered stygian by the clouds that lowered overhead. It had become necessary to light the carriage torches in their reflective holders.

On their arrival at Whiteleaves, some minutes later, they were greeted in the gold saloon by the Earl of Clarendon, garbed as an Egyptian pharoah, and his daughter, the goddess, Diana. James caught his breath. Clothed in gossamer sprinkled with glitter, her red curls adorned with a crescent moon, she was pure witchery. Silver sandals flashed on her feet, and in her hand she carried a delicate bow and arrow. More arrows could be seen protruding from a small quiver slung over her shoulder.

"James!" she cried out in pleasure. "That is"—she swept a low bow—"your most august majesty."

"Indeed, James," boomed the earl, "you lend a certain cachet to the gathering. And these"—he turned to the other two gentlemen—"this must be Mr. Newhouse. You make a splendid Attila, sir, though I suspect that's not much of a compliment. And Professor, you are magnificent! Welcome, all of you."

Several guests were already present, and James observed that he was acquainted with most of them. He circulated about the chamber, greeting a Red Indian, a harem girl, a Venetian doge, and assorted pirates. He kept Rufus by his side, and the warrior beamed in genial incomprehension, accepting with alacrity the wines presented to him by passing footmen.

Some thirty couples sat down to dinner, and James was pleased to note that he had been seated next to Hilary.

It was not until much later, when the dancing had begun, however, that James was able to converse with her with any degree of privacy. He had gone to considerable lengths to insure that the dance she saved for him would be a waltz, and now, as he placed his hand on the small of her back, it seemed to him that he was gathering a creature of fire and cloud into his arms.

Hilary's reflections as she stepped into his embrace were not quite so fanciful, as she was barely able to refrain from sneezing into the musty folds of James's robes, and she experienced some difficulty in keeping his beard out of her mouth. However, these insignificant details fled from her mind when he placed his arm about her waist. Dear heaven, she could feel the heat of his hand through the thin fabric of her gown.

And he was so very close! She imagined she could feel his heart beating against her own. It seemed to her that their pulses combined to throb in rhythm with the music and their feet took on a magic of their own as they whirled about the floor.

"You make a beautiful goddess of the hunt," he murmured. "Diana herself could look no more lovely in the moonlight."

His words were so uncharacteristic that Hilary glanced up quickly, and immediately wished she hadn't. His chocolate-brown gaze held a spark of something in their depths that she dared not try to identify. She felt the heat rise to her cheeks and strove for a light answer.

"Be careful, sir. You know what happens to mortals who dally with the deity of the hunt."

"Do you plan to transform me into a bear and toss me into the skies?"

"Sirrah, does the deity discuss her plans with a mere mortal?" she asked playfully, aware that her own eyes must be giving away her feelings.

"Ah, but I am not a mere mortal. I am Lear, mighty king, and father of three impossible daughters."

"Nonsense. Even such as you are dust beneath the feet of Diana, Ruler of the Moon and Stars."

James smiled, and, to her dazed senses, it seemed a smile of such tenderness that she almost gasped with the surge of longing that swept through her. When the music stopped, she stepped back abruptly, as though fleeing from her own emotions. She gazed distractedly about the room and became aware of a strange figure lurking and bobbing on the perimeter of the dance floor.

"Who in the world is that odd little man?" she asked, pointing discreetly.

James turned to observe a personage, as wide as he was tall, whose face was almost totally obliterated by a bushy wig and a truly astonishing beard. He appeared to be garbed as King Arthur, for on the wig teetered a large crown of what looked like iron, and around his neck hung a heavy, brazen torque in the Celtic style. His costume consisted of layered perceptions of Arthurian fashion. A woolen tunic drooped over fur leggings, the whole covered by a swirling cloak. Atop this lay—a wolf skin, for God's sake?

"Good Lord, I have no idea," James replied. "Although he seems slightly familiar. Could it be the vicar, trying to outdo last year's performance as a shock of wheat?"

"Oh, no Reverend Thomlinson is much taller. See, I believe that is he over there—dressed as Friar Tuck."

When the dance concluded, Hilary's hand was immediately solicited for a country set and James watched her whirl away on the arm of an American frontiersman. He wondered if she would indulge him later in a stroll on the terrace. By now the earlier mutter of thunder had progressed to an ominous rumbling, but James envisioned the methods in which he might protect his lissome companion from the elements. Hastily, he expunged them from his mind. He merely, he assured himself, wished for some quiet conversation with Hilary.

His gaze swept the room, but she had disappeared. He supposed he should ask someone else to dance. That's what one usually did at these functions, wasn't it? On the far side of the room, Robert had joined in the country dance, animal skins flying and chains clanking with abandon. James smiled. At least someone was fulfilling his social duties.

James glanced again about the great ballroom, looking for

Rufus, but did not see him, either. At last sight, the warrior had been having a very good time. Too good, perhaps. He had obviously been imbibing rather heavily, for he gesticulated expansively and weaved as he made his way about the room. Lord, thought James, he hoped Rufus wasn't making himself sick.

As if in answer to his concern, a footman materialized at his elbow.

"Sir, Lady Hilary wished to convey to you the intelligence that, er, Rufus has been taken ill."

"Oh Lord," exclaimed James. "Is he all right? Where is he?"

"He has been taken to the Tapestry Bedchamber, and Lady Hilary requests that you join her there. If you will follow me, sir?"

The servant turned and led James into the corridor and to a nearby wing. Here they came upon a heavy wooden door. The footman gestured James inside, then bowed before closing the door again behind him.

James found himself in an ornate bedchamber, hung with rich tapestries and featuring a huge, tester bed. Upon this structure, like a slain warlord, reposed Rufus, obviously completely unconscious and breathing stertorously. At the side of the bed, Hilary vainly tried to undo the lacings that held Rufus' armor together. Behind her, through the window, thunder sounded close, and intermittent flashes of lightning rendered the scene somewhat macabre. Rain could be heard spattering against the panes.

"James!" Hilary cried, looking up. "I'm so glad you have come. I cannot rouse him, but I don't know if that's due to his overindulgence or whether he's seriously ill. Do you think he is all right? I've sent for the doctor. He's a guest here tonight, you know."

"Mm. I think I saw him earlier, dressed as—Moses, I think it was. I believe Rufus is suffering merely from plunging too enthusiastically into the blushful Hippocrene. Lord, I should have known better than to let him loose in a room full of flowing wine."

James completed the task of removing Rufus' armor and covered the old soldier with a quilt. The doctor, when he arrived a few moments later, confirmed James's diagnosis, merely advising that Rufus be allowed to sleep it off.

"I don't think he should be left alone, do you?" asked Hilary anxiously. "I'll stay here for a while."

"I think we should both stay," James averred. "He might be hard

to handle when he awakes." He left unsaid the fact that if Hilary
were not among the dancers below, he had no desire to join them.
He turned once more to Rufus.

"His breathing seems a little easier, but he is still very pale."

Rufus stirred uneasily and Hilary bent over him.

"Oh dear," she murmured as he began to thrash about on the
bed. His eyes remained closed, but he was in obvious distress.
"Now what? Do you think—?"

"I think you'd better get a jug," said James tersely. "He's about
to cast up his accounts."

Hilary's gaze swept the room, and she grabbed a delicate porce-
lain basin from the washstand. As James slipped his arm under
Rufus' shoulders to lift him, she thrust it under the warrior's chin
in the nick of time, for the next moment he unburdened himself of
the seemingly endless quantity of wine he had consumed earlier.

At length he lay back against his pillows, still unconscious, his
face as white as his bed.

"Well," said James prosaically, "that ought to make him feel better."

"Ugh!" Hilary moved again to the washstand, this time to dip a
towel into a water-filled pitcher. Returning to the bed, she wiped
Rufus' mouth gently. "Poor old fellow. The one time he gets out to
enjoy himself, he puts himself out of commission. Goodness, how
are we going to get him home?"

"Oh, he should come around before too long, though it might be
a good idea to help the process along."

He bent over Rufus and applied the damp towel to his forehead
and cheeks, tapping him lightly as he did so.

"Come on, old fellow. Time to return to the land of the living."

Rufus groaned and his eyelids fluttered, but he did not awaken.

"I think he could probably stand some hot coffee." James
reached for the bellpull nearby, encountering Hilary's fingers on
their way to the same mission. He hadn't realized they were standing so close, and the sudden awareness of her proximity in this intimate circumstance made his heart race.

Rufus was momentarily forgotten as the two gazed for a long
moment into each other's eyes. Hilary knew a deep trembling
within her as James reached to adjust her headband. His fingers
brushed warmly against her temple.

"We can't have the moon goddess wandering about with her crescent askew," he whispered unsteadily.

"N-no."

He was going to kiss her! Somewhere beyond the pounding of her heart, the thought drifted across her consciousness that James picked the oddest times to become amorous. A man lay in a drunken stupor not two feet away, and the smell of his unpleasant upheaval still lingered in the room. None of this seemed to matter, though, as everything in her prepared to participate in this most welcome of gentle assaults. She raised her face as James bent his head to hers.

It was at this supremely inopportune moment that the bedchamber door opened abruptly. Hilary and James sprang apart from one another to behold an inordinately large group of costumed guests, their eyes wide with various expressions of shock and satisfaction. It was a moment before Hilary was able to discern the individual components of the assembled horde. Prominent among them was Lord Clarendon. At his shoulder stood the doctor, the doctor's wife, Squire Beddoes, Mrs. Strindham, and Mrs. Thomlinson. In the rear, bobbing about in an effort to view the proceedings, was the plump, bewigged, and bearded little stranger they had observed earlier.

"Hilary!" gasped the earl, rushing into the room to enfold his daughter in an embrace. "Are we to wish you happy at last?"

"How marvelous!" chimed Mrs. Thomlinson, her hands clasped to her bosom. "I *knew* the rumor of your imminent betrothal was true!"

Lifting her head, Hilary glanced wildly at James, only to intercept an angry spark of darkest suspicion in his eyes.

Chapter Twenty-four

For an instant, Hilary held James's gaze in a horrified realization. Her father spoke again.

"W-what?" stammered Hilary, feeling as though she had just stumbled into a nightmare.

The earl spoke in a tone of unwonted sternness. "You are alone in a bedchamber with a man. I can come to no other conclusion."

"Oh! But—" cried Hilary, unable to utter a coherent protest.

James spoke in a voice she had never heard before.

"My lord, you are vastly in error. There will be no wishing anyone happy, for there is to be no betrothal. I am sorry to disappoint you, but the scene that you chose to interrupt so erroneously is completely without significance. Lady Hilary and I are merely giving aid and comfort to our friend. He is a stranger in a strange land and we did not wish to leave him alone in his distress."

Lord Clarendon turned to dismiss the crowd of curious guests from the room, and when only he and James and herself remained, Hilary tried to step forward. She seemed unable to move, however, frozen in a fog of humiliation and disbelief. She stared in anguish at James, whose contemptuous gaze swept over her like a cold tide. Dear God, he thought she had taken advantage of Rufus' indisposition to lure him into the Tapestry Room with the express purpose of compromising him!

"No—" she whispered blindly, but her father continued.

"I'm afraid, my dear," he said gravely, "the fact that the professor is unconscious makes the situation all the more perilous to your reputation. To be caught by such a large number of persons with a man not your husband, in a bedchamber whose only other occupant is another male—dead to the world . . . There is only one satisfactory interpretation. The rumors have been spreading for some time now of Mr. Wincanon's interest in you. I had thought them false, but now—well, they will serve to allay any hint of scandal."

James stared at the earl, disbelieving and sick. He glanced again at Hilary. She looked sick, too, as well she might. She was not even trying to dispute the earl's words. Dear God, he had been utterly duped. A slim gamine with eyes of copper and hair like fire and the mind of a scholar had not only pierced his defenses, but had stolen the heart he had thought inviolate. She had taken the very breath from his body, leaving him stunned and helpless.

And empty.

For, as he had known from the beginning, it was all a sham. Her erudition was real, but the soul that lay beneath it was fool's gold.

The brandy-colored eyes that gazed so luminously into his lied like those of a courtesan.

"You may interpret the situation as you choose, my lord," declared James, his face pale and set. "I have not asked your daughter to marry me, nor do I intend to. Now, if you will excuse me, I believe it is time I took my leave."

Lord Clarendon made no attempt to stay his daughter, as she moved to follow James, but said to James, "We will speak later, sir."

In the corridor, Hilary turned to James, a desperate prayer in her heart. She must make him understand!

"I am so sorry about this, James," she said in a rush, and now that she had found her tongue, the words tumbled out. "I don't know what possessed Father to troop upstairs with half our guests in his wake, but his inference is utter nonsense. Evidently," she noted bitterly, "everyone has just been waiting for us to make a declaration. Our absence from the ballroom must have served as some sort of signal to them. Please, believe me, I shall make it clear that you are in no way obliged to marry me, nor have I any intention of allowing him to announce our betrothal."

"I am pleased to hear you say so, Lady Hilary." His voice was like ice in a winter sea, and Hilary shivered. "I, too, have been wondering how he happened to pay a visit to the Tapestry Room at that particular moment. And now, if you will excuse me, I believe it's time I took my leave."

Hilary bit her lip. James obviously believed she had engineered the whole scene. Lord, did he think she had enticed him into the embrace she was sure he had intended? At the very least, he believed she had made sure her father and several guests would happen upon them.

James swung away from her and strode toward the stairs. Hilary followed, suppressing the tide of sickness that welled up within her.

Listening to her faint footfalls behind him, James thought he had never known such a sense of betrayal and humiliation. By God, he'd been right about Hilary from the first. The realization struck him like a blow.

How could he have been so stupid as to allow himself to trust her? After the years it had taken him to craft a wall around his heart, he had behaved like the veriest moonling, falling under the spell of fiery curls and eyes like golden pools.

Well, thank God he had come to his senses in time. If my lady thought she had him trapped, she had quite another think coming.

They had by now reached the hall, and Hilary turned to him.

"I will return to Rufus," she whispered through dry lips, "and I'll see that someone stays with him through the night."

"Thank you." James kept his tone cool and distant. "I shall return tomorrow morning to collect him."

Desperately, Hilary grasped for a measure of insouciance.

"In the meantime, I shall speak to Father in an effort to effect a measure of damage control."

From the rigidity of his bow, Hilary realized that her effort to put a light face on the matter had failed miserably. She opened her mouth to speak again, but at that moment, Dunston materialized with James's cloak, which he draped ceremoniously over the royal robes.

James bowed formally. "Good night, then, Lady Hilary. I—" He was interrupted by a thunderous pounding on the manor's entrance door. Dunston proceeded majestically to answer it, and in a moment his mellifluous, if somewhat outraged voice drifted to them across the marbled expanse of the hall. "I am sorry, sir, the family is entertaining this evening, and I fear none of them is at home to visitors."

"Never mind all that."

James turned in surprise at the sound of the voice that issued from the driving rain outside.

"I understand that James Wincanon is among the guests, and I must speak to him."

The figure pushed his way past Dunston, rain streaming from the crown of his somewhat disreputable beaver hat. In his hand, he carried a small metal canister, pierced with several small holes.

"Cyrus!" exclaimed James. "What the devil are you doing here?"

Hurrying toward his friend, he peered outside. There, parked before the great doorway, stood Cyrus's old wagon. It contained a bulging object covered with a tarpaulin.

Cyrus, ignoring Dunstan's affronted snort, strode into the hall, dripping with every step. He stared at James for a puzzled moment, taking in the velvet robes and the beard, then bowed quickly to Hilary.

"Get your oilskins out, James," said he said jubilantly, "and come with me to the tower. I trust the soldier is on the premises, as well. I have solved the problem! At least," he amended, "I have contrived another method which may do the trick, but my procedure must be accomplished now. Move, man!" he ordered peremptorily. "I'll explain on the way. Go round up your Roman."

James swung to Hilary. He hesitated a moment. He could not look at her without experiencing a wave of pain, but he forced himself to speak crisply. "I don't know what he's babbling about, but I think we'd better do as he says. Will you find Robert? I'll go roust Rufus. I may need a couple of footmen to haul him out of bed, if he's still hors de combat."

Hilary said nothing, but lifted her hands in a pleading gesture. After a moment, she swung about and departed hastily, signaling to Dunston. James raced up the stairs, but upon entering the Tapestry Room he was brought up short by an incredible scene.

Rufus was still stretched out on the bed, but he was partially awake. Just above him hovered the pudgy King Arthur James had noticed earlier and who had been part of the group come to witness the fruition of Hilary's little plan. Also in the room were two burly men, garbed in dark clothing. The long windows of the chamber stood open, allowing the curtains to billow in the wind and the rain. The king was apparently trying to pull Rufus from the bed. He swung about at James's entrance, causing his crown to tumble to the coverlet. The golden wig immediately followed suit, which, though half his face was still covered by his beard, left his features clearly discernible.

"Cheeke!" shouted James in disbelief.

"Damn you, Wincanon!" snarled Mordecai, leaping from the bed. Since he was severely encumbered by his many layers of clothing, he landed on the floor with an ignominious thud. Scrambling to his feet, he faced his antagonist. Behind him, Rufus mumbled grumpily and attempted to sit up.

"What the devil are you about, you unconscionable toad?" James advanced on him, but Mordecai's companions moved forward menacingly.

"What does it look like I'm doing? I'm removing this unfortunate gentleman from your clutches." Mordecai gestured to one of his cohorts to stand between him and James.

"My *what*?"

"You heard me. You see, I've been following your activities, James. I know all about your Roman soldier."

"What!" James uttered the word explosively.

"Oh, yes. Did you really think you could keep your secret from a man of my intelligence? I've been watching every move you made—including your efforts the other day in that ruined tower. You were trying to create lightning, weren't you?

"I was crouched nearby and I heard every word you all said. At first I thought you must have gone mad. A legionary of the first century—traveling through time? But I came to believe the truth of it, and I must say I was appalled at your knavery."

"*My* knavery!"

"The man is a treasure beyond price to the antiquarian community," trumpeted Mordecai virtuously, "and you're keeping him bottled up like a specimen on a shelf. It is my duty as a scientist to see that his knowledge of ancient Britain is made available to the world at large. And you can't stop me!"

James advanced threateningly on the imitation king. Mordecai squeaked faintly and dodged behind his protector. The second man, surging from his position at the window assisted in effectively preventing James from reaching his target. The man raised a beefy fist, but at that moment, Dunston, accompanied by two stalwart footmen, entered the room, Hilary on their heels.

"James, what's toward? Cyrus is waiting, and—oh!" Hilary stopped abruptly on observing the scene taking place in the bedchamber.

Mordecai sent a glance of concern toward the footmen, but stood his ground. He watched as Hilary advanced into the room.

"Ah, the little lady." He smirked. "I understand I am to wish you happy. But did not James come up to snuff soon enough for you? I must congratulate you, my dear. Luring James up here was a masterstroke. What a picture you made—all blushing innocence in the arms of poor, deluded James—with a mob of country gentry to witness the tender scene."

James, after one look into Hilary's wide, anguished gaze, growled unintelligibly and launched himself at Mordecai in a blind rage. Instantly, he was grasped by Mordecai's henchmen, one of whom delivered a blow to the back of his head that brought him to his knees.

At that point, Rufus came fully to his senses. It took him only an instant to comprehend what was afoot. Rising from the bed-clothes, he stood atop them, swaying, but undaunted. He drew his sword, and Cheeke, glancing over his shoulder at him, turned pale. Another glance, this time at the footmen and Dunston, advancing into the room, prompted him further. With a shouted command to his companions, he edged past James, still in the grip of the two bullies. With an agility surprising in one of his girth, he ran for the windows, and in an instant had disappeared into the depths of the rainstorm. His hirelings abruptly lost interest in the proceedings, and in James as well. Thrusting him into the arms of the advancing servants, they, too, scurried out through the window.

As soon as James had recovered his equilibrium, he gave pursuit, but by then, nothing could be seen from the windows through the gathering murk. He turned back into the room to face Hilary, standing utterly still, her face the color of parchment. Rufus, Dunston, and the footmen blurred into insignificance as he stared at her. She had thrown a serviceable woolen cloak over her costume, and with it, she wore sturdy boots of jean.

"I—I returned to the hall, and—you were not—I wondered what had become of you," she whispered, her fingers groping blindly as though the world had gone dark around her. Their gazes met and locked and James felt his heart turn over in his breast.

Suddenly, between one breath and the next, James felt a burden lifted from him. He knew in that instant—he *knew* that Hilary had not schemed to entrap him.

Dear God, he'd been so wrapped up in his cynical theories on the female sex, that he'd let a pearl beyond price slip through his fingers, for he knew that Hilary was aware of his unworthy suspicions and that she was terribly hurt. Cheeke's final words shouted inside James's head.

What was he to do now? thought James, frozen in a morass of guilt and regret. Hilary, too, seemed unable to move or speak, but after a few seconds, she whirled and fled from the room.

"Sir. Sir?" It was Dunston, speaking at his elbow. "It appears the miscreants have left the premises. Do you wish to notify the magistrate?"

"What?" asked James blankly. "No—no that will not be necessary. I think we won't have any more trouble from them. Ah, thank you for assistance, Dunston. I think that will be all for the present."

With a stately bow, Dunston exited the chamber, waving the footmen on ahead of him. James turned to Rufus. He knew there was something he should be doing, but his thought processes were mired in such a black depression he could not seem to function. He stared at Rufus.

"What is it, lad? Do you want to go after those bastards? They did me no harm, but it was a near thing. If you hadn't come in just then, with me still in the arms of Bacchus, they'd have whisked me out of here with no trouble. Lad?"

James stared at him blindly. "Hilary?" He was unaware that he'd spoken aloud. "No! Cheeke—"

"What in Hades are you mumbling about?" Rufus snorted, thrusting his sword back into its sheath. "Did the foul Cheeke say something about your lady?"

"She's not my lady," mumbled James despairingly. It was the truth, wasn't it? She had never been really his and in a split second, he had lost whatever chance he might have had to capture her heart.

With a shuddering sigh, he forced his mind to the matter at hand. "Come along, *optima*," he said dully. "It appears you have another appointment with destiny."

Chapter Twenty-five

With Rufus babbling excitedly at his side, James returned to the hall. Hilary stood waiting with Cyrus and Robert. At James's entrance, she moved toward him stiffly.

"I am here to help," she said, her voice sounding rusty and unused. "But perhaps I am not needed. If—" She turned to go, but Cyrus stayed her.

"Of course, you're needed," he snapped. "I'll need all the help I can get for this."

Hilary's eyes turned to James. They still held that lost look, and James knew an urge to go to her, to gather her in his arms and tell her he'd been a fool and could she forgive him.

"Shall I—" she began.

"Of course," he said, his own voice sounding strange in his ears. There was so much he wished to say to her. He loved Hilary Merton, by God, and it was high time he did something about it. So far he'd done damn little to make her love him, but once they got Rufus off to his own place in the cosmos, he would devote his entire fund of energy toward that goal. Please God, he could convince her that there was something in him to love, though at the moment, he couldn't think of a thing.

But right now there was no time. Dropping his gaze, he turned to Robert. His secretary had moved toward Rufus, who swayed suddenly. Only the hurried assistance of Hilary, Robert, and James, prevented him from falling to the floor. They half carried him to a settee placed at the edge of the hall's expanse. By now, he was white and perspiring.

"Gods!" he panted. "Don't know what came over me. I feel like week-old rat turds."

He fell against James, who had seated himself next to Rufus. The warrior's eyes rolled back into his head and he seemed to fall into a semiconscious state.

"I don't understand," James whispered to Hilary and Robert. "This is the worst I've ever seen him, I think." He raised his eyes to Cyrus, who had hastened from his place near the door to join them. "I assume this plan of yours involves another attempt to create lightning—I'm not sure he can survive being struck by lightning again."

"Well," began Cyrus, "I don't intend to create it, but—"

"It seems to me," interposed Robert, "that he may not survive anyway. We've got to try something." His boyish face was hard with concern, and it was apparent that he, too, had grown fond of the old soldier in the past few weeks.

"If we're going to try my experiment," Cyrus declared urgently, "we must move now, while the storm is raging. It must be directly overhead when I set off the rocket, and it's nearly at that point now."

"The rocket?" echoed his listeners in unison.

"I'll explain on the way." Cyrus's voice was high with impatience. "Here"—he handed the small, metal canister he still carried to James—"keep it dry. And be careful. I had a servant fill it with hot coals while you were retrieving the soldier. Come on—we must get him into the wagon."

Accepting the oilskins and umbrellas produced with superb aplomb by Dunston and his minions, the little group swathed Rufus carefully. Then, in a combined effort, they bundled him out into the body of the wagon. Once he was settled, they climbed in, and Hilary, additional blankets in hand, stretched over him, covering most of his body with her own. James, carefully cradling the canister, sat next to Cyrus, who held the reins himself. Robert took a place near Hilary.

To no one's surprise, Jasper galloped up just as they were about to set off. As usual, he seemed oblivious to the rain that pelted him, flooding his eyes and ears. He barked joyously as Cyrus called, "Gee-up!" as though the whole scenario had been created for his express entertainment. When the wagon moved forward, Jasper lumbered along in its wake, splashing like a grampus and offering encouragement with an occasional, gurgling woof.

"Yes, I plan to set off a rocket," explained Cyrus, shouting against the noise of the storm. "I remembered something I read some years ago about the properties of saltpeter, when mixed with sugar."

"Sugar!"

"Yes. I know it sounds unlikely, but together, along with sulfur, they create a powerful propellant. I have the rocket all set up back there." He gestured to the tarpaulin-covered object, against which Rufus lay. "What I propose to do is, when the storm is directly over the tower, I shall fire it off, straight up into the cloud. I have a wire attached to its base, and I'll place the other end against the same shovel we used before, near Rufus. With any luck, the electricity in the cloud will be attracted to the wire. It will travel to the ground and—boom!"

"My God," breathed James. "You'd be calling lightning from the skies! Do you think it will work?"

Cyrus shrugged. "It might, and then again it might not—but I can't think of anything else."

James shivered and shrank inside the warmth of his oilskin. Despite his concern for Rufus, and his hopes for the success of Cyrus's experiment, his thoughts kept returning to Hilary. What was he to do to regain her trust?

Behind him, Hilary adjusted a blanket about Rufus' shoulders. Try as she might, she could not keep her mind on the old soldier and his monumental woes. She was possessed by the scene in the Tapestry Room. Dear God, James thought her a scheming adventuress! She would carry to the grave the expression of contempt on his face as her father and the crowd of guests had pushed into the Tapestry Room.

Well, why would he not have thought the worst? She and James had known each other for just over a month. Certainly not long enough to know that she would never do a thing like that. In fact, it was just the sort of thing he would immediately suspect her of, given his not unwarranted distrust of her sex. She could try to explain to him, she supposed, that she was blameless. She could try to make him understand.

No, by God, she would not. Short acquaintance or no, they had become friends—or, at least she thought they had. James should know without being told that she would never be part of something so despicable. How could he have jumped to such a conclusion without a moment's consideration?

She allowed her anger to build. How could she have been so foolish as to fall in love with him? she asked for the hundredth time. Her heart had been inviolable for so many years, and now she had somehow let it slip into the fingers of a man who had let it fall into the dust. What was she to do? Clinging to the half-a-loaf theory, she had looked forward to a mild friendship with him once he returned to London. She had thought they might correspond intermittently for a few years, and perhaps they would see each other on her infrequent forays into the city. Now, he would not want to so much as share a cup of tea with her.

She could not at all define the look he had just sent to her. His features had been virtually invisible, but the tension between them had been palpable. He had seemed to come to some sort of decision, and she knew all too well what that decision must be.

Perhaps it was all for the best, she told herself in a belated attempt at wisdom. She could never have hoped for his love, and now he would be out of her life—if not her heart.

She had got through most of her six and twenty years of life without James Wincanon. She supposed she could muddle through the rest on her own, as well.

But she feared it would be incredibly painful.

Straightening her shoulders, she turned her attention back to Rufus. Please God, whatever Cyrus had in mind would work and Rufus would return to his own world, and his old life—and, hopefully, his health. Right now, he seemed to be no better. Occasionally, he opened his eyes, but only for a few seconds. He muttered unintelligibly once or twice, but showed no sign of returning to complete consciousness.

She lifted her head to discover that they had arrived at the tower. Cyrus's first move, after clambering down from the wagon, was to light several lanterns under cover of an umbrella held for him by Robert. Their beams seemed weak against the stormy blackness that surrounded them, but they gave enough light to carry out their tasks.

Carefully avoiding any contact with James, Hilary assisted in removing Rufus from the wagon. He seemed to recover himself slightly as they led him inside. Jasper, enjoying his outing among such convivial company, romped beside them.

"The tricky part," said Cyrus, carrying the canister and avoiding with some difficulty Jasper's enthusiastic assistance, "is to make sure everything stays dry. We'll keep everything covered, and all hands will man the umbrellas. You must, every one of you, follow my instructions implicitly. Yes, just prop him up on that stone bench by the wall. Lady Hilary, see to him, please. Now, James, you and—Robert, is it?—will help me bring in the rocket."

Without waiting to see if his orders were being followed, he turned and made his way through the driving rain back to the wagon. The time interval between the lightning flashes and the subsequent crashes of thunder were becoming shorter. Lifting the rocket, under its tarpaulin and the umbrellas, the scientist and his assistants carried it into the tower. Under Cyrus's anxious direction, they set it upright near Cyrus.

Hilary, from her place at Rufus' side, watched anxiously. The warrior was recovering his senses, but he was very weak. Just sitting in an upright position seemed to take all his strength. He grasped Hilary's hand.

"I've been listening," he gasped. "We're going to try it again, are we?"

"Yes." Hilary tried to infuse her tone with optimism. "And this time I'm sure it will work."

To her surprise, Rufus nodded.

"Yes, I believe it will," he murmured, patting her fingers. "You must not worry."

How odd, Hilary thought, that it was he who was offering her reassurance. She thought she heard a soft chuckle from somewhere in the storm, but she could not be sure. She *was* sure, however, that something was moving outside the tower, past the wagon that now stood empty. She tried to peer through the curtain of rain, but could see nothing. Her gaze went to James, who had again been summoned to Cyrus's side. As though aware of her scrutiny, he turned to her, but did not speak.

Not that she could have heard him had he done so. The storm had increased in intensity, howling and tearing at their clothing like an infuriated beast. Fumbling under the tarpaulin, Cyrus drew out a length of wire.

"Copper," he explained perfunctorily. "One end is attached to the rocket. This one"—he handed it to Robert—"you will attach to the shovel." He pointed to the implement, lying where it had been left after their previous, abortive attempt.

When Robert had completed his task, and moved the shovel close to Rufus, Cyrus drew a deep breath.

"Now, then. We must light the fuse. Hand me the canister," he commanded James. "Everyone hold your umbrellas over the rocket—and me. Do be— For God's sake!" he blurted explosively. "Get that damned dog out of here."

Jasper, unfazed, stared interestedly up at Cyrus, his tongue lolling happily. He appeared completely oblivious to the lightning streaking across the sky and the roar of the thunder that accompanied it. He thrust his dripping muzzle inquisitively under the tarpaulin.

"Jasper!" Hilary cried. "Bad dog! Go away!"

Jasper glanced at her in affronted surprise, but turned with no diminution of spirit and trotted out of the confines of the tower.

"All right," barked Cyrus. "As you were."

When he and the rocket were completely sheltered, Cyrus removed the tarpaulin and held up one of the lanterns so the others could view his masterpiece. The device was revealed as curiously shaped, and composed of metal canisters, similar to but larger than the one containing the hot coals. They were strapped together around a thick wooden rod, which protruded outward and down from the rocket. The wire was tied to the rod. The top of the contrivance was pointed, and around the whole was smeared a black, gooey substance.

"Gunpowder paste," said Cyrus. "The canisters contain the propellant and the nose"—he gestured to the pointed end of the rocket—"is made of glazier's putty." He glanced around the group complacently. "Simple, but, I trust, effective."

"Do you really think this will work?" asked James, his voice noticeably lacking hope.

"The chances are slim," admitted Cyrus, thrusting the wooden rod into the ground. "The storm center is directly overhead, but it would be better if we were closer—on a mountaintop, perhaps. Once the wire enters the cloud, it will be in the electrical field, and may very well attract a charge that should, in turn, be drawn down the wire. A lightning bolt, if you will." He glanced around. "Are we ready, then?"

James turned to Rufus. *"Optima?"*

"Yes, James, I've been ready for some days now." With an effort, he stood. Solemnly, he shook James's hand. "It has been a pleasure knowing you, lad, and I wish you well with your villa, and"—he glanced at Hilary—"with your other, er, project."

He turned then and bent over Hilary's hand. "My lady, I wish I could take you back with me to meet Maia; you would like each other. I wish you every happiness, and—and I shall miss you."

"And I you, Marcus Rufus Minimus," replied Hilary brokenly. "I hope you and Maia will share many years of happiness together—and a son."

Rufus blinked and swung hastily to Robert. "And you, my boy. Perhaps you will be a governor of this province one day—or at least a procurator. You won't forget an old soldier, will you?"

Robert shook his head wordlessly and gripped Rufus' hand. Rufus then turned once more to Cyrus to signify his readiness. Cyrus, who had been wrapping the loose end of the copper around the shovel blade, stepped over to the rocket. He reached for the canister.

"All right," he said sharply. "Keep the umbrellas over me until I light the fuse. Once it's going nicely, everyone run like the devil."

A heavy mist had settled on the scene and Hilary shivered, remembering this same phenomena had accompanied the lightning flash that had brought Rufus from his own time to the present. The lantern light was now almost completely ineffectual as Cyrus removed the lid from the canister, and with a small pair of tongs drawn from his pocket, he removed a red-hot coal. This, he applied to the fuse. It sputtered for several long, agonizing seconds, but at last, to involuntary cries from those present, it caught. Rufus glanced around once more, then lifted a clenched fist to his breast in a salute.

"James!" he called. "When you go back to the villa, examine the shrine—very carefully!"

James nodded abstractedly and, placing an arm around Hilary, drew her into the scant shelter of the rubble surrounding the tower entrance. The rocket ignited and shot skyward in a burst of sparks. As it did so, a bulky figure hurtled into the tower.

"No!" screamed Mordecai Cheeke, plummeting toward Rufus. He reached for the wire leading from the shovel to the rocket. "You cannot leave. I must—"

But his sentence was never completed. A furry streak, yowling in rage, flung itself against him, pushing him against Rufus. As Mordecai flung his arms about the startled warrior, a white-hot streak of flame descended from the clouds above the tower, striking the ground below with an earth-shaking roar.

Hilary was torn from James's arms and hurled against the far wall of the tower. She was seared by the instantaneous heat of the bolt and for a moment, thought she would be consumed. The smell of singed fur and a terrified howl filled the air. Then, again as it had happened before, all became still. The mist cleared, the rain stopped, and all that could be heard was a continuous whimper issuing from Jasper's throat and the sound of footsteps approaching the tower from outside. Cautiously, Hilary peered toward the place where Rufus had stood. He was gone!

And so was Mordecai Cheeke.

Chapter Twenty-six

"Hilary!" James's voice called out of the darkness. "Hilary, where are you? Are you all right?"

Hilary glanced about, but could see nothing in the blackness that enveloped the scene. A large tongue licked her cheek, and Jasper's wet, furry bulk pressed against her. She buried her face in his fur. Thank God he was all right!

"Yes," she called. "Are you?"

"Yes, and Robert—and I think, Cyrus, as well." A muffled grunt confirmed James's assessment.

A moving light caught Hilary's attention, and she discerned a cloaked figure entering the tower.

"Dorcas!" she exclaimed. "I might have known," she added to herself. "Does the old woman never sleep?"

Dorcas continued on her path into the tower, pausing to bend over a still-immobile Cyrus. Hilary struggled to her feet.

"Ah, my daughter," chided Dorcas in her oddly youthful voice. "You and your friends are at it again, are you?" A wry smile further creased her lined face. "At least this time you did not try to create lightning—you merely drew it down from the skies." She patted Jasper's head.

"And this time we were successful," replied Hilary, unable to keep a measure of satisfaction from her voice.

Dorcas' smile widened. "Were you, then?"

"Yes, Rufus was sent back to his own time by the lightning bolt. Or—at least, he is gone. We can only assume he is back home—and that he will see a return to health."

"Oh, yes, he will live to be an old man, I am sure of it."

Hilary frowned uncertainly at the old woman's words, oddly

echoing those of Rufus earlier. "So, everything has turned out well," she added brightly.

"You are pleased then, daughter—at last—with your gift?"

"My gift?"

The old woman lifted her face to the moon, just now emerging from a tatter of cloud. "Why, yes. Did you not sacrifice to the Nameless One?"

"Sacrifice? The Nameless—? Why, of course not. Why would I do anything so foolish? I'm not— Oh! You mean the seedcake? But that was only a whim. I thought of the old spirits who might still— Not that I believe in any such nonsense. I—"

Dorcas halted her with a stern gesture. "Be careful, daughter," she said sternly. "Do not mock what you do not understand. Do you really think it was your pitiful little device that sent the soldier back to his place in time? Be humble, daughter, and be grateful for the gift from the mist, for it brought you your heart's desire, did it not?"

Before Hilary could reply, Dorcas turned with a swirl of her black cloak, and the next moment had disappeared into the darkness of the forest.

Really, mused Hilary, moving in the direction of the men's voices, the old lady was getting stranger every time she came into view. Her heart's desire? How absurd. Why, she could not even recall why she had left the slice of seedcake on the alt— Oh, yes, she had been thinking of her forthcoming meeting with the famous James Wincanon. For goodness' sake, she had merely wanted the meeting to go off propitiously. Which it hadn't, of course. Why, if it hadn't been for the appearance of Rufus—

She halted abruptly in her reflections. If Rufus had not dropped almost literally into her lap, she and James would never have become friends—even if only temporarily. Was that what Dorcas meant? And what was that about their own pitiful devices? Good Lord, what had the old woman been implying? And how old *was* she, anyway?

Hilary hurried toward a light that shone dimly inside the tower. The source was Cyrus's lantern, which he had lit upon struggling to his feet. He lifted it high in the air to examine the interior of the tower. After a moment, he let out a whoop and performed an impromptu jig.

"It worked!" he sang, capering like a demented stork. "It really worked. I did it! I brought lightning down out of the clouds!" He paused and looked around once more. His voice dropped to a whisper. "And—and, by God, the soldier is gone! James, your theory must have been right. He *was*—"

"Yes, yes," interrupted James. "He was from the past, and now he's been returned—safe and sound, I trust. But what about Cheeke?"

"Eh?" asked Cyrus blankly.

"Did you not see him? Although, I must say, it happened so quickly, perhaps I imagined—"

"No," cried Hilary. "I saw him, too. He ran in and tried to disconnect the wire. Jasper jumped up on him. But he's not here now. Good Lord," she gasped in dawning horror. "Do you suppose—"

"I saw him, too!" interrupted Robert excitedly. "He was trying to keep Rufus from leaving! Jasper leaped at him and pushed him, practically into Rufus' arms. When the lightning struck, Cheeke must simply have been swept along for the ride."

James uttered a small, rusty chuckle, and as the others gaped at him in surprise, the chuckle grew to a broad laugh and then a belly-wrenching guffaw. In a moment, as the implications of what had just happened surged through her mind, Hilary, too, began to laugh. A few seconds later, Robert joined in. James moved to Hilary's side and without thinking, encircled her with one arm. He ruffled Jasper's ears vigorously with the other.

"Jasper, I don't know why you weren't sent backward in time as well, but I'm glad you're still with us. You are a pearl among canines and I promise you, you shall have steak every day for the rest of your life, courtesy of one grateful antiquary."

He turned to laugh down into Hilary's face, but a moment later, his face closed. He dropped his arm and stepped abruptly away. Hilary's heart sank. Even in this moment of exhilaration and the release of pent-up tension, James had not forgotten his hostility. The constraint between them seemed a physical presence and she put a hand up in a gesture of defeat.

"Well, that's that, then," declared Cyrus. "James, may I beg a bed at your house for the night? It's a bit late to start back to Gloucester, and I want to begin writing up my notes while the whole thing is still fresh in my mind."

"You may have a bed, old friend, indeed you may have unto half my kingdom. You have not only restored one of the emperor's finest to his place in time, but you have rid me of the curse of my life."

He began to laugh again. "I do hope Mordecai made the trip in one piece. I wonder how he will fare in second-century Britain?"

The next moment, as he intercepted the answering mirth in Hilary's eyes, once again the laughter died from his own. "We will, of course, escort Lady Hilary back to her home." He began to move toward the wagon, but Robert interposed himself in his path.

"That won't be necessary, sir. It appears that Mr. Cheeke left us a gift." He gestured to the showy curricle that stood some distance from the wagon. "I do not believe he will have any further use for it, so you may as well appropriate it. Mr. Bender and I will make our way to Goodhurst in the wagon."

"Oh, no," gasped Hilary. "That is—I don't think—"

"Cheeke's curricle will serve nicely," interrupted James, a light in his eyes that Hilary could not interpret.

Watching her, James felt his heart leap. He had not expected an opportunity to be alone with Hilary. The ride to Whiteleaves would not take long, but he intended to make every moment count. First of all, he must make Hilary forgive him. After that—well, he would not press his suit, of course, for it was much too soon. Indeed, the thought of doing so caused his stomach to drop to a place somewhere below his knees. No, he would behave in a logical manner. He would approach her gently, with circumspection. Time enough to speak of love—weeks from now—when he had put in some much-needed spadework.

He eyed her doubtfully. She did not seem overjoyed at the prospect of the short journey home with him. He thought back to that split second when his world had tumbled about his ears. How could he have been so stupid, even for a moment?

Judging from Hilary's reaction in the Tapestry Room, his feelings of betrayal and humiliation must have been writ large on his face. What must she think of him? His first move in his campaign to win her heart must be to assure her that, except for that one small flicker of doubt, his faith in her had never wavered.

His heart fell. One flicker of doubt? It was like asking her to overlook a swift stab to the heart.

But he must make her forgive him, and when he did, he would set out to transform himself from the scholarly, acid-tongued pedant with whom she had become accustomed to a dashing, articulate, sincere, heart-pierced swain. Lord, he didn't even know anyone like that, let alone filling the bill himself. He staggered slightly, almost overcome by the panic that swept over him. He could face a room full of academicians with complete aplomb, but the thought of conveying his feelings—feelings he had never experienced before, to one, peppery female left him weak with fear.

Pinning what he hoped was an engaging smile to his lips, he handed Hilary into the curricle. Jasper fell into place behind them and they started off.

Hilary peered at him in the dim lantern light. She did *not* want to drive to Whiteleaves with James. She could not bear another second of his contempt, though she was determined not to offer excuses for a nonexistent transgression. From his expression, it was obvious that he was still very angry. In fact if— She paused in her reflections. Good heavens, what was the matter with him? What she had taken for anger had looked more like some sort of grimace, as though he had just bitten into a peach to discover half of a large, disgusting bug there.

They rode in silence for some minutes until at last, Hilary said tentatively, "I expect the ball is still going on. It would probably be better if we enter through the rear of the house."

"Yes."

The conversation, such as it was, lagged.

James said something then, of which Hilary could only discern the words, "Your hair."

"My hair? What about it?" she asked, puzzled.

James cleared his throat. "It—it looks very nice tonight. As it always does," he added hastily.

Hilary stared at him in blank incomprehension. She knew that in the darkness, it must be impossible to see her hair, which in any event must look like a fox fur left out in the weather too long. What in the world was he doing talking about her hair?

At her continued silence, James gulped audibly. "I liked your costume tonight, too. It was very—pretty."

At this, Hilary swung about in her seat to face him.

"James, what on earth is the matter with you? Whatever are you nattering on about?"

There was a moment's pause before James replied with great dignity and some irritation, "I am trying to do the pretty, devil take it."

If Hilary had not been so astonished, she would have laughed aloud. The words, "empty blandishments," and the name, "James Wincanon" could hardly be uttered in the same sentence, yet here he was, in all his eminent scholarliness, spouting absurd flattery. The question was, of course, why?

"Why?" she asked baldly.

In response, James drew the curricle to the side of the lane and turned to face her. He stared at her for a long moment, searching her face in the moonlight.

"Because," he said at last, "I suppose I am trying to make amends. And not doing very well at it," he added.

"Amends?" She held her breath. Surely she had not imagined the condemnation she'd read in his face in the Tapestry Room. But—amends?

Oh Lord, thought James. Now, he was in for it. He had not meant to bring up the Tapestry Room fiasco. At least not until he had softened Hilary in a suitable manner.

With which he was having little success, so far.

Unthinking, he grasped both her hands in his. "Yes, amends. I—I did not behave well when your father and the others burst into the room. When Cheeke spewed his unconscionable lies about you, I should have flattened him out and pushed him through the carpet."

"His lies?" Hilary's voice quavered almost undetectably.

"Well, of course!" exclaimed James, all righteous indignation. "You—you don't think I believed you responsible for our—our compromising situation, do you?"

She said nothing, but gazed at him with a clear, direct stare.

James squirmed.

"You're not going to let me wriggle out of this, are you?"

"No—though if truth be told, I am at a loss to understand just what it is you're trying to wriggle out of." She lifted her brows questioningly, her gaze becoming almost painfully intense.

"The fact that I—I betrayed you," he blurted. "God, I almost wish I could be other than honest with you. It sickens me to admit it, but I did—just for a moment—believe you had arranged the whole situation. I believed it because I wanted to," he added painfully.

"You—you *wanted* to?" The anguished disbelief in her voice made him flinch.

James opened his mouth, and closed it again abruptly. His grip on her hands tightened spasmodically. At last, he spoke in a strained voice.

"You may not have noticed it, but I am rather prideful."

Hilary blessed the darkness that helped conceal her confusion. "Yes," she gulped, "I had noticed that."

He released one of her hands to run it through his hair. The gesture did nothing to improve his appearance, which, to put it kindly, resembled that of a distraught owl.

"I don't know if I can explain this, Hilary—my dearest Hilary— but I had some rather deeply imbedded notions concerning the female sex, and—"

Hilary, whose heart during this dialogue had threatened to jump from her breast, calmed suddenly. A mounting sensation that she only vaguely recognized as joy, filled her being. From the stillness of the night around them, from the damp, earthy scent of the forest—from the spirit of the wood itself, she seemed to draw an ancient feminine knowledge that confirmed the growing certainty that grew within her like a newly nourished plant.

"And"—she interrupted gently, her breath suspending itself somewhere between her soul and her life itself—"you could not allow yourself to believe that a woman could desire nothing from you but your—your friendship."

"Oh, the devil with my friendship," he blurted angrily. "My God, Hilary, it took me long enough to realize it, but I fell in love with you, and if you want to know the truth, it terrified me."

"I know," Hilary replied gently, lifting her hand to smooth a tendril of brown hair that had fallen across his forehead. She had no idea from what well of inner cognition her surety sprang, but it was as though someone whispered to her of an ancient power. A sensual song of infinite, eternal wisdom swelled within her, dispelling all doubt with a sort of glorious benediction. "And now?"

"And now," James breathed hoarsely, "I seem to be consumed by the most appallingly primitive desire to drag you by the hair into my cave and keep you there for the rest of our lives and have at least seven children with you."

Smiling, Hilary lifted her face. "I must say that sounds like a most appealing program," she whispered, listening to herself in some astonishment.

James gaped at her as though in equal surprise, but lost no time in gathering her into an embrace that drove the breath from her. He bent to cover her mouth with his in a kiss that was searching and urgent and demanding. A searing heat leaped from that contact and spread through her like a summer storm sweeping through a meadow. She arched into him, reveling in the feel of him and the scent of him, that had now become as familiar and necessary to her as the air she breathed.

She became aware of the mounting fire in her blood. She moved within his arms to mold herself even more tightly to his lean strength. Abruptly, James drew back from her, just enough so that he could look into her face.

"Lord." He laughed shakily. "I had not planned to do this for a month, at least. I planned a sedate, logical, step-by-step courtship."

"Ah, you—you scientist, you," sighed Hilary from within the curve of his arm. Then—"Courtship? I thought perhaps this was a seduction."

"Mm," replied James, his fingers straying to the laces at her bodice. "What would give you that idea? You think me a cad, then? A shameless ravisher of virgins?"

"You mean you're not?" asked Hilary allowing a tinge of disappointment to creep into her tone. James scattered butterfly kisses on her rainwashed cheeks.

"All in good time, you shameless hussy. First we will stand up together to plight our troth in a very large church, in front of a very large group of family and friends. Then we'll see about ravishment and seduction." His demeanor changed abruptly to one of anxious solemnity. "You are going to marry me, aren't you?"

"Yes, my dearest love. As soon as ever such a ceremony can be arranged."

James smiled and availed himself once more of her lips. "I expect I shall be obliged to seek out your father when we get to Whiteleaves."

"He will fall on your neck."

"I suppose. It can't have been easy watching one's daughter decline into a meddling, unlovable old spinster. He will no doubt be grateful to me for taking you off his hands.

"I am not old!" Hilary cried indignantly.

"Do not argue with your affianced husband," returned James primly. "And with all that perfectly frightful red hair to boot," he murmured hoarsely, his lips returning to hers to smother a squeak of protest.

For some moments, nothing was heard except the chorale of the night, accompanied by the benign rustle of the ancient oaks that surrounded them and Jasper's investigative snuffles as he patrolled the area.

At last James released Hilary. "I think," he said unsteadily, "we'd best be on our way—before I make a wife of you ahead of the calendar."

As the curricle began to move forward once more, Hilary murmured, "I wish Rufus could have known about—about us. I think he would have been pleased."

James chuckled. "I think he had an inkling, despite what he categorized as my lamentable lack of enterprise."

"Your lack of—"

"Yes, according to him, we should have been wed long ago." He prudently chose to omit Rufus' advice on the baking of buns.

"Was he truly a gift, then?" murmured Hilary wonderingly.

"I beg your pardon?"

"Nothing," said Hilary with a shaky laugh. Perhaps one day she would tell him of her childish seedcake prayer and the ancient, imponderable forces she had set into motion. Right now, she would let him continue to believe that a scientific miracle had brought them a traveler from the past and subsequently returned him to his home. "But I think you are right, my love. Halloween is almost over, and it is time we left this realm of mystery and witchery to return to the real world."

"As long as my real world contains you, I have no objection, my love."

As the curricle moved off once again, Hilary glanced over her shoulder once more at the Roman tower, a ghost of vanished centuries, gleaming palely in the moonlight. She breathed a swift, silent prayer of thanks to whatever deity had seen fit to bless her on this magical Al Hallows' Eve, and to the handmaiden who had served her for so many centuries.

Epilogue

The disappearance of Rufus caused little stir in the neighborhood. He was, after all, a foreigner and thus of no account. Mordecai Cheeke was another matter. It was Sir Harvey Winslow, Cheeke's host, who first reported him missing, and the full magesterial resources of the shire were brought to bear in the disappearance.

Mordecai had apparently found it prudent that evening to conceal his intentions even from his servants. The stable hands at Benchley Park, Sir Harvey's abode, knew only that he had taken out his curricle, giving no clue as to his destination. The head groom at the Park made no mention of anything extraordinary in his appearance, so he must have donned his King Arthur apparel just before arriving at Whiteleaves.

After a hurried conference among the witnesses to Mordecai's contretemps with the forces of nature and science, it was decided that there was no reason for them to come forward with the truth. After all, who would believe them? There had been no criminal intent, James pointed out, if one discounted Jasper's rather pointed hostility. Cyrus averred that he would just as soon avoid any tedious inquiries into his part of the program. One never knew what pettifoggery might come forth from the minions of the law, whose views on scientific experimentation sometimes bordered on rank superstition. Robert's contribution to the discussion was the opinion that there was nothing anyone could do to bring the fat little weasel back, anyway—which was all to the good.

Hilary attended the sessions among the conspirators, but merely nodded serenely and said that she would be pleased to concur with whatever the gentlemen decided. She found herself wholly occupied with the parade of visitors that appeared at Whiteleaves in the wake of the Halloween Ball to wish her happy and to offer suggestions for her coming nuptials. In all the investigative flurry that took place during the weeks following Mordecai's departure into the past, no hint of a connection was discovered with the presence of his most notable rival in the neighborhood. It would be unthinkable, in any event, for anyone to question the eminent James Wincanon in such a matter.

Thus, the abrupt departure of Mordecai Cheeke from the haunts of men remained a mystery, much talked of in the neighborhood for years to come.

It was some weeks before Hilary and James, with Jasper at their heels, returned to the Roman villa. Jasper once more lent his dubious assistance. It was not until they had been working for some hours on the triclinium mosaic, frequently interspersed with more pleasant activity, that Hilary bethought herself of Rufus' final admonishment.

She picked up trowel and rake and moved to the little shrine just to the north of the villa. There she worked in the area where she had seen Rufus digging, until she was obliged to turn her attention to Jasper, who was apparently trying to tunnel under a large rock nearby.

"Jasper," she scolded gently, "what have I told you? Why, what in the world . . ." she exclaimed, bending for a closer examination. "James!" she called suddenly. "Come look at this."

When James reached her side, she pointed silently at the rock. Following her direction, he was astonished to see his own name etched faintly in its surface, accompanied by a crooked little arrow, pointing straight down. The scratches had been made recently.

He exchanged a glance with Hilary.

"What in the world can this signify?" she queried. "Do you suppose Rufus carved it? And to what purpose?"

"Ump. I have no idea, but I suppose there is one way to find out."

He picked up a shovel and began digging in earth that seemed freshly overturned. It was not until he had progressed to more than a foot below the surface that a dull chink signaled the presence of something metallic below the soil. A few minutes' more digging and much tugging brought forth a chest, about four feet square. It was made of wood, most of which was rotted away, but was so heavily banded that for all intents and purposes, it was constructed of iron.

"Oh, my," gasped Hilary.

James anticipated some difficulty in opening the chest, but to his surprise, the clasp opened and the lid swung up effortlessly.

"It looks to me," James mused aloud, "as though someone opened this not too long ago."

"Rufus!" exclaimed Hilary.

"No doubt, and—good God, look at this!"

Reverently, he drew from the chest an object wrapped in a heavy oilskin. Unwrapping it, he drew in a sharp breath. Hilary fell on her knees to the earth beside him.

"It's—why, it's a helmet!"

"Yes, and extraordinarily well-preserved. And look here. Tucked in with it. A *pugio*—a dagger. And—yes, it is the one Rufus wore at his side." He ran his fingers along the hunting scene carved on the shaft. "I believe," James murmured, "the helmet, too, must have belonged to Rufus."

"Yes! Do you remember the day Rufus spent so much time here, near the shrine? He must have uncovered the chest then and realized that he, himself had buried it after his return from our century."

"No wonder he was so sure he would be sent back home safely. Oh—here's something else," he observed as a small object fell to the ground to lie glittering in the morning sun. Picking it up, he examined it carefully and then began to laugh. He handed it to Hilary, who after gazing at it, puzzled, for some moments, also uttered a delighted whoop.

"It's a quizzing glass!" she cried. "And bless me, if it isn't Mordecai's."

"Good old Rufus! He sent us a message to let us know that Mordecai made the journey as well. One can assume, I think, that he arrived in one piece."

"I wonder what became of him after that?"

"I neither know nor care, except to hope fervently that he ended up as a slave to a tyrannical master."

James rummaged further, giving a startled cry as he drew yet another wrapped parcel from the chest.

"Dear heaven!" breathed Hilary, as the sunlight glinted dully from a assortment of metal objects. "James—this is badly tarnished, but I'm sure it's—it's a cache of crafted silver!"

Indeed, on further inspection, the package proved to contain two large silver trays, three smaller ones, four serving bowls, a half-dozen goblets, and several spoons. Through the grime and oxidation of centuries, the metal was still clearly identifiable.

"But where do you suppose Rufus got all this?" Hilary frowned in disbelief. "It would have been worth a fortune then. It would be costly even today," she added.

"And why would he bury it here?" James continued. He glanced again into the hole created by the removal of the chest. "Wait—there's something else down here as well."

Reaching into hole, he brought forth two marble slabs, one large and one small, and both were inscribed. James ran his fingers over the markings on the smaller.

"It says, 'My father instructed me to place this replica of his tombstone in this hiding place. He said to give his most—um—heartfelt greetings to James and Hilary and perhaps he will see you someday in the Elysian fields, where happy spirits roam. In the meantime, he hopes you will find a use for these tokens of his regard.' It's signed, 'Marcus Minimus Rusticus of Corinium.' "

James exchanged a long, wordless look with Hilary before picking up the tombstone.

" *'DIS Marcus Minimus Rufus,' "* he said. " *'Amicus Hadriani Caesar.'* Well, well—friend of the Emperor Hadrian. Apparently our old friend rose in the world after his return home. Let's see," he continued, stooping over the tombstone once more. " *'Veteranus Legio Il Agustus Annorum LXXX.'* Good Lord, Rufus lived to be eighty! Or at least thereabouts. The Romans used to round the age off to the nearest five years."

" *'HFC,' "* said Hilary, reading the last line of the inscription. "What does that signify?"

"It stands for *'Heres Faciendum Curavit,'* or 'His heir had this stone set up.' "

Hilary sighed happily. "Rufus and Maia did have a son together. And from the looks of it, one who must have been most dutiful. A source of great pride to his father, no doubt." She picked up the helmet and laid her cheek against it. "And, he did live to be an old man. I'm so glad. Oh, James, he knew what an archaeological find these things would be. Every other Roman helmet I've seen from this time period is incomplete, with pieces missing and marred by scratches and gouges. This one is whole and beautiful. It is a treasure. Just think what it will look like when it's polished."

James took the helmet in his hands. "It was his parade helmet, made for show and not for fighting. See—it is carved with battle scenes and would cover nearly all of the warrior's face. It's a beauty," he whispered. "I wonder if he made it himself?"

"It certainly seems more than likely."

"The detail is astonishing. And the silver"—James gestured to the serving pieces—"will make a magnificent display in the British Museum. But"—he bent to peer closer at one of the large trays—"Hilary, see here! The reliefs appear to be mostly mythological subjects, but look at this man. He's obviously a farmer, standing before his villa and if that villa isn't this villa, I will personally eat this shovel. And the dagger at his belt—it's the one Rufus left for us here."

He lifted the dagger, comparing it with its silver counterpart.

"Good heavens." Hilary, too, bent to examine the dagger. "Do you suppose Rufus was trying to tell us that he became so successful that he was able to purchase this place? Maia must have been ecstatic!"

"Well, his tombstone does say 'amicus Hadrian Caesar.' The old sly boots must have taken advantage of his childhood relationship with the emperor. Hadrian must have seen fit to grant him some sort of munificence."

Hilary moved close to rest her head on James's shoulder. "I'm so glad to know life turned out well for him—and Maia. I wonder if he didn't purchase this particular villa just so he could bury these things to speak to us through the ages, knowing we would find them."

James hugged her lightly. "Or perhaps he was the builder. What a mystery is the circle of time. Rufus visited the future and left a message for us to find a treasure that had not even been created yet." He turned to press a kiss on her temple, just there where a silky feather of red hair covered a fluttering pulse. "Do you suppose, my love, man will ever invent a machine to carry him back and forth between the ages?"

"James, you go too far." Hilary sniffed, at the same time nestling closer in James's arms. "Next you will be thinking men will fly to the moon someday."

James gazed skyward for a moment, his eyes narrowed.

"A ridiculous notion, to be sure, my love," he murmured, turning her in his embrace to give more careful attention to the little curl and its surrounding terrain.

Jasper, eyeing them through half-closed eyes, gave a weary sigh and rolled over to dream doggie dreams of lame rabbits and meaty bones, uncaring of the cosmic events that had taken place over his massive head.

SIGNET REGENCY ROMANCE   (0451)

ENDURING ROMANCES

☐**THE DUKE'S DILEMMA by Nadine Miller.** Miss Emily Haliburton could not hope to match her cousin Lady Lucinda Hargrave in either beauty or social standing. Certainly she couldn't compete with the lovely Lucinda for the hand of the devastatingly handsome Lord Jared Tremayne who was on the hunt for a wife. The duke couldn't see Emily as a wife, but she did manage to catch his roving eye as a woman.   (186753—$4.50)

☐**THE RELUCTANT HEIRESS by Evelyn Richardson.** Lady Sarah Melford was quite happy to live in the shadow of her elder brother and his beautiful wife. But now that she had inherited her grandmother's vast wealth, all eyes were avidly upon her, especially those of three ardent suitors. She had to decide what to do with the many men who wanted her. For while money did not bring happiness, it most certainly brought danger and, hopefully, love.   (187660—$4.99)

☐**THE DEVIL'S DUE by Rita Boucher.** Lady Katherine Steel was in desperate flight from the loathsome lord who threatened even more than her virtue after her husband's death. Her only refuge was to disguise herself as the widow of Scottish lord Duncan MacLean, whose death in far-off battle left his castle without a master. But Duncan MacLean was not dead.   (187512—$4.99)

☐**THE RUBY NECKLACE by Martha Kirkland.** Miss Emaline Harrison was the widow of a licentious blueblood after a marriage in name only. Around her neck was a precious heirloom, which some London gentlemen would kill for. So it was difficult for Emaline to discern the true motives and intentions of the seductive suitors swarming around her. Such temptation was sure to lead a young lady very dangerously, delightfully astray.   (187202—$4.99)

Prices slightly higher in Canada